"It doesn't matter how many hoops you throw at me. I'm going to jump through all of them.

"If you want to play games, I'll play. We're still headed in the same direction. It'll just take longer to get there."

"No."

"We're going to be together. No matter how scary that feels to you right now."

"No." Her automatic denial sounded hollow and, frankly, pathetic, but it was the best she could do. "We're not."

She heard Andrew's harsh, frustrated sigh. "Have it your way. Like I said, if you want to play games, I'll play, but…I play dirty."

Of course he did.

Books by Ann Christopher

Kimani Romance

Just About Sex
Tender Secrets

ANN CHRISTOPHER

is a full-time chauffeur for her two overscheduled children. She is also a wife, former lawyer and decent cook. In between trips to various sporting practices and games, Target and the grocery store, she likes to write the occasional romance novel featuring a devastatingly handsome alpha male. She lives in Cincinnati and spends her time with her family, which includes two spoiled rescue cats, Sadie and Savannah.

If you'd like to recommend a great book, share a recipe for homemade cake of any kind or have a tip for getting your children to do what you say the *first* time you say it, Ann would love to hear from you through her Web site, www.AnnChristopher.com.

Tender
SECRETS

ANN CHRISTOPHER

KIMANI
ROMANCE

To Richard

 KIMANI PRESS™

ISBN-13: 978-0-373-86087-6
ISBN-10:   0-373-86087-0

TENDER SECRETS

Copyright © 2008 by Sally Young Moore

www.kimanipress.com

Printed in U.S.A.

Dear Reader,

Do you like secrets? Can you keep one? I have one to share, if you're willing....

Andrew Warner, the millionaire CEO and heir of WarnerBrands International, is about to fall in love. Passionately, hopelessly, desperately in love.

It doesn't matter that he doesn't believe in love or that the object of his affection is the worst possible woman— Viveca Jackson, the enigmatic reporter determined to write an exposé about his family. He couldn't care less that Viveca has her own agenda, one that may reveal the skeletons in the darkest corner of his closet. Even the potential loss of his fortune and birthright seems like nothing compared to his growing feelings for this one impossible woman.

And here are a few other things you may want to know about Andrew Warner: he's charming, determined and ruthless. When it comes to seduction, he's a consummate master, and he's not about to let their competing interests keep them apart. Not when he sees the smoldering desire in Viveca's eyes every time she looks at him.

Andrew knows that if he waits...and charms...and seduces, Viveca will come to him willingly. After all, the explosive chemistry between them can only be denied for so long. When she surrenders—and she *will* surrender—he'll spend the rest of his life loving her to the very best of his exceptional ability.

Assuming, of course, that their secrets don't tear them apart first.

Happy reading,

Ann Christopher

P.S. Don't forget to look for Eric Warner's story, *Road to Seduction,* in February 2009. He's about to see his best friend, Isabella Stevens, in a sexy new light....

Deep in my soul that tender secret dwells,
Lonely and lost to light for evermore,
Save when to thine my heart responsive swells,
Then trembles into silence as before.
—Lord Byron

A man keeps another person's secret better than his own; a woman, on the contrary, keeps her own secrets better than those of others.
—Jean de La Bruyère

No one keeps a secret like a child.
—Victor Hugo

Chapter 1

Viveca Jackson had never been a voyeur, reluctant or otherwise.

Until now.

She'd been having a lot of firsts lately.

Like being offered a book deal. She'd gotten the thrill of her life a month ago when she'd picked up the phone in her microscopic East Village apartment and her agent told her that an editor wanted to buy her book. Viveca was writing a family history about the Warners, who were Columbus, Ohio, royalty.

Even more exciting, Arnetta Warner, the family matriarch, wanted to participate in the writing of the book.

It was the opportunity of a lifetime.

Viveca had never dared hope that in one fell swoop she'd get the chance to build her career *and* ruin the reputation of the Warners, the family that had destroyed *her* family, but there it was, falling neatly into her lap.

Nor had she ever before taken a leave of absence from her job as a reporter for the *New York Times,* but she'd arranged the time off, sublet her apartment and flown to Columbus for a six-month stay at Heather Hill, the Warner estate.

Who'd ever have thought the Warners would open the doors of their palace to Viveca while she engineered their long-overdue comeuppance?

Was this divine justice? It sure felt like it.

She'd certainly never seen such a staggering display of wealth. In the Warners' world, uniformed butlers answered front doors, and houses weren't houses. They were estates with pretentious names like *Heather Hill* and with soaring, domed ceilings, curving staircases, silk wallpaper, damask drapes, crystal chandeliers and priceless antiques.

Unbelievable, really. Sickening.

The butler—Franklin Bishop, he'd said his name was— led Viveca down a long, windowed hallway and into a library to wait for Mrs. Warner. She studied him, liking his quiet dignity. He wore a crisp white dress shirt, starchy enough to stand by itself on the floor, dark trousers and black shoes polished to a mirrored brilliance that almost hurt her eyes.

"If you give me your car keys," he said in an accent that had originated somewhere in the Deep South, his lightly lined brown face crinkling into a welcoming smile, "I can get your luggage and put it in the cottage."

"Oh, no," she began automatically. She hated to think of the old gent lifting those heavy bags, but then she gave herself a swift mental kick in the butt. Why not enjoy the trappings of living with the filthy rich? The Warners owed her that much and more.

But…she still couldn't inconvenience this nice man.

"I can bring them in later," she told him. "Really."

He held out one weathered palm. "Give me those keys right now."

Not wanting to injure his pride, she handed them over and tried to be gracious about it. "Thank you."

"Tea or coffee?" he asked. "You must be thirsty."

"Oh, no," she began again.

He raised a salt-and-pepper eyebrow, and his lips twitched around a repressed smile. "You trying to put me out of my job?"

"Ah, no," she said. Now she felt sheepish.

"Good." He nodded with satisfaction. "I'll bring you some Darjeeling. You'll like that."

"Thanks. Have you been with the family long?"

"Oh…about a thousand years. They couldn't get along without me."

Viveca was still laughing when he winked and left. She reminded herself that in six months, when she finished the research, she'd have to return to the real world, where people handled their own luggage and got their own tea.

Yeah. That'd be an easy transition. Not.

Turning in a loose circle, she gawked openly, something she'd tried not to do in front of Mr. Bishop. She'd thought libraries like this existed only in movies, but she'd been wrong. Thousands of colorful leather-bound books lined thirty-foot-high bookshelves on opposite walls. A staircase on one side of the room led up to a second level, which had a narrow, railed walkway.

Books, books, books.

There was nothing she loved more. If only there had been a plate of brownies with thick, gooey icing on the coffee table, she would have thought she'd stumbled onto heaven on earth. What she wouldn't give to have the run of a library like—

Laughing voices and the splash of water outside broke her train of thought.

One of the French doors, she noticed for the first time, was ajar and let in the sweet, heavy fragrance of roses from some unseen garden and the smell of chlorine. Viveca crept to the doors and peeked out.

Blinding June sunlight scorched her eyes for a second or two, but then an amazing scene came into focus. She saw an enormous, glittering sapphire pool surrounded by columns and statues of various Greek gods, lush potted trees and flowers, and them.

No, *him*.

She gasped because there was no way to hold in her stunned appreciation of such a man. Or was he a god? She wasn't sure, having never seen anything like him before.

She'd researched him, of course. Andrew Warner, the thirty-five-year-old CEO of WarnerBrands International and heir to the Warner family fortune. He was one of *Queen City* magazine's most eligible bachelors, Yale graduate, blah, blah, blah.

Meaningless words that couldn't possibly prepare her for *this*.

Rising out of the pool just twenty feet away, Andrew Warner was *glorious*. There was no other word for him. That first glimpse of him froze Viveca into place, and she could no more look away than she could resurrect the dead.

She had a dazed initial impression of a flashing white smile, startling against the healthy honey-with-cream color of his skin, and curly, dark hair flattened against his head.

But then she noticed his body and her gaping mouth went dry.

Water streamed down his long limbs as he sauntered

over to an occupied lounge chair and sat beside his female companion's legs. *Tall,* Viveca thought. He was very tall. Muscular, too, with wide, sculpted swimmer's shoulders, a round butt, powerful thighs and shapely calves. A soccer player's calves. Dark hair dusted across his chiseled chest, tapered through the ladder rungs of his abdomen and disappeared into his blue board shorts.

Watching him grab a towel and run it over his head, Viveca felt a strange, tight knot form low in her belly.

The woman laughed, and Viveca's gaze slid unwillingly to her. Viveca refused to acknowledge her negative response to the woman, who was a shade or two darker than Andrew and had a sleek, precision-cut bob.

She'd been lying on her stomach, wearing only the bottoms of a skimpy red bikini, but now she flipped over and sat up. Viveca was treated to a startling glimpse of large, jiggling, walnut-tipped breasts that stuck straight out like twin *Hindenbergs,* impervious to the effects of gravity.

Don't watch this, Viveca told herself sternly. *You're spying on people in a private moment…you don't want to see this…you don't—*

She did.

Dismayed and fascinated, Viveca stared as the woman scooted down to the end of the lounge chair, wrapped her arms and legs around Andrew Warner, and pressed—undulated—against his back.

Viveca whimpered involuntarily. Unwelcome images and questions burned through her mind, demanding answers…

What did it feel like to touch that man? To press against that hard, perfect body? To make love with him?

In answer, Viveca's breasts peaked.

Even without touching her, Andrew Warner aroused

her more than her few and infrequent boyfriends ever had. This was not good.

Viveca watched as Andrew frowned and pulled away from his companion. The woman laughed, tossed that gleaming hair and, whispering in his ear, snaked her hands down his chest, kneading and caressing.

Viveca couldn't breathe, knowing she should look away and knowing she wouldn't. Slowly…slowly…the woman's hand slid lower until finally it stroked his crotch.

The woman cooed with obvious appreciation.

Viveca gasped again, loudly, and this time there was no splashing water to drown out the sound.

Andrew's head whipped around—naturally he had the perfect hearing of a bat—and Viveca's reflexes failed. The panicked voice in her head screamed directions at her to hide, but her uncomprehending feet and legs did nothing.

Andrew Warner, her enemy and the sexiest man she'd ever seen, looked directly at the French doors and saw her. And Viveca couldn't do anything other than gape.

For one endless, agonizing, pulsing moment, they stared at each other, connected by a force as powerful as it was invisible. Looking into his bright eyes, Viveca felt a succession of his emotions—surprise, curiosity and something darker.

Viveca was mortified and felt her cheeks flame with enough wattage to light the Vegas strip for a year. In the lamest move of her life, she leapt behind the curtains until she was out of his line of sight, a tactic only marginally more effective than rearranging deck chairs on the *Titanic*.

Safely hidden, she slapped a hand to her forehead and squeezed her eyes shut, as if that could block out what she'd just seen, or her reaction.

Stupid, stupid, stupid.

What had gotten into her?

Outside, Andrew spoke, his voice deep and commanding. "Stop it. Get dressed."

The woman said something whiny, and then was silent.

Breathe, Viveca told herself. After a few seconds her galloping heart rate returned to something approaching normal.

Rattled, she slumped back against a bookshelf, rubbed a hand over her churning belly, pushed Andrew out of her mind and focused on the reason she'd come *here,* to the heart of the enemy.

Justice for her family.

The Warner family had untold millions, private jets, lavish estates and spoiled playboys, and they deserved none of it. For this simple injustice, she'd hated them for half of her thirty years. Hated their glorious living and, most of all, their overwhelming sense of entitlement, as though they thought God had smiled on them, would smile on them forever and to hell with the rest of the world.

Viveca looked to the portrait above the enormous marble fireplace: Reynolds Warner, the late patriarch of this godforsaken family and as imperious as Henry VIII, stared out at her with a fiery gaze.

The painter had captured every bit of the man's energy and power. Staring up at him, Viveca couldn't believe he'd been dead for more than twenty years, or that all that intensity could ever leave the earth.

He was the one who'd killed her father, even if he hadn't done it with his own hands. *He* was the corrupt villain who'd built a company on the broken backs of his workers. *He* was the one whose legal but immoral policies had poisoned the corporate culture of WarnerBrands International.

He was the one whose name she most wanted to smear.

He had spawned a dynasty of men every bit as spoiled and entitled as he'd been, and engineered the fairy tale of a loving, beautiful family, much like the Kennedys, committed to good works and public service.

But the Kennedys had had dirty linen, and Viveca was here to air the Warners'.

She knew just where to start, too. She'd already arranged an interview with one of Reynolds Warner's mistresses.

Soon the world would know just how dishonorable the Warners really were. How corrupt their private lives. How all that glittered wasn't gold with them, no matter how they seemed to shine and glow.

Anger, hot and vicious, shuddered through her.

How dare they laugh and play and swim in beautiful pools when their clothing company was nothing but a glorified sweatshop? When her father, God rest his soul, had worked his fingers to the bone for them, and then lost his arm in one of their death-trap machines?

Remembering sobered her up immediately, until all Andrew Warner's intoxicating but unwanted effects left her body and only the familiar, seething rage was left.

Oh, yes, she remembered…

The day the phone rang when she was fifteen. Mama's screams. The hushed whispers of relatives. The day, weeks later, when Daddy came home from the hospital, minus his right arm and his will to live. The day he started drinking.

Mama's constant tears, Daddy's shame as he tried, and failed, to dress himself, her parents' anger when the Warner family paid Daddy's medical bills, gave him a small settlement check, and sent him on his way to provide for his family as best he could.

And there were more painful memories.

The loss of their apartment and the laughter that had made the place a home. Daddy's alcoholism and early death from liver cancer. Mama's death the following year.

How many other accidents had occurred inside WarnerBrands factories before they finally shipped their operation overseas, where they could maim and kill without government interference? How many other lives had the Warners ruined? Hundreds? Thousands? Did the Warners know, or care?

They *would* know. Once Viveca got finished with them. That was why she was here. To expose their true nature.

She'd given up on revealing their unscrupulous business practices. They were too clever now, too powerful, and they knew how to walk the line and keep things just this side of legal.

But the soulless Warners had a soft underbelly—their personal lives. Viveca would expose them for the corrupt bastards they were, and she would do it with their help.

Viveca had waited, and worked, her whole life for this opportunity, become a reporter in the hopes of one day exposing the Warners for what they were. She'd neglected her personal life so she could work toward the chance to avenge her dead father, but it was worth it because she'd sold the book proposal.

How beautifully her plan was coming together.

"Viveca?"

Jarred back to the present, Viveca smiled and stood in time to see Mrs. Warner sweep in from the hallway.

"So nice to meet you, Mrs. Warner."

Willowy Arnetta Warner, trailing the light scent of jasmine, shook Viveca's hand in a bone-crushing grip that belied her seventy-plus years. Her piercing eyes were a light, icy brown that perfectly matched her twinset. Fat

Barbara Bush pearls offset her café-au-lait complexion and short, natural silver hair. She must have been quite a beauty back in her prime, Viveca thought. She'd seen ancient black-and-white photos of Mrs. Warner's graduation from Howard University, and they didn't begin to do her justice.

"So nice to meet *you,* Viveca." The sharp, crisp voice held only the vaguest hint of a Southern accent, but of course she'd left New Orleans more than half a century ago. "Sorry I kept you waiting. Is Franklin getting you some tea?"

"He is."

"Good." Mrs. Warner waved a diamond-laden hand at the sofa, and they sat. "I'm so excited about the book."

"So am I. I can't wait to get started."

"Take a day or two to get settled in the cottage. There's an office there, or you can work in here."

Mrs. Warner pointed to a desk in the corner, on top of which sat a banker's box filled, no doubt, with records. Viveca's pulse rate picked up as she saw the wealth of information waiting for her. Records hid skeletons, and she was skilled—and determined—enough to find them.

"You'll want to interview everyone, I assume?"

"Yes."

"My family bible is here, and Reynolds's over there." Mrs. Warner indicated the books stacked on the desk. "Mine is over a hundred years old."

"Oh, my."

"And I have other documents… Well, you'll see."

"You've been very thorough. That's wonderful."

Mrs. Warner smiled fondly up at her husband's portrait. "The Warner family has a proud history, and I—"

Without warning, the French door swung open, and

Andrew Warner stepped into the room, his girlfriend following while he held the door for her.

Viveca shrank back against the sofa cushions and paralysis set in.

They'd both managed to find more clothes, for which Viveca said a thousand silent thank-yous. The woman now wore a wispy sarong around her slim hips and the top of her bikini, although the cups only covered one-third of her breasts, if that.

Viveca wasn't too startled to notice that the white T-shirt covering Andrew's massive shoulders did nothing to hide his assets.

Smiling, he went straight to his grandmother and kissed her cheek. "Hello, Grandmother."

"Andrew." Arnetta frowned up at him. It wasn't a grumpy but affectionate frown, Viveca noticed, but the annoyed look of someone who'd glanced up to discover a muddy dog headed her way. "What are you doing here? Who's running my office?"

His smile widened, revealing no hint of concern. "It's Saturday. Every six months or so I like to take a day off."

"Maybe you're losing your edge."

Mrs. Warner's tone now carried a faint hint of a taunt, and Viveca wasn't the only one who noticed. Andrew's amusement evaporated and those wide shoulders squared, which was quite an impressive sight.

"Maybe I want a life."

Grandmother and grandson exchanged a chilly look that dropped the temperature in the room by at least thirty degrees.

"And who is *this?*" Mrs. Warner turned her assessing gaze on his girlfriend, who nervously adjusted the shoulder strap of her beach bag and flashed a toothy but pretty smile.

"This is my, ah, friend." Andrew drew the woman closer. "Grandmother, meet Brenda Jones."

Brenda had extended her hand to Mrs. Warner, but now her million-dollar smile faded and her face colored up like a lobster just out of the pot. "Jeffries, Andrew," she said in exactly the kind of breathy sex-kitten voice Viveca expected her to have. "Brenda *Jeffries*."

"*Jeffries*. Right." Andrew hung his head for a minute, managing to look as repentant as a choirboy on his way to confession. "Sorry, honey. My mistake."

Brenda uncompressed her lips, apparently deciding her two seconds of pouting had been more than enough punishment for Andrew. She smiled beatifically at him, but he'd already turned to Viveca.

Viveca wasn't ready.

By now, she'd had several seconds to adjust to his physical presence, but it hadn't been anywhere near long enough. Once he trained the high beams of his intense gaze on her, thinking even the most rudimentary thoughts became impossible. Whatever outrage she'd felt toward him on behalf of all womankind died a quick death.

She stared while her brain and knees turned to mush.

His face would have been pretty if not for the hard edge of barely contained ruthlessness about him, as though he'd only recently been civilized and would give society's rules a chance as long as they didn't interfere with his agenda. None of his features escaped perfection. Dark, curly hair, heavy brows, straight nose and X-rated body. A whole that was exponentially more than the sum of the parts.

Worst of all were the incredible midnight-blue eyes that Viveca knew were a gift from his biracial mother. Unbelievable eyes. Cynical, piercing, dangerous eyes with every bit of the intensity of his grandfather's. His lush, decadent mouth was designed for things she'd never experience and therefore didn't want to think about. A deep cleft in his chin kept him real and human.

Though she doubted her legs would support her, she stood up. It was the polite thing to do, but also a mistake. Up close, this close, his body heat, penetrating gaze and sheer size coalesced into a thrilling sexual cocktail she had no business noticing. Their gazes held, and in that moment there was nothing but him and the wild thrill of having his attention. Anything else was invisible and irrelevant.

She waited, heart thundering.

His discreet, thorough gaze slid over her filmy peach silk pantsuit, lingering for half a second on the hint of lacy camisole covering her cleavage. Viveca reminded herself that this meaningless inspection was the Andrew Warner equivalent of a dog peeing on every hydrant in the neighborhood—pure instinct, with no conscious thought—but she stood a little straighter anyway.

Finally he looked back into her eyes. His narrow-eyed, tight-jawed disdain made her wince. "Who are *you?*"

The dark, velvety tone called to mind endless, pleasure-filled nights. Swallowing hard, Viveca needed a moment to think. "Viveca Jackson."

"And you are…?"

"A reporter for the *New York Times.*"

"Really."

He studied her face, no doubt calculating and assessing. A beat or two passed while her cheeks flamed and she worried that he'd expose her as a Peeping Tom, which was no less than she deserved.

Finally he grunted a dismissal. Peeling his gaze away from Viveca, he took Brenda's arm and propelled her toward the door to the hallway. "Let's go. I'll walk you out."

"Andrew." Mrs. Warner sounded like the queen addressing a subject from her throne. "Don't leave. Since you're here, I want to tell you about my little project."

"Don't worry." His unreadable gaze returned to Viveca. "I'll be right back."

Undone, Viveca watched them leave and wondered how long her respite from Andrew would be.

"Andrew runs the company and chases women." Mrs. Warner oozed disapproval. "It's past time for him to find a nice girl from a good family and settle down. Do something with his life."

"Oh."

Viveca felt an odd pang of sympathy for Andrew, who ran his demanding grandmother's company and, according to *Fortune* magazine, did a darn fine job of it. Apparently, being CEO of a huge multinational corporation didn't qualify as "doing something with his life" in Mrs. Warner's book.

Keeping her jaws clamped shut, Viveca decided not to mention the obvious, that Andrew hardly acted like he was in the market for a bride. Which was just as well, since a man like him attracted women the way ice cream trucks attracted children. Viveca put the likelihood of him ever marrying and being a faithful husband well in the negative digits.

Just then Bishop returned carrying an elaborate porcelain teapot and service, which he settled on the coffee table. "Here we go."

"Thank you, Franklin," said Mrs. Warner.

Smiling placidly, he handed the women heavy linen napkins and poured tea into two paper-thin china cups. Mrs. Warner peeked inside a fragrant basket of steaming brown muffins and frowned.

"What's *this?*" Mrs. Warner made *this* sound as if Bishop had presented them with cow patties.

"Low-fat pumpkin muffins." Bishop smiled at Viveca as he passed her one of the cups on a saucer.

Mrs. Warner blinked at the muffins, possibly hoping she was seeing things. "I asked for cinnamon rolls today. With pecans. I told Cook."

"These are better for your heart." Bishop arranged the sugar and cream to his satisfaction and put muffins on plates for each of them.

"I don't want a low-fat pumpkin muffin." Mrs. Warner's frigid tone sounded vaguely plaintive now. "I want cinnamon rolls. Please bring them out."

"Okay."

Bishop's response was pleasant and immediate, but Viveca wasn't fooled. Watching him turn toward the door, she stifled a laugh, willing to bet her last dollar that Mrs. Warner would be waiting until the next ice age before Bishop showed up with any cinnamon rolls.

Viveca had just taken her first fortifying sip of tea when Andrew reappeared and clapped Bishop on the back.

"Hello, Scooter," Bishop said.

"Don't call me Scooter," Andrew said good-naturedly. He walked to the other end of Viveca's sofa and started to sit.

"Andrew." Mrs. Warner kept her head lowered as she added lemon to her tea. "You're not about to sit on my good sofa in those wet trunks, are you?"

Andrew froze, straightened, and gave her a mocking little bow. Selecting a straight-backed mahogany chair instead, he turned it around, straddled it and rested his forearms across the top.

"What a nice…*friend,* Andrew." Mrs. Warner sipped from her cup. "When does she get her driver's license?"

Viveca hastily took a sip of her own tea, scalding her tongue in her effort not to laugh. Andrew did laugh, and the sight of that thrilling, dimpled smile trapped Viveca's breath in her throat and sent sparks of heat skittering over her skin.

She looked away, determined not to stare again.

"Brenda's a little young, but she has her charms," he said.

"Yes." Mrs. Warner raised one eyebrow. "Two enormous charms."

Andrew laughed again. Viveca kept her gaze lowered.

"So what are you and Viveca Jackson cooking up, Grandmother?" All business now, he stared at Viveca with cool interest.

"Viveca's writing a biography about us."

Andrew's skin paled and his head whipped around to face his grandmother. "Like hell she is."

Chapter 2

The sudden sharpness in Andrew's voice startled both Viveca and Mrs. Warner, and they stared, openmouthed, at him.

Mrs. Warner recovered first. "Why *wouldn't* I do it? We have a proud history. Your grandfather took a little clothing store and turned it into a billion-dollar company. Other people have written about us. Why shouldn't we leave our record?"

"Personal lives are *personal*." Andrew, his face grim and tight, leapt up from his chair and paced in front of the coffee table. "Once you start opening the door and letting the press—"

"Viveca isn't wearing her reporter's hat, Andrew." Exasperation crept into Mrs. Warner's voice. "She's a biographer, not a tabloid hack. She's not here to draw blood. Why are you so against the project?"

"You can't trust a *reporter*." He pointed a finger at

Viveca as he spat the word out. "She'll lure you in, you'll tell her all of our business, she'll write some exposé on the lifestyles of the rich and famous or something, and then our reputation'll be ruined."

"Yes." Mrs. Warner dabbed at her lips with the napkin and then smoothed it across her lap. "And you wouldn't want to ruin *your* reputation, would you, Andrew?"

Andrew ignored the veiled reference to his womanizing. He stopped pacing and dropped to one knee in front of his grandmother's chair, crowding her crossed legs. "You need to think carefully about this." The raw urgency in his voice made the fine hairs on the back of Viveca's neck stand up. "These things never turn out like you expect."

"Now you listen to me." Mrs. Warner's icy tone left no room for argument. "She's already sold the proposal to a publisher. It's done. Eric supports the project. Why can't you?"

"Because I'm not your little puppet like my cousin is."

Viveca froze, not that anyone was paying any attention to her. Mrs. Warner and Andrew, both rigid with rage, stared at each other, locked in a silent battle of wills. Neither blinked.

"Eric has the good sense to pick his fights. That's something you haven't learned yet. Maybe it's time I gave Eric a shot at running the company."

Andrew didn't flinch. "Be my guest. If you think anyone else can show you the kind of profits I have, knock yourself out."

Her bluff thus called, Arnetta's face went beet red in a dead giveaway. Andrew was invaluable to the company and she knew it. Viveca silently awarded game, set and match to Andrew. Still, she had to hand it to the old woman, who seemed to have antifreeze flowing through her veins. Mrs. Warner recovered quickly. "The book is a done deal."

"No, it's not." Andrew sat back on his haunches and squared his jaw. He rose, pivoted and dropped back into his chair. "I'm going to stop you."

Mrs. Warner now looked supremely unconcerned as she sipped her tea. "Of course you won't. Viveca will want to interview all of us, and I expect you to cooperate."

Andrew's flaring nostrils and red face threatened imminent doom, as though they were in the final seconds of the countdown to his explosion. Watching the two of them, Viveca wanted to clap with glee. Only fifteen minutes into her stay and she'd already glimpsed at least two simmering rivalries—one between Andrew and his grandmother, and another between Andrew and his cousin, Eric.

She'd hit the mother lode with this family: seething emotions, jealousies, and competing agendas. Six months of this, and she'd have enough material for a six-volume set.

"I'm a good writer," Viveca told Andrew. "I've always tried to be very thorough and—"

He turned his frigid stare on her, choking off the end of her sentence. "I don't believe anyone was talking to you."

Viveca fumed and glared. What a miserable human being he was. Taking him down would be one of the highlights of her life.

"Oh, stop it, Andrew." Mrs. Warner stood, smoothed the bottom of her sweater and edged around the coffee table toward the door. "Viveca doesn't need to be attacked, and I have a meeting at eleven. So you'll just have to cause trouble some other time."

"This isn't over, Grandmother."

Mrs. Warner pretended she didn't hear him. "Viveca,

make yourself at home. Once you get moved into the cottage, you can set up in here. Feel free to explore a little if you want to. Andrew can show you around, if you can stand him for that long."

Andrew stiffened and glowered.

"Franklin will serve you lunch, and you'll eat dinner with us, of course," Mrs. Warner continued. "Dinner's at eight. Eric will be here, so you'll get to meet him. Oh, and my eightieth birthday party is coming up at the end of next month. Mark your calendar."

"I wouldn't miss it."

"I'll be back this afternoon."

Mrs. Warner looked over her shoulder at the muffin basket and Viveca felt the woman's silent battle. The older woman wavered between hunger and showing Franklin Bishop who was the boss in her house. Hunger apparently won. Mrs. Warner squared her shoulders, swiped a muffin and swept out of the room, her nose in the air.

Viveca would have laughed, except that Mrs. Warner's departure meant that she was now alone with Andrew, and that was a very bad thing. She experienced a strong prickle of unease, feeling vulnerable, like a lion cub whose mother had gone off to hunt.

She watched warily as Andrew unfolded that big body from his chair and came to stand in front of her. Swallowing her anger and ignoring her continued mortification— how could she have spied on him?—she tried a rueful smile and prayed it would work.

"I'm a little tired from my flight," she lied. "I'll just go to the cottage and unpack—"

"Oh, I don't think so." A slow, humorless smile turned up the left side of that amazing mouth, and she knew she was dead in the water. "We have a few things to talk about."

* * *

Though he'd been blindsided by news of this so-called book project, Andrew had already started to recover and to scheme. First on his agenda was getting rid of this woman, which was a shame.

The fascinating and beautiful Viveca Jackson, still flushed with embarrassment, didn't look any too happy to be alone with him, nor did she look as if she wanted to hop the next plane back to New York, but he didn't care.

Life as he knew it was at stake, and he would kill or die before he let this woman discover the truth. The secret he had to protect at all costs—he wasn't the Warner heir. Hell, he wasn't even a Warner.

His grandmother didn't know. If she did, she'd most likely disown him in favor of his cousin Eric, her favorite. Only Bishop knew his secret.

Everything Andrew had, and was, hung in the balance. WarnerBrands International, the company he'd nurtured and developed. His job as CEO. His inheritance of ninety million, give or take. His power, prestige and birthright. All could be gone in the blink of Viveca Jackson's pretty brown eye.

He'd never let that happen.

Though the job and the lifestyle had begun to suck him dry, he would never let them go. He was Andrew Warner, corporate titan, WarnerBrand International's savior, and that was all he was. Being Andrew Warner was his only reason for taking up space on the planet.

Fighting was in his blood, tainted though it was. So was winning. Diplomacy could work, though, so he'd give peace a chance…for about five minutes. Then he'd take off the kid gloves if he had to. One way or the other, though, he was throwing Viveca's shapely little butt back on a plane before the sun set tonight.

And that was unfortunate because, had circumstances been different, he would have liked to have gotten to know her much better.

To say he'd been surprised to look up and see her, poorly hidden behind the curtains, watching Brenda grope him, would be the understatement of the year. More surprising had been the naked heat he'd felt radiating from her in waves, as if she wished *she'd* been the one doing the groping.

They'd stared at each other for the longest, most sexually charged moment of his life. He'd caught a shadowy, unsatisfying glimpse of her wide eyes and pretty face. He'd seen enough of her ripe, curvy figure to see that it was shorter and fuller than Brenda's, but also God-given and not store-bought.

For that one moment out of time, he'd fantasized that the hand and bare breasts pressed so tightly against him had belonged to *her,* whoever *she* was.

The want had only intensified when he saw Viveca up close and got a good look at her numerous and remarkable assets. She had smooth caramel skin he desperately wanted to taste. A tumble of black corkscrew curls he wanted to touch. Dark cat eyes he wanted to make glaze over and close with ecstasy. Perfectly bowed lips he wanted to kiss and bite. A fantastic bounty hidden under that demure suit he wanted to claim.

But it wasn't meant to be. He had to get rid of her. Now.

Her fine brows flattened into a frown, and she abandoned her fake, sugary smile. "I don't think we have anything to talk about—"

"Then you can just listen."

"—and if you have something to say it can wait until later, can't it? It's not polite to—"

"Polite?" Intrigued, he gave in to the impulse to ruffle

her feathers. "You didn't seem all that worried about manners a few minutes ago when you were spying on my little, ah, private moment with Brenda."

Bingo. Her color rose until she looked as if she burned with a hundred-and-five-degree fever. She probably wanted to slink off and hide behind the sofa, but he knew, even before she raised her chin in defiance, that she was too proud to ever let him best her.

"I'm sorry about that." Her voice was cool with righteous disdain. "If I'd known I was stumbling onto a peep show, I wouldn't have glanced out at the pool."

"You barely knew there was a pool out there." He took a large step forward, breaching the invisible boundaries that surrounded her like a barbed-wire fence, and enjoyed the flare of panic behind her bright eyes even as she stood her ground. "Your attention was focused on other things, wasn't it?"

She winced but recovered quickly. "Not really." Taking all the time in the world, a study in nonchalance, she turned, picked up one of the framed family portraits from the side table and examined it. "I was just wondering if Brenda's, ah, *assets* work as flotation devices in the pool."

Audacity was, unfortunately, a quality he admired, as was courage. She seemed to have both in spades, and that attracted and irritated him.

"Really?" Trying not to smile, he needled her because she was so easy to provoke and so…*unexpected.* "I could've sworn you were staring at *me,* not Brenda."

Though she kept her head lowered over the picture, she went perfectly still and he knew his sharp little arrow had hit the bull's-eye again. She replaced the photo, and her gaze, furious and glittering now, flickered back up to his.

"You're very obnoxious, aren't you?"

"I say what I want." If she expected him to apologize, she could forget it. "I get what I want. Period. Remember that."

"Well, what do you want to talk about that's so important?" Abandoning all pretext of playing nice, she perched on the edge of the sofa, her back rigid, and glared.

"Well, Viveca." He sat on the chair nearest her, stretched out his legs and studied his nails. "As I mentioned earlier, I think this whole book project is a stupid idea and I want you to drop it."

"No."

"Why would you want to do it, anyway?" He needed to learn anything he could about her. "Working in New York at the *Times* has to be much more exciting."

"I've taken a leave of absence. I like writing nonfiction, and I'd like to move my career in that direction. This book is a huge coup for me. Any other questions?"

"What about the rest of your life?" A strange, unwelcome knot tightened in his gut as a new thought occurred to him. "Don't you have a husband or boyfriend—"

"My personal life is none of your business."

Annoyance surged. His position—as heir to a fortune and CEO of a *Fortune* 1000 company—entitled him to a certain amount of respect, and he usually got it. One quirked brow from him was generally enough to make men and women alike snivel like children. Why didn't she? Who was she that she thought she could talk to him this way in his grandmother's house?

"I don't see any rings. And if you were with me I wouldn't let you—"

"*Let me?* I'm a grown woman, in case you hadn't noticed."

Oh, he'd noticed. Her beautiful face and generous bosom, heaving now with anger, were constant reminders.

So was her faint, exotic scent, which reminded him of fruit, like Brenda's, but was otherwise a world apart. Brenda smelled like apples and cucumbers, but Viveca smelled like mangoes, coconuts and something more sensuous.

Resisting the strong urge to follow his nose into her hair or the smooth column of her neck was becoming harder by the second.

The frustration and deprivation pissed him off.

"Go home to New York." His jaw flexed and his teeth ground down around the words he didn't really want to say. "Work on something else."

"No." She got up and walked to the door.

He stood, too, and scanned through his limited options. Talking to his grandmother again would do no good, and if he knew anything at all about the Silver Fox, which he did, it would only make her dig in her heels even more. Ditto with trying to reason with Viveca. But…maybe throwing a little money at the problem would make it go away. Money spoke volumes, and he had plenty to spend.

"A hundred thousand."

Pausing, one heeled foot over the threshold into the hall, and one foot still in the library, she looked back at him. *"Excuse me?"*

"You can't be making that much as a reporter. I'll pay you a hundred K to drop the project. You can take the next plane out and be home by dinner."

It took her a while to get her jaw off the floor and splutter her outraged answer, but it finally came. "Maybe you're not up on current events, but I just told you I'm going to do the book."

"Two hundred, then."

Her searching gaze, narrowed and sharp, intensified. "Let me get this straight. You're willing to write me a check for two hundred thousand dollars just to get me to go away? Just like that?"

"That's right."

"Why not three?"

Irritation tied all his muscles into tight little pulsating knots, but blowing up at her was not an option, no matter how badly he wanted to. If he lost his temper, she'd write the damn book just to spite him.

"Think of everything you could do with this money, Viveca." He kept his voice reasonable and soothing. "Travel. Save. Buy a vacation house in the Hamptons."

She tilted her head, studying him, and he started to believe she was actually considering his proposal. But then one side of her mouth hitched up into a disquieting, calculating smile. His hopes sank.

"No one's ever tried to bribe me before. It makes me wonder what you're hiding."

Keeping his face blank while he lied, not blinking or looking away from that piercing, brown-eyed gaze, was one of the hardest things he'd ever done. "I'm not hiding anything. I just think my grandmother isn't quite up to a project like this at her age."

"Is that right?"

"She had that heart attack last year, and I think she's biting off more than she can chew. And I don't trust you not to sensationalize our story to try to sell a few extra books."

The half smile slipped from her face and was replaced by a glare so chilling he was amazed he didn't see little puffs of steam from her breath when she spoke again.

"There's something you should know about me, *Andrew*." She squared her shoulders and enunciated each syllable with military precision. "I don't take bribes. Here's something else you should know. I don't back down from challenges. Oh, and here's one more thing. You're really pissing me off."

He watched her with anger, fascination and unwilling admiration. She was quite a woman, and he was sorry they were on opposite sides of this issue. Long after he'd put her on a plane back to New York, he'd wonder what those lips tasted like, how soft her thighs were and what she'd say next.

"I like you, Viveca." He meant it, and it wasn't just the lust talking, either, which disturbed him. He crept closer, irresistibly drawn to those wide, dark eyes. "You're heading down the wrong path with this book, and I'm going to stop you, one way or the other, but it's not personal."

"I don't care whether you like me or not."

He laughed, both because he couldn't help it and because he couldn't remember when he'd had this much fun sparring with someone.

Viveca's breath hitched and her gaze lingered on his face—his mouth—giving him the small satisfaction of knowing that underneath the cool facade, she wasn't immune to him.

More than that, she wanted him. He'd seen the signs often enough in his life to know what they meant—her breathlessness, bright eyes and husky voice all screamed that she wanted him, even if she didn't like him.

Realizing this, and considering how explosive a night in bed with Viveca Jackson would be, his secret suddenly seemed less important.

He inched closer. He noticed the way her breasts heaved as she tried to get her erratic breathing under control, and need tightened his gut.

"Any other time, Viveca, I'd really enjoy getting you to like me, too."

"What's to like?"

Laughing again, he said, "Most women can find something."

"Yes, well, I'm not most women, and I'm certainly not *Brenda*—"

"I can see that."

"—and your little smile doesn't work with me."

"You noticed my smile?"

He knew this was another direct hit because her cheeks flamed. His mind, which was having a very difficult time staying on task this morning, veered off again.

So much passion in this one woman. Right now she'd like to use it to smash his grinning face, sure, but what other uses could he find for it?

"I'm leaving." She brushed by him on her way to the door.

That inadvertent but electrifying contact with Andrew's body sealed her fate. Rational thought went out the window, replaced by hot lust and blind need. If there was some option available to him other than touching her, he couldn't think what it was.

"No, you're not."

Reaching out, he caught her arm and swung her lightly around. The momentum brought her up against his chest, and he greedily latched on, holding tight around her waist and ignoring her startled squeak.

Reeling, intoxicated with the feel of her, he tried to think.

"Viveca…I really need to…"

The words trailed off because it was way too hard to speak when she was in his arms. Lowering his head until his lips hovered half an inch from hers, he spent a moment drowning in her wide, surprised eyes. Her hot, sweet breath feathered his mouth as she panted. Realizing he'd made her that excited, he hardened to full readiness and waited.

He wouldn't take; she had to give.

After a moment's hesitation, she closed her eyes and surrendered.

When she mewled helplessly and tipped her chin up that last fraction of an inch to meet him, he shuddered with triumph and the kind of raw excitement that could knock a grown man to his knees.

Before she could change her mind, he kissed her.

Chapter 3

The kiss raged out of control from the moment of contact. Frenzied, hot, wet, it consumed him with a heat he'd never experienced before and didn't know what to do with now.

He clung to her, more than half out of his mind.

She didn't tell him no, so he let his hands do what they wanted, which was everything. He ran them over the slippery silk covering the arc of her back then up into the cottony softness of those curls at her nape, across her warm satiny cheeks and back into her hair again, tilting her head so he could deepen the kiss the way he needed to.

It wasn't enough. He had to touch her…taste her…possess her.

The pleasure was bottomless. Strong enough to kill him. Too strong to endure and come out the other side in one piece. And then it was gone.

That warm, supple body went rigid beneath his fingertips, and she wrenched away. Horror widened her eyes, and one of her hands flew up to cover her mouth.

Yeah, he couldn't quite believe it, either, he thought, looking away. Not the heat between them, or the fever for her that still burned white hot in his blood. A full, painful erection taunted him, demanding a relief that wouldn't come. Worst of all, he suspected that if she smiled and crooked her little finger at him, he'd happily sign his fortune over to Eric.

If only she'd let him make love to her. If only she'd give herself to him with the passion she'd just shown. Damn, he was seriously screwed.

None of this made any sense. He wasn't a teenager, nor was he over—or *under*—sexed. He'd been pleasantly anticipating sex today with Brenda, a woman he'd had his eye on for a while. Now, though, Brenda had lost all appeal and looked about as appetizing as a peanut-butter-and-salami sandwich on rye. One glimpse of Viveca and Brenda was forgotten, her last name deleted from his memory banks.

That was a scary commentary on Viveca's power over him. Scarier was the fact that his every muscle—every nerve ending—still vibrated with frustrated tension.

What had this complete stranger—this *enemy*—done to him? He never lost control. *Never.* Not over his mind or his actions, and certainly not over his vastly experienced body.

This could never happen again. Whatever it took, he had to get rid of her. Reacting on pure instinct, desperate to douse the spark of panic that had flared deep in the pit of his belly, he turned back to her, smirked and said the first hurtful thing that came to mind.

"Why don't I take you home with me for a couple of hours? I can give you something to remember Columbus by before I put you on a plane back to New York."

That beautiful face contorted with fury as she cried out. Her hand came up and, before he could even blink, she slapped him hard across the face.

"Rough can be sexy, too." Manufacturing a smile, he rubbed his jaw and shrugged. "Whatever you want is fine with me, Viveca."

They stared at each other. Actually, Viveca glared and he imprinted her face on his memory because he knew he'd never see her again and didn't want to forget anything about her.

"*Bastard*," she said, finally.

That was the funniest thing he'd heard all day. "You have no idea."

Agitated, confused and disgusted with herself, Viveca spent the afternoon unpacking in the antiques-filled cottage and trying to forget the lust for Andrew Warner that still throbbed in her lips, breasts, belly and sex.

The humiliation she'd felt when he issued his leering, insulting invitation was exactly what she deserved for being such an idiot. Within half an hour of laying eyes on him, she'd had the two most embarrassing moments of her entire life, and she was no better than the simpering, brainless Brenda.

To make matters worse, she was positive that she and the kiss meant nothing to him. No doubt he'd already forgotten about it and had scheduled a romantic Saturday night with Brenda or someone else like her.

The thought made her want to smash things, but she would get over it. She would avoid Andrew and execute her plan. Period.

At exactly seven-fifty, when dusk had just begun to fall, Viveca left the cottage and took the cobblestone path back to the main house. Over the sound of her footsteps, she heard a car engine die, and when she got to the intersection of the path and the driveway, she saw a tall man in dark pants and a blue dress shirt get out of a black Mercedes SUV.

She realized right away that he must be Eric Warner. He was the son of Mrs. Warner's second son, Gifford, and therefore Andrew's cousin. Seeing her, he turned, smiled and waved.

Why this one family should be blessed with two such astonishingly handsome men when there were so many unattractive people in the world, Viveca didn't know. But if Andrew Warner was the best-looking man she'd ever seen, Eric Warner was a close second.

The cousins couldn't be more different; Andrew was moody and fair, but Eric was dark and smiling, with a black skull trim, mustache and goatee, and walnut skin. He had his grandmother's light brown eyes, and his flashing smile was as warm and open as Andrew's was arrogant and suspicious.

His body was another long-legged, wide-shouldered, X-rated dream.

"Viveca?" He strode toward her with his hand outstretched, managing to convey so much delight one would have thought he'd discovered an abandoned satchel stuffed with thousand-dollar bills.

"Yes." Smiling—how could she not smile with such a greeting—Viveca shook his hand. "I'm so glad to meet you."

Before either of them could say anything else, another car, a dark Maybach sedan, half a million dollars' worth of vehicle, raced up the driveway and screeched to a halt several feet from them. Viveca's pulse kicked back into overdrive.

The engine died and Andrew, glowering as usual, got out and surveyed the scene, then walked around to the back passenger-side door and opened it to let out a young boy of about eight.

"Who's that?" Viveca whispered to Eric.

"A boy he mentors. He's in foster care."

"Oh." This incontrovertible evidence that Andrew Warner had a heart after all had the perverse effect of making Viveca feel sulky.

The boy wore jeans and a T-shirt and had curly black hair. He wore glasses and had his nose stuck deep into one of those handheld computer games. Without looking to see where he was or where he was going, he submitted while Andrew put a hand on his shoulder and steered him in their direction. His small thumbs fluttered over the beeping game like a hummingbird's wings.

Andrew held Viveca in his sights as he approached. With each passing second, his expression grew darker until finally he seemed to be nothing but a pair of angry, slashing dark brows and a scowling mouth attached to a body. He looked as if he meant to kick someone's—or maybe every-one's—butt.

Viveca braced for the worst.

Well, no.

First she registered how spectacular he looked.

Then she braced for the worst.

He'd dressed in a starched white dress shirt and dark trousers, what should have been a forgettable outfit but somehow wasn't. She was glad he'd changed out of his swimming trunks and managed to cover up that chest and those shoulders, but his current attire was no improve-ment in the sexiness department. It was worse.

If he ever wore a tuxedo she'd have to run for cover.

As he came closer, she saw that he'd ruthlessly tamed all those thick black curls, which were flecked here and there with gray. His intoxicating cologne, which the breeze carried straight to her unsuspecting and unprepared nostrils, was a potent combination of spice and musk designed solely to seduce.

"What's up, Nathan?" Smiling at the boy, Eric held up a hand for a high five.

"'Sup?" The boy, never looking up from his little computer screen, held up one hand and smacked Eric's palm.

"This is Viveca," Eric told him.

"'Sup?" Nathan said again.

"Ah," Viveca stammered. Forcing herself to look away from Andrew, she smiled at the boy. "Nice to meet you."

"You, too."

"What's up, man?" Eric said to Andrew.

Grunting in the general direction of his cousin, Andrew focused on Viveca. She resigned herself to the impending inspection, dreading the effect she knew it would have on her overheated body, but it was worse than she'd expected. Despite all her best efforts to remain impervious to all things Andrew Warner, something awakened deep in her belly, and it was delicious and fluttery and overwhelming.

Andrew's hard, glittering gaze took a ruthless inventory as it flickered over her body, noting the sleeveless little black dress with wide straps over her bare shoulders, square neckline that showed more than a hint of cleavage, knee-skimming hemline and sexy sandals. He absorbed it all, every tiny detail, with excruciating thoroughness.

Finally he looked her in the face and his flashing eyes told her he wanted to wring her neck. "What the hell are you still doing here?"

"Walking to dinner."

"I told you to leave."

"Oh, I remember." She kept her tone cheerful and

smiled because she knew it would infuriate him. "I decided not to. I don't need a vacation home in the Hamptons."

Bull's-eye.

His cheeks took on a ruddy flush; his nostrils flared; his jaw pulsed.

Energy, hot and dangerous, vibrated between them. Though it should have been entirely negative and asexual—just hate, nothing more—it wasn't. Not even close.

It dawned on her then, a realization of the worst possible kind—she'd learned nothing since kissing him this afternoon. Despite everything she'd told herself, all the stern warnings she'd recited in her head about the evils of Andrew Warner, she wasn't immune to him.

"This isn't over, Viveca."

He wasn't just talking about his attempts to get her to stop researching the book, and she knew it. *This* meant so much more—the chemistry between them, his attempts at seduction and her unwilling and uncontrollable response to him.

This meant all of the things she'd hoped to avoid.

Against all reason, goose bumps shivered over her skin, and she cursed Andrew Warner for causing them. Satan incarnate couldn't be this tempting or thrilling. This was not about seduction, she told herself.

It was about justice, and she wouldn't forget that.

"No." Raising her chin and preparing for the fight yet to come, she agreed with him for what she suspected would be the last time ever. "Not even close."

Turning her attention to Nathan, she tried to pretend Andrew didn't exist.

Chapter 4

Dismissed.

Andrew stared at Viveca's bare, toned back and tried to remember when in his life anyone had had the balls to dismiss or snub him. *Never.*

What a piece of work she was, chattering and laughing with Eric and Nathan, challenging Andrew, staying when he'd told her to go, wearing a dress sexy enough to make a grown man drool.

Was this a joke? A reporter dismissing him?

Who the hell did she think she was?

And why did he feel something suspiciously like relief to see her still here?

Unfortunately, he wasn't as good at ignoring Viveca as she was at ignoring him. Watching her inspect Nathan's Game Boy, Andrew was vaguely aware of Eric coming to stand beside him, arms crossed, an amused, annoying grin on his face.

"You've got a problem with Viveca?" asked Eric.

"I've got several problems with her."

Eric laughed. "What's the big deal about the book?"

"I think it's a bad idea. Private lives should stay private. Once you open that door to the public, you can't shut it again. Everything becomes fair game. Plus Grandmother's health isn't all that great, so—"

"Her health is fine."

"—I'm not going to cooperate."

"Interesting." Eric's appreciative gaze stayed on Viveca, lingering too long for casual interest as far as Andrew was concerned. "She's not that hard to look at, though, is she?"

Andrew grunted, not liking the direction the conversation was taking.

"I, for one, plan to enthusiastically cooperate with anything Viveca wants."

Eric grinned the kind of shifty grin that made jealous husbands look for their shotguns, and Andrew went still while some strange new emotion washed over him. It was hot and cold at the same time, fierce, primitive and overwhelming.

He didn't like feeling it. Not at all.

Turning, he stared at his younger cousin. Eric was probably what would pass for his best friend—if he had close friends, which he didn't—but just as frequently Eric was the bane of his existence. His chief rival, the constant thorn in his side, the competition always nipping at his heels trying to gain on him.

He went to Phillips Exeter, Eric went to Choate. He went to Yale, Eric went to Princeton. They both got MBAs. He became CEO of the company, and Eric was senior vice president, waiting…always waiting for his chance, his call to move up to the big league.

Grandmother made no bones about the fact that Eric

was her favorite and she didn't give a damn that Andrew was the oldest male grandchild, the anointed one.

As for women, well, they were fair game in the perpetual contest between them. There'd been a time or two when they'd both had their eye on the same woman, and it was each man for himself. If Eric won the prize, Andrew didn't really care because there'd never been anything that special about a woman, and there was always another one willing to hop into his bed the second he smiled at her.

Andrew had made peace with these facts about his life years ago, and had no problems with competition. The world thrived on it, and so did he.

What Andrew was feeling now, though, had nothing to do with competition and everything to do with the fact that he would skin Eric alive and feed the bleeding strips of his flesh to the giant goldfish in Grandmother's pond if Eric so much as accidentally brushed a corner of Viveca's dress with his hand.

Unsmiling, he held his cousin's gaze so that Eric got it and there could be no later claims of confusion or misunderstanding. Keeping his voice level and civilized when such primal feelings wanted to run free was difficult but he managed it as he pleasantly told Eric something he'd never told him—or anyone—before.

"She's off-limits."

Eric's jaw dropped and he gaped as if Andrew had started speaking Cantonese. When he recovered his shock, he apparently decided, as Andrew had known he would, that he didn't like being told what to do, and squared his shoulders, spoiling for a fight. "Who says?"

"I say."

There was nothing special about his inflection, and

Andrew didn't raise his voice by so much as half a decibel, but it didn't matter.

Eric, getting the message—that there was violence in his immediate future if he looked twice at Viveca—held his hands up in surrender and stood down. "Knock yourself out." An amused grin worked at his lips.

Adrenaline still pumping, Andrew thought that maybe a fight was just what he needed. They were pretty evenly matched, and throwing a punch or two would go a long way toward lessening his frustration with the book project, Viveca and, most of all, himself. "Just so we're clear."

Eric, to his surprise and growing irritation, shook his head, grinned and spoke with exaggerated concern. "You poor guy."

Yeah, Andrew thought savagely. *A fight would be real good.*

Except that Viveca had just wrapped up her conversation with Nathan and turned back to them.

"Well," she said brightly to Eric, gifting him with a spontaneous smile that was more spectacular than the pink-and-purple-streaked sunset on the horizon. For Andrew she had only an annoyed sidelong glance that, Andrew supposed, was an improvement over being completely ignored. "Should we go inside? I'm starving."

Eric smiled back at her.

Andrew wanted to kill both of them: Eric for receiving such a smile and her for giving it. Especially when Andrew knew she'd never in a million millennia smile at *him* that way.

"Let's go," he barked, trying to take charge of the situation if not his runaway hormones. "Grandmother'll be mad if we're late."

Eric and Viveca exchanged a silent, raised-eyebrow,

what-a-jerk look that had Andrew's temper flaring like a sun spot. Keeping his expression bland, he fought the urge to shove his smirking cousin away from Viveca and face-first into the row of hedges lining the driveway. With one hand on Nathan's shoulder, Andrew led the procession toward the house.

Before they got to the path leading to the front door, though, another car turned into the lengthy drive. Recognizing it, Andrew's heart sank like Atlantis to the bottom of the ocean.

Only one person in the world, as far as he knew, drove a car like that—a custom-painted, pale pink Porsche Carrera, an abomination of every unwritten vehicular standard of taste and respect.

The car stopped and Brenda got out, unfolding her long-legged body from the low-slung car like a giraffe climbing out of a Radio Flyer wagon. Slipping off her enormous dark sunglasses and the colored scarf she'd had wrapped around her head, she swept toward them, grinning.

"Hi, baby." Throwing her arms around him, she kissed him wetly on the cheek with her red lips, leaving a smudge of lipstick that felt like an oil slick. "Am I late?"

Andrew, Eric, Nathan and Viveca all gawked at her.

Maybe it was the car. Maybe it was the blue dress, which was filmy, low-cut and tight. Maybe it was the platform stilettos, which might have been all the rage in New York and L.A., but which would scratch Grandmother's gleaming hardwood floors.

For Andrew it was surprise, twenty percent of which was because he hadn't expected her, and eighty percent of which was because he couldn't believe he'd found her attractive as recently as that morning. Whatever the reason, he couldn't get his tongue to work.

"Ah," he said finally, pulling her off to the side, aware of their audience watching them with open curiosity. "Hi. What're you doing here?"

"Well, remember when I called you earlier, and you said you couldn't get together tonight because of this dinner?"

"Yeah."

"Sooo…I invited myself." She beamed as though she'd presented him with the best gift imaginable. "Since this is my last night in town. Bishop told me I was always welcome."

"I…see."

Andrew cursed Bishop and himself. He had planned to call her tomorrow and meet her for breakfast or coffee. He would have told her that while he had enjoyed their interlude together, he was way too busy for any kind of relationship. He'd go his way, she'd go hers and that'd be that, or so he'd thought.

Now here she was, showing up with an appetite and expectations about the future that he had no intentions of fulfilling. Not to mention the fact that getting through a dinner with her and Viveca at the same table would be weird, to say the least.

Plus Brenda was a dingbat of the highest magnitude, a quality that hadn't mattered when he'd planned to keep her busy in bed, where communication skills were optional. Sitting across the dinner table from her, trying to carry on a conversation, was a different kettle of fish altogether. Given his choice, he'd sooner jam fork tines under his fingernails. But he didn't have any choices and was stuck, stuck, *stuck*.

Her megawatt smile faltered. "You don't mind, do you?"

"Not at all," he lied, thinking, among other things, of Grandmother's impending horror when she saw Brenda enter her house in that getup. "Let's go."

They all turned up the path and he glanced at Viveca, who was still ignoring him.

But then fortune smiled on him a little and he received his only consolation for what was sure to be an awkward evening. A vivid flush was spreading across Viveca's cheeks, almost as if she were jealous.

Viveca found herself sandwiched between Eric and Bishop at the enormous table, which was set with china and crystal so fine it would have passed muster at a White House state dinner. Across from her sat Andrew, Brenda and Nathan. Mrs. Warner presided at the head of the table.

It was an exquisite setting, all romance, elegance and class. It was perfection, the portrait of family unity and Southern hospitality until Viveca remembered one crucial fact—everyone here, with the possible exceptions of Nathan and Bishop, disliked at least one of the other guests.

Andrew, for instance, regarded Viveca with unconcealed animosity, the personification of brooding irritation. There was not one second of the interminable evening that she didn't feel his intense gaze on her face.

"I hope you like baked potato soup, Viveca."

Mrs. Warner, ever the gracious hostess, smoothed her linen napkin on her lap and gave Viveca a beatific smile. Viveca caught herself glancing at Andrew, gave herself a stern warning to ignore him, and smiled back at Mrs. Warner. "I love it."

"Wonderful. Here it is now. We'll follow it up with a nice medium-rare filet." Mrs. Warner looked around as a server marched in from the kitchen carrying a tureen. With a flourish, the server raised the lid, ladled some soup and poured it into Brenda's bowl.

It was red.

Mrs. Warner gaped at the bowl, putting Viveca in mind of Pharaoh seeing the Nile River run with blood for the first time, and then the old woman's lips thinned to a razor's edge.

"Bishop." She turned to the man Viveca had already realized was more a member of the family than a servant. "What happened to the baked potato soup?"

Bishop, who'd been enjoying his roll, dabbled a little more apple butter on it and took his own sweet time about chewing. After what seemed like ten minutes, he looked up and lowered his knife.

"Well," he drawled, "I had Cook take out the potatoes and the cheese and the sour cream and the bacon and put in some tomatoes and some onions and some—"

Mrs. Warner's nostrils flared ominously. "This is *gazpacho*."

"I reckon it is," said Bishop. "Better for your heart."

Mrs. Warner glared at Bishop, who ignored her and went back to his roll. When the server crept forward and ladled soup in Mrs. Warner's bowl, Mrs. Warner leaned back in her chair and gave the gazpacho a narrowed glance, as though she'd been given a big scoop of vomit.

The server, looking nervous but relieved that he'd survived the dangerous mission of serving his boss unwanted food, scurried back through the double doors into the kitchen, where it was safer.

After a long moment spent staring down at her bowl, Mrs. Warner overcame this blow to her dignity and appetite. She cleared her throat, reached for her spoon and took a bite.

The signal to begin the course thus given, Viveca and the others exchanged discreet glances, kept their heads lowered to hide their smiles, and commenced eating.

"Tomatoes are good for you." Nathan, who'd finally put down his Game Boy, spoke happily to the table at large in between loud slurps of soup. "They have antioxidants. That's good for cancer. But did you know tomatoes are fruits—"

"Well, I—" said Mrs. Warner.

"—because they have seeds on the *inside?* Not the *outside.*"

"Oh, *no.*" Brenda, looking startled and swallowing hard, grabbed her napkin and wiped her mouth. With apparent embarrassment, she gave a quick smile and leaned closer to Andrew to speak in his ear. "My soup is cold," she said in a stage whisper.

Andrew's cheeks colored. For some unaccountable reason, his gaze flickered across the table to Viveca and then skittered away. "It's supposed to be cold."

"Oh." Brenda gave her bowl a dubious look.

Viveca focused on her soup and tried not to snort.

Next to her, Eric sniggered. "Andrew likes 'em smart," he whispered.

Viveca choked back a laugh. "What about you?"

"Let's just say my best friend in college, Izzy, carried me."

"Is that right?"

"I'd've flunked without her. No doubt."

"Viveca." Mrs. Warner's voice was loud and determined as she turned away from Brenda, who was now dubiously swirling her spoon through her soup. No doubt Mrs. Warner meant to restore some dignity to her dinner party even if it killed her. "I've been wondering about your family."

Viveca froze, her spoon hovering in midair. "My family?"

"Yes. Are you related to Senator Jackson? He's a dear friend of ours."

Viveca blinked. *Was this a joke?* "Uh, no."

"We have a senator in our family, you know. Jonathan Warner. He'll probably run for president."

"That's wonderful," Viveca said.

"Hmmm." Mrs. Warner's brow furrowed. "What about Dr. Peter Jackson, the chief of surgery at Columbia Presbyterian? I served on the ballet board with him when he lived in Columbus. Any relation?"

"No."

Undaunted, Mrs. Warner plowed ahead. "The Vernon Jacksons of Atlanta?"

Viveca had been teetering between amusement and annoyance, but now annoyance won by a nose. Was this how the other half operated? By examining guests' pedigrees before serving them their entrees? If Viveca told her the truth, that her family was poor, would she get Spam instead of the promised filet?

"No." Viveca raised her chin. "I'm from the Brownsville Jacksons in Brooklyn."

"I...see." Looking pensive, Mrs. Warner took a sip of her soup.

The sarcasm was obviously lost on her, as were Viveca's defiance and wounded pride. Viveca could almost see the wheels turning in the woman's mind, almost hear her thoughts—*Brownsville...Brownsville...is that near Park Avenue?*

Cheeks burning with repressed anger, Viveca reached for the iced-tea pitcher and caught Andrew watching her. *For the love of God, why was he always watching her?*

"Ignore her," Eric muttered in Viveca's ear between spoonfuls of soup. "It's not like she came over on the *Mayflower.*"

Viveca shot him a grateful smile and nodded. Andrew frowned at them.

"And what do you do, Brenda?" Having realized Viveca was a peon of no social importance, Mrs. Warner evidently decided to give Brenda a chance. Turning to the woman, who now seemed to be enjoying her gazpacho, Mrs. Warner favored her with a cool smile.

Brenda brightened under the attention and spoke with an unmistakable note of pride in her voice. "I'm a hand model."

Silence.

Mrs. Warner, Viveca and Eric exchanged discreet, uncomprehending glances. Andrew, looking as though he wanted the sleek hardwood floor to open up and swallow him whole, rested his head against the back of his chair, closed his eyes and shook his head. Nathan crunched enthusiastically on a slice of celery.

Several beats passed before Mrs. Warner recaptured her placid smile and asked the obvious question. "A…*hand* model, did you say?"

"Yeah. You know." Grinning, Brenda raised her hands up by her face, flicked her wrists with a dramatic flourish and presented Mrs. Warner with ten perfectly manicured, waggling fingers. "I model in print ads and commercials. Rings, mostly, but also lotion. Oh, and dish liquid. That's a big source of income for me."

"I…see." Mrs. Warner reached for her wine goblet and took a generous sip.

"My fingers are really long and thin, and I don't have knobby knuckles." Brenda lowered her hands and examined them with a loving eye. "I have to take good care of them. Lots of moisturizing, no dishwashing, no letter-opening. A paper cut would just be tragic."

"I can imagine." Eric nodded with rapt attention, but one corner of his mouth twitched. Seeing this, Viveca bit the inside of her cheek and fought not to laugh.

Andrew, his eyes still closed, gave his head another infinitesimal shake.

"I'm shooting a commercial this week," Brenda concluded.

"How nice for you, dear." Smiling weakly, Mrs. Warner drained her goblet and reached for the wine bottle cooling in its bucket.

Viveca watched as Andrew opened his eyes and, turning, studied Brenda with an unreadable expression. Brenda was busy smiling at Mrs. Warner and didn't notice, but Viveca certainly did. An ugly feeling twisted to life in her gut. She told herself it wasn't jealousy, but if it *wasn't,* why did she suddenly want to take the nearest fork and spear it through Brenda's perfectly smooth hand?

Just then Andrew looked over the table at Viveca and their gazes locked.

Thinking of how he'd kissed her this afternoon, nearly made her come just from the strength of her lust for him, and how he'd no doubt be having sex with Brenda later that night, Viveca silently cursed him.

Just then, a new distraction arrived in the form of that same beleaguered server bringing in the entrée and setting it on the table. The poor man lifted the platter's lid gingerly, as though he were afraid it covered an armed nuclear warhead waiting to take them all out. Underneath was a lovely arrangement of some sort of white fish with a cream sauce and capers. It did not look like filet mignon.

Mrs. Warner had also noticed this discrepancy. Catching the server squarely in her sights, she glowered at him while Andrew reached for a fork and began loading Nathan's plate.

"I'll just, ah…" The server gestured over his shoulder

toward the kitchen and then, abandoning all pride, turned, broke into a trot and disappeared back through the swinging door.

With this victim gone, Mrs. Warner turned and focused her Glare of Death on Bishop, who sipped his wine, unperturbed. "Bishop."

Bishop smacked his lips and looked around at her, his eyes widening as though he were surprised to discover that anyone else was at the table with him. "Yes?"

"What happened to my filet?"

Bishop craned his neck, peering at the platter. "Looks like filet of fish to me."

Mrs. Warner rested an elbow on the table, lowered her head, closed her eyes and pinched the bridge of her nose. After three beats she opened her eyes and spoke to Bishop in a voice that was calm, but barely audible.

"You know perfectly well," she said, "that I ordered *steak* for dinner."

"Oh, you don't want steak." Bishop, ever the gentleman, served Viveca a filet, and then took one for himself. "Try some of this nice Dover sole."

Mrs. Warner gaped at him while everyone else tried not to smile.

This was, Viveca thought, the funniest dinner she'd ever attended.

There were a few minutes of blessed silence during which everyone filled their plates and began to eat. Viveca knew the peace couldn't last, but it was nevertheless something of a shock when Mrs. Warner spoke to her again.

"Did I read that you went to Columbia, Viveca, dear? I know you went to school in New York."

Viveca cringed but managed to plaster a smile on her face. "I did. I went to Baruch College."

Mrs. Warner gave her another one of those politely puzzled looks. "I don't believe I've heard of it."

"It's part of the New York City university system."

Mrs. Warner gasped, no doubt having put two and two together and realizing that Viveca had gone to a public school. "But you went to Columbia for graduate school," she persisted.

"Grandmother," Andrew said. Eric coughed and Bishop cleared his throat.

Viveca had had enough. She put her fork down, wiped her mouth and replaced her napkin in her lap. When she was done with that, she held her head high, drew her line in the sand and dared Mrs. Warner to cross it.

"Mrs. Warner," she said, keeping a pleasant smile in place, "you're going to have to get used to the idea that my family isn't old or famous or wealthy. We were poor. My mother did people's hair and my father worked in a factory. We lived in a pitiful little apartment that was smaller than this dining room."

Mrs. Warner's face turned red. "Oh, I didn't mean—"

"I worked two jobs and barely scraped up enough money for public college, and then I did it again for public graduate school. I was not born with a silver spoon in my mouth, and I did not have an Ivy League education."

It occurred to Viveca then that she was the center of attention and should probably shut up, but she had no intention of sitting by quietly while the old woman tried in vain to find something socially redeeming about her.

"I guess what I'm saying, Mrs. Warner, is that I'm not ashamed of my humble beginnings and I hope they don't bother *you*."

Though she was the world's biggest snob, Mrs. Warner, like most snobs, would die a million violent deaths before she'd admit it. Stammering only slightly, her color high, she emitted a tinkling laugh that didn't suit her at all.

"My dear," she said, reverting to gracious hostess mode, "we all have humble roots if you look back far enough."

With that, Mrs. Warner reached for her fork and dove into her Dover sole.

"Nice," Eric murmured in Viveca's ear, but Viveca barely heard him because her attention was now riveted on Andrew who had, she knew, listened to her little speech with rapt attention, his goblet of wine hovering near his lips. There was no mistaking the admiration in Andrew's half smile, or the new respect shining in his eyes as he raised his goblet an inch or two in a private toast, just for her.

The act was so warm, so intimate, that everything else fell away and only the two of them and their secret messages and yearnings were left in the world. Viveca almost felt as though he'd trailed his fingers low across her belly, or opened his mouth over her breast. A delicious shiver skittered up her spine.

Holding her gaze, he drank, exposing the strong, smooth column of his throat.

Viveca felt a responsive ache of longing, one so powerful that reminding herself how much she hated him did absolutely nothing to dispel it.

Chapter 5

After dinner, Andrew got rid of Brenda as gently and firmly as he could, a task that Brenda didn't make easy. All during the excruciating conversation, he told himself that dumping Brenda had nothing to do with Viveca, but it was a lie. The juxtaposition during dinner, of Brenda's flakiness with Viveca's beauty, grace and unshakable pride and courage, had only sealed Brenda's fate. Not that he had freed himself to pursue Viveca. He hadn't.

But…drawn like iron shavings to a magnet, he went to wait for Viveca. The cottage looked cozy tonight with its fluttering curtains and interior lights glowing with warmth. Through one mullioned window he glimpsed the table in the kitchen and had the rogue thought that he wanted to sit there and eat dinner with Viveca. Through another he saw the bedroom with its enormous, fluffy wrought-iron bed, and had the forbidden but delicious thought that he wanted to be in it with a willing, passionate Viveca. Desperately wanted, but he wouldn't think about that now.

He climbed onto the porch and sank into the creaky white wicker swing to wait and outline a revised plan, which was simple.

He would cooperate with the book after all.

Having had a few hours to think about it, he'd decided he'd overreacted with the whole *bribe her to go back to New York* tactic. Surrendered to his knee-jerk reaction when he should have kept his wits about him.

Now he'd calmed down and looked at the situation with a cool head. What was the big deal, really? None. Let her investigate all she wanted. She wouldn't find anything. To the best of his knowledge, which was pretty good, only two living people knew the true story of his paternity, and neither he nor Bishop was talking.

So let Viveca do her worst; she couldn't hurt him.

As an insurance policy, he could hire a private detective to check out Viveca. Just in case worse came to worst. See if she had any little secrets she wouldn't want made public—maybe allegations of fabricating a story while a reporter for her college newspaper, for example, or a shoplifting charge that could embarrass her.

Everyone had a past and a closet with a skeleton or two—himself being a prime example—and Viveca was surely no different. If she did, his investigator would discover them.

Thus armed, Andrew could strike a deal if she stumbled upon the truth, and she'd no doubt be much more willing to agree to his terms. He'd keep her secrets quiet, and she'd drop the book.

He didn't like the idea of trying to find dirt on her, but what else could he do? Confess that he wasn't the rightful heir to the family fortune when he'd given this family, and the company, an entire life's worth of sweat and blood? When he'd helped make it the empire it was today? He didn't think so.

It wasn't his fault that his mother had been an unfaithful wife, and he wasn't about to be punished for her transgressions.

He was the *legal* heir, no question. His father had been Grandmother and Grandfather's eldest son, and he'd been married to Andrew's mother at the time of Andrew's birth. He'd accepted Andrew as his son and never challenged his paternity publicly or in court, even though he'd'd've been well within his rights to do so.

So there were no blotches on Andrew's name, no challenges to his authority or birthright, and there never would be.

Swaying lazily, his arm draped over the back of the swing, he thought about his plan. He'd allow the book, investigate Viveca and play dirty to protect what he'd earned.

Just then, he heard footsteps, the *click, click, click* of high heels on cobblestones. Excitement hummed through him, an inappropriate reaction to the pending arrival of his enemy if he stopped to think about it, but he didn't think.

He waited, willing her to move faster, walk quicker, come to him.

Finally she appeared through the trees and his uncontrollable pulse galloped. For long seconds she didn't see him, and that gave him what he wanted—the chance to stare, to study, to wish.

Those wild corkscrew curls fluttered in the breeze, framing her face and trailing across her cheeks. That smooth bare skin gleamed in the moonlight, patches of silver over brown, begging to be stroked and worshipped.

Those breasts, softly rounded and full, bounced gently as she walked.

Watching her, his gut tightened and suddenly he was hard and ready. He wanted her. He wanted her every way a man could want a woman. His blood burned with it; his body ached with it; his soul hungered for it. The latter was his biggest problem because he felt more than physical want for Viveca.

Look at how she'd dealt with Grandmother's snobbery over dinner. She was clever, brave, proud and strong. A perfect match for him and...

Wait, wait, *wait.*

Where the hell had *that* thought come from? That was the scariest thing about Viveca—she made him think crazy thoughts, but he wanted her anyway.

Too preoccupied to notice him, her face tight and pensive, she kept her eyes lowered as she walked. He wondered what she was thinking about, if she was okay and, most of all, if he took up a tiny percentage of the thoughts in that smart brain.

The swing creaked when she was ten feet away, catching her attention for the first time. She looked up and their gazes locked. For one millisecond she allowed herself an honest reaction before she reverted to hating him, and in her expression he saw desire, need and all the unruly, inconvenient emotions he was also grappling with.

That was when it hit him.

Even as he watched her scowl and lock her feelings safely away behind those bright dark eyes, even as he reminded himself that he couldn't trust her, even as he remembered the painful truth that she hated his guts, one thought came to him, blowing all his plans and intentions straight to hell—he *needed* her.

There was something about this one woman that touched him, spoke to him, and he would not deny himself, regardless of the consequences.

Just like that, a new plan was born, one at which he had to succeed at all costs: seduce Viveca and, if there was time, protect his fortune.

Viveca approached the porch warily, feeling as though she'd conjured Andrew out of thin air. Unsettling images of him and Brenda—naked, twined and moaning—flooded her exhausted brain, promising a miserable night of sleeplessness. Each mental picture was a knife directly to her foolish heart, a grave wound. He was probably with Brenda right now, touching Brenda right now, undressing Brenda right now.

Or so Viveca had thought.

But there he was, waiting for her, and Brenda was nowhere in sight.

She was not glad, Viveca told herself fiercely, even though the pain in her chest eased and she could breathe again, as though she'd just surfaced from diving fifty feet into the ocean and taken her first fortifying gasps of air.

It was a lie, of course.

Once the initial shock of seeing him wore off, she wished him gone.

It was late, she was tired and each charged encounter with him left her feeling that much more agitated and unsettled. His mere existence was an aphrodisiac and seeing him, breathing the same air, made it worse. She wondered how long she could fight and whether she had the heart to resist, when what she wanted to do was surrender. Surviving yet another interlude with him seemed like a losing proposition.

What could he want now?

He's not for me, she reminded herself. *Not for me...not for me.*

But why not?

That foolish, self-destructive little voice in her head wouldn't shut up. In the moonlight, with a glass of wine or two under her belt, seeing that face, those intense eyes, that body, it was hard to remember exactly *why not,* but she tried.

Eventually the long list of reasons came back to her— he was a jerk, he used seduction as a weapon, he was a player and he was an enemy.

Oh, and one more thing.

She was so furious that she'd had to endure an evening with *Brenda*—the kind of woman he really liked, the kind of woman Viveca could never be, would never want to be. Brenda, the woman he'd no doubt kissed and touched and screwed, and probably would kiss, touch, and screw later on tonight—and that made her want to smash his face in with the nearest wicker chair.

"What do you want?" She climbed onto the porch. "It's late."

"I want to talk to you." He spoke quietly and calmly, making her seem hysterical by comparison, and patted the empty spot next to him on the swing. "Sit down."

Right. As if she'd ever come within touching range of him again. "I don't want to sit down." God, that was childish. Taking a deep breath, she did her best to sound like the calm adult she normally was. "And aren't we all talked out?"

"No." Resting his elbows on his knees, he clasped his hands and looked down at them for several long beats. When he raised his head again, his gleaming dark eyes held enough regret and sadness to keep a priest in a confession booth for years.

"I'm sorry about what I said earlier. About giving you something to remember Columbus by. That was crude. And unnecessary."

"Is that right?" She blinked and tried not to reveal how surprised she was by this out-of-left-field and seemingly sincere apology. "How polite of you."

"There's more."

"Why am I not surprised?" Crossing her arms over her chest to provide the only poor protection available against his glittering gaze, she watched as he stood, put his hands in his pockets and leaned against the screen door. "Want to up your offer to four hundred K?"

His eyes crinkled at the edges, but he didn't unleash the full smile and all its devastation. "No. I've given up on trying to get rid of you."

Well, now wait a minute. What the hell was going on here? Had someone come and switched the Andrew Warner she knew and mistrusted with a pod person?

Things couldn't be this simple and easy. Not in this lifetime. She'd read about his reputation as a fight-to-the-death businessman and seen enough of him today to know he didn't just give up.

"What? Are you supporting the book now?"

"Yeah, actually. But the real reason I don't want to get rid of you is that it'll be hard to seduce you if you're in New York and I'm here."

Chapter 6

Viveca froze.

It was amazing the way he did it. Brilliant, really. Looked at her with those hot eyes, murmured to her with that husky voice, radiated sex and want. And despite everything she knew about him, she could almost believe that he *did* want her. That every word that came out of those lush lips was not a lie.

Or maybe it wasn't a testament to his brilliance at all.

Maybe it was all about her stupidity.

"Don't even try it." She brushed past him to reach for the knob and escape inside the cottage, where she could lock the door. "I'm not falling for your whole seduction gambit."

He moved suddenly, blocking her, and then he was in her face, all glittering eyes, controlled tension and scorching body heat. Paralyzed, she stared up at him, waiting, not daring to blink.

"If you had *any* idea how good you smell and how hard it is for me to keep my hands in my pockets right now," he said, his voice rough, low and urgent, "you wouldn't come this close to me."

A beat or two passed during which the rest of the world disappeared and even the crickets seemed to stop chirping.

Viveca stared, her weak body trembling with lust, too conflicted to know what to do. She wanted to move away from him, maybe to Nepal or Jupiter or somewhere farther away where she couldn't *feel* him, but she also wanted to stay where she was, to stand her ground and show him he couldn't run roughshod over her.

Most of all, she wanted to move into his arms, coil around him, and take every inch of him as deep inside her body as he could possibly go.

In the end, she stood her ground.

"Stop pretending." Her voice shook, betraying her turmoil, but it was a blessing that it worked at all right now. "I know you don't want me to write the book, and you'll use every dirty trick you can think of to stop me from uncovering whatever it is you're hiding. But you don't need to do this whole ridiculous seduction thing. It won't work."

"Won't work?" He swayed closer, crowding and tempting her until she felt she would crawl out of her skin if she didn't rub against him. "I'm being honest with you, baby, so—"

"Don't call me that."

"—why don't you try being honest with yourself?"

She tried to snort with disbelief, to laugh, but it was as impossible as bringing the saber-toothed tiger back from extinction. "Honest? *You?*"

Again that half smile, that glimmer of amusement before he reverted to the deadly seriousness of pursuing his goal. "Yeah. Even though it's inconvenient, and even though it's the last thing I should be thinking about, and even though I can't figure out how this could all work, I want you. And I'm giving you fair warning—"

No, she thought with growing panic. She didn't want to hear this.

"—that I'm going to do everything in my power to get you."

This was too much for Viveca. White-hot rage sprang from nowhere until she shook with it. "Want me?" She wheeled away, desperate to lash out and somehow break his spell over her. "Wow. How touching. Does Brenda know you're here right now doing all this *wanting?*"

Eager to see his reaction to this mention of his lover, she turned back in time to see him pull one hand from his pocket and run it over the top of his head and down the back of his neck, radiating tension, frustration and earnestness in equal parts.

"Brenda's gone. I won't be seeing her again."

Viveca gaped. She couldn't believe the lies that poured out of his mouth, one after the other without end.

Her brain screamed warning after warning at her, but her stupid heart, or maybe it was her vanity, apparently needed to be burned to believe there was a fire. Fool that she was, she wanted to believe him. Almost did believe him.

This whole scene just got worse and worse, her emotions more and more unmanageable, but she could not lose control here. The thing she had to remember was that it didn't matter whether he screwed Brenda, anyone else or everyone else.

He was nothing to Viveca and never would be anything to her except a walking representation of an old score she needed to settle. That was all. That had to be all.

"It's none of my business anyway," she began.

"I know how it looks," he said. "You think I'm trying to manipulate you, and you think I'm bed-hopping, but you're wrong. She and I never even had sex. I was going to, sure... But then I saw you."

Another unbelievable lie she wanted to believe. "I don't care who—"

"Don't care?" His voice rose for the first time since they began this whole ridiculous conversation. "You're such a liar."

"I am *not*—"

"Viveca." He shook his head and spoke in a chiding tone, as if to talk her out of pursuing a position so outlandish that it was an embarrassment to both of them. "You blush when you look at me. You can't breathe. You kissed me this morning. Did you think I didn't notice?"

"You're unbelievable." Her humiliation complete, Viveca turned her hot face away, unable to look him in the eye for another excruciating second. Andrew crept closer, back into the danger zone, until her skin prickled with awareness and desire.

"There's no one else," he murmured. "No one else."

Angry tears burned her eyes, but she ruthlessly blinked them back. Revealing a weakness to this man would be fatal, and she was in a precarious position as it was.

"Does it bother you at all," she said, looking back over her shoulder, "that I think you're a despicable human being?"

Once again he surprised her, this time with a subtle show of emotion: his nostrils flared; his jaw throbbed; something unhappy flickered behind his eyes.

"Yeah, it bothers me. But not enough to stop wanting you."

She couldn't maintain eye contact, not when he looked at her like that, all wounded pride and bleeding heart, and all a lie. Looking skyward, up into the dark night, she hoped some inspiration would come to her, but the stars were silent and she was defenseless.

Taking a breath, she reached deep inside for the last dregs of her courage and self-respect.

"Well." She tried to sound nonchalant as she spoke over her shoulder. Rummaging in her purse, she found her keys, pulled open the screen door and unlocked the inner door with fumbling hands. "I think I've got it all straight now. Number one, you now inexplicably support the book project. Number two, Brenda's gone and you're such a saint you never touched her even though she served herself up like a roast pig with an apple in her mouth."

"Viveca," he said, unsmiling.

"And finally, you *want* me and I should just…what? Surrender my panties right now?"

He went very still and made a threatening sound, somewhere between a snarl and a growl.

"Does that about cover it, Andrew? Did I miss anything?"

"Yeah." There was a terrifying new edge in his voice. *"This."*

Moving quickly, unleashing what she knew was just a little of his limitless power, he stepped forward. He jerked his hands out of his pockets, touched her and was suddenly everywhere at once, inescapable and driving her wild.

Pulling her back, he pressed against her so that their entire bodies molded together, her back to his front, and the hard ridge of his erection settled between the two halves of her butt.

Viveca gasped with what should have been outrage instead of lust. The reverberations of the contact shuddered through both of them, a force as tangible as it was powerful.

In that instant she knew what it would be like if they made love. His heat…his strength…his unyielding body inside hers…and cataclysmic pleasure, the kind that ruined a person forever.

"Don't," she said, but the very last thing in the world she wanted was for him to let her go.

Crooning, he ran his lips along the sweet, *sweet* curve between her neck and shoulder, shooting one wave of unbearable pleasure after another through her, weakening her knees and making her wet. She was lost. Gone.

With Andrew's hands on her, avenging her father meant nothing. Ruining the Warner family name meant nothing. In the entire universe, only two things mattered—Andrew and the way he made her feel.

Against everything she'd planned, everything she wanted to believe about herself, everything she was, she pressed closer, tilted her head to the side and gave him silent permission.

With a rumbling purr in his chest, he took immediate advantage, nipping her hard enough to hurt and to thrill. Worse, his hands ran free, caressing arms, shoulders and hair before finally settling in, one on her throbbing breasts and one just about her sex.

He stroked her, over and over again. Endlessly, expertly.

Her body sang. Her mind went dark.

His lips skated up the side of her neck to her ear and his voice, rough with need, filled her head. "This thing…between us…it's already started."

A little clarity returned, enough for her to know she shouldn't concede this point but not enough to make her pull away. *"No."*

"Shhh." He bit her ear, and that terrible hand tightened over her breasts, rubbing back and forth, one nipple…the other nipple…until she sagged against him. "It doesn't have anything to do with the book, and you know it. It has to do with you and me. And even if you dropped the book and got on the next plane to New York, even if you moved to Taiwan tomorrow, I would follow you and we would still end up like this."

On *this,* his hand slid lower over her dress, unerringly circling around the most sensitive spot in her body, and she knew she shouldn't spread her legs for him, but she did anyway because she *had* to.

Raw pleasure rippled through her belly, powerful and delicious and yet a mere shadow of what she knew she'd feel if she had him inside her. She cried out, insensible.

"Wouldn't we, Viveca?"

She shook her head, too undone to speak.

Now his lips left her ear and slid across her nape. She swayed, her muscles going lax. Between her thighs she felt the responsive tightening of inner muscles, the siren's call of the most sensual experience of her life if only she would let herself go.

"I want you to understand, baby." The extreme tenderness in his voice was almost worse than anything else that had happened this entire day. "The next time I touch you like this, we're going to make love. You're going to give yourself, and the word *no* will never come out of your mouth."

As suddenly as he'd touched her, he let her go.

With no prior warning, it was over. One minute he was everywhere and the next he was gone, out of her reach even if she could've managed to move one of her heavy arms to hold him. Dazed, she teetered on the edge of an orgasm so bright and powerful it would light up the night sky.

Wobbling a little, robbed of the most intense physical sensations she'd ever felt, cold and empty without him, Viveca turned. Three feet away now, he held her gaze and she saw hot passion, unwavering determination and, worst of all, a need that matched her own.

He backed away slowly…one step…two steps…as though it was agony to leave her and he wanted to do it in stages. After a minute he turned his back and left her alone with her guilt, which was immediate, and her regret, which was bottomless.

Two excruciatingly painful weeks passed, during which Viveca tried to work and tried harder to forget about Andrew Warner, who'd apparently already forgotten her. Two weeks of daily interviews with Mrs. Warner and wading through boxes of documents, and nightly dreams of her infuriating grandson.

On that second Sunday morning, after a long, sleepless night filled with scorching dreams of Andrew Warner, his hands and lips gliding across her body, his eyes, his hair, his skin, and the aching need he created—but did not satisfy—between her thighs, Viveca woke to a body taut with sexual tension and frustration.

She was still hot and bothered an hour later, after she'd showered and dressed for breakfast with Mrs. Warner and was walking up the path to the main house. Still feeling agitated when her cell phone vibrated in her skirt pocket and made her jump.

Fishing it out, she kept walking. "Hello?"

"It's me."

Her feet glued themselves to the gravel and refused to move another step. The bane of her existence, reappearing out of nowhere, sounding wide awake and reporting for duty on what was sure to be another day of trying to drive her right out of her mind.

"A-Andrew," she stammered. "Hi."

"Hi."

She wished she could do something about her heart, which seemed determined to jump out of her chest and run a marathon. Unwanted, unblockable images came to her mind and refused to go quietly away: the things he'd last said to her, how she'd been tempted to believe him, the way he'd touched her, the way she'd responded.

Something delicious tightened low in her belly.

Unable to walk, she looked up at the brilliant blue sky and then over at a riotous garden filled with more pink and yellow roses than ten florists could use at a hundred weddings, seeing nothing…waiting…waiting.

"How are you?"

There he went, acting like he cared and pulling strings. Her stupid, feeble body responded like the puppet it was, aching in all the wrong places at the sound of that low, sexy voice. She supposed she ought to be grateful Andrew didn't command her to jump off the nearest cliff. No doubt she'd have one foot off the edge before her brain registered that it wasn't such a good idea.

"I'm fine. *Great.*"

"I'm not fine. I've been trying to stay away and not scare you to death, but…two weeks is about all I can manage." He swallowed audibly. "More than I can manage, actually."

Viveca wanted to say *bull,* but the sincerity in his voice was hard to ignore. "Listen," she said, determined to set things straight once and for all. "About what happened—"

"You regret it, I know. If I touch you again, you'll slap me. That about cover it?"

The wind went right out of her sails. "Well…yeah."

"Great. Now that that's out of the way, I want to come by and show you around the estate today. Maybe around eleven?"

Yes, she wanted to say, but *yes* was impossible. "Bishop has already shown me around. And…it's a bad idea anyway."

He didn't answer but she wasn't fooled into thinking this was the end of the matter. She could almost feel his clever mind purring like the engine from Brenda's Porsche, considering strategies and formulating plans.

"I've got to go, Andrew."

"Wait," he said. "There's something you need to understand, and the sooner you understand it, the better."

"What's that?"

"It doesn't matter how many hoops you throw at me. I'm going to jump through all of them. If you want to play games, I'll play. We're still headed in the same direction. It'll just take longer to get there."

"No."

"We're going to be together. No matter how scary that feels to you right now."

"No." Her automatic denial sounded hollow and, frankly, pathetic, but it was the best she could do. "We're not."

She heard Andrew's harsh, frustrated sigh. "Have it your way. Like I said, if you want to play games, I'll play, but…I play dirty."

Of course he did.

Grateful for the reminder, which she'd sorely needed, she hardened her heart. Though she'd had a moment or two of weakness and had actually let herself think, for half a millisecond, that maybe he did feel something for her, she would never let him get to her again. She would *not* be a lamb happily led to slaughter by this man. Ruthless was the name of the game, and she was more than his equal.

"I play dirty, too, Andrew."

Chapter 7

Armed with her digital voice recorder and ready with another round of questions, Viveca found Mrs. Warner, just back from church, on a walled terrace off the east wing of the house overlooking a meadow. The sun shone, birds chirped, a breeze ruffled the leaves, and there was, unbelievably, a doe and her fawn grazing at the far edge of the grass, near the trees.

"Viveca." Mrs. Warner, smiling broadly and dressed in her smart, blue silk church suit, waved as Viveca emerged from the music room. "Just in time for brunch."

Viveca could see that. Spread on the heavy white tablecloth was enough food for the buffet line at Golden Corral. Piles of bagels and bowls of flavored cream cheeses, lox, onions, capers, fresh sliced fruit in most colors of the rainbow, more of the low-fat pumpkin muffins, juices, milk, coffee, tea, yogurt… The treats went on and on.

Viveca blinked, her smile frozen in place, exhausted by the effort of trying to pretend this was a perfectly normal proposition. At least a hundred dollars' worth of food at the table for three people. This was how Andrew Warner had grown up, while in Brooklyn she'd been eating Hamburger Helper without the hamburger because that was all Daddy could afford to buy on his salary as a WarnerBrands International serf.

"How was church?" Viveca asked.

"Wonderful. The choir—we've got the best gospel choir, Viveca—sang 'O Happy Day.' That was one of my husband's favorite songs."

Looking misty-eyed, Mrs. Warner spread blueberry cream cheese on half a bagel, the picture of brave widowhood even though Reynolds Warner had been dead for more than twenty years. Even though tales of the man's abrasive, borderline-abusive personality and womanizing were legendary.

"Why don't you tell me more about him?" Viveca placed her digital voice recorder on a clear spot on the table and turned it on, and then filled her own plate with a bagel and fruit. "We've talked about your courtship, but what was he like in business?"

"A workaholic, of course." Mrs. Warner beamed with pride. "You don't get where he got without working your fingers to the bone. Tough, but fair. Wonderful to his factory workers. He liked to think of them as part of his extended family, his responsibility as well as his pleasure. He served them donuts every Friday as a treat, you know. To keep morale up. And they loved him for it."

Donut Fridays.

Ah, yes, Viveca remembered them well from the time or two when she'd gone with her father to the hellhole they called a factory. The overhead fluorescent lights, the endless rows of workers at sewing machines, the noise, the lint flying through the air that tickled her nose and covered every available surface. The workers hunched and stooped, arthritis no doubt taking root in their backs and fingers, the detail work probably ruining their eyesight.

Negligible pay, the barest medical coverage, a laughable pension. But they'd had donuts. Donuts made it all worthwhile.

Sickened by this woman's disconnection from anything resembling reality, Viveca put down her knife. Reynolds Warner had been a blight, a parasite, a disgrace to his people. If he'd ever done anything to help his workers in any material way, Viveca's research hadn't revealed it. Many of the articles she'd read remembered him the same way: as a betrayer who could have uplifted thousands of poor workers but instead chose to line his own pockets with the profits rather than invest them in projects to improve his employees' quality of life.

And here sat his willfully blind widow, gushing about him as though he'd been Nelson Mandela.

Viveca could only stare.

The silence seemed to make Mrs. Warner uncomfortable. Dabbling at her lips with her napkin, she shot Viveca a sidelong, assessing glance. "The press was unkind to him, of course."

Unkind was putting it mildly. "How do you explain that?"

Mrs. Warner laughed and the sound was harsh and unexpectedly cynical on such a beautiful morning. "Reynolds was a successful black businessman who was years ahead of his time. People were jealous."

Right. Jealousy was behind all the stories. Not the truth. Never the truth with the Warners. Did this woman actually believe what she was saying? Was that it?

Only one thing was clear. Interviewing Mrs. Warner would always be an exercise in futility. The woman was incapable of any true insights or critical thinking where her sanctified husband was concerned.

Still, Viveca was being paid to go through the motions, so she may as well pretend Mrs. Warner's propaganda was useful. Feeling adventurous—*let's see what new parallel reality Mrs. Warner will create now!*—Viveca changed the topic.

"What was he like as a husband?"

As though a switch had been flipped, Mrs. Warner began to glow like a bride on her march down the aisle. Her cheeks flushed; her eyes brightened; years fell off her face. "He was wonderful. The perfect husband."

Though Viveca hadn't expected any sort of honest assessment, this was still a bit much. Without breaking a sweat, Viveca could think of three or four friends who would insist that the words *perfect* and *husband* should never be used in the same sentence. "Is that right?"

"Oh, yes. He was very romantic. Jewelry for every special occasion—I'll show you my collection later, it's in the safe—never forgot a birthday or holiday." Mrs. Warner sighed dramatically, her gaze fixed on some distant point over the meadow. "He worshipped me. We were very happy. I miss him every day."

"I can see that." Viveca tried to sound sympathetic, but the investigative reporter in her just could not let all this bull pass unchallenged. "Mrs. Warner." She gathered her thoughts and tried to broach the subject diplomatically. "I did a lot of research before I got here."

"Of course, dear." Ever placid, Mrs. Warner sipped her coffee.

"There were rumors." Viveca paused. "Lots of rumors."

That delicate jawline tightened as Mrs. Warner smoothed the napkin in her lap, her head bowed. Finally looking up at Viveca, her eyes flashed brown steel. "Lies."

"I…see."

They stared at each other while Mrs. Warner conveyed all sorts of subliminal messages without ever saying anything. She'd heard the rumors, Viveca realized, but considered them beneath her dignity and would therefore not respond to them in any meaningful way. Mrs. Warner also expected Viveca not to mention them in the precious book—or there would be fierce retribution, probably the withdrawal of her cooperation.

Viveca couldn't have cared less. The book was not going to be a candy-coated primer on the glories of Reynolds Warner. Not in this lifetime. Viveca had never pretended otherwise, to her publisher or to Mrs. Warner. Let Mrs. Warner withdraw her support. Big deal. The book would be unauthorized rather than authorized, but either way Viveca had enough independent sources of information that there *would* be a book.

They might have continued their undeclared staring contest forever if a smiling Bishop hadn't come onto the terrace just then. "Eric's here, ladies." Sure enough, Eric trailed behind, looking rugged with a weekend beard, shorts pressed to a razor's edge, and a polo shirt. "Came to eat up all the bagels."

Grinning, Eric pecked his grandmother on the cheek, then Viveca. He leaned over the table, grabbed a plate and stacked it with more bagels and calories than Viveca ate in a week. He then sank into the chair nearest Viveca and took a huge bite of bagel.

Standing, Mrs. Warner threw her napkin in her seat. "You'll excuse me for a moment. I'm running to the powder room." She glared at them each in turn, silently defying anyone to challenge her with so much as a crooked grin. When she got to Bishop, he raised one eyebrow in a clear, though silent, rebuke.

Mrs. Warner lobbied him a final, withering look, said, "I'll expect those cinnamon rolls tomorrow, Franklin," and flounced off in a dramatic exit worthy of Gloria Swanson in *Sunset Boulevard*.

Bishop loaded a stack of plates onto a cart, winked and grinned at Viveca, and left. Viveca and Eric looked at each other and burst out laughing.

"What'd you do to the Silver Fox?" Eric asked.

"'Silver Fox'? That's appropriate."

"Andrew's nickname for her."

Viveca's smile died. She refused to have anything to do with Andrew Warner—even in absentia and even if it was only laughing at one of his jokes—if she could help it. Making busywork, she grabbed a knife and spread some of the nearest cream cheese on her bagel.

Then she pointed to her voice recorder. "Can I ask you some questions?"

"Sure."

"What are your memories of your grandfather?"

"He was a tough son of a bitch."

This bit of unexpected honesty surprised Viveca. "How so?"

"Everything was a mountain to climb. A challenge to win. A competitor to destroy. Never anything soft with him, no gray. Only black and white." Eric frowned. "Either you were a winner or a loser. A somebody or a nobody. A Warner or a nobody." Shooting Viveca a rueful sidelong look, he grinned. "No offense."

"None taken." Sipping her coffee, she thought of

Andrew again. What would it do to a young boy, to know that he had the weight of a dynasty on his shoulders? How had that shaped Andrew? Had it ruined him? "What was it like growing up with that kind of pressure?"

"Hard. It wasn't until I got to college and spent some time in Cincinnati with Izzy's family that I realized most families weren't like ours."

The tight line of Eric's jaw said it all, as did the way he stared down at his lox, stabbing it with his fork. Apparently he hadn't been excused from his grandfather's demands and expectations just because he was the spare rather than the heir.

"Again with this *Izzy.* She's pretty special, eh?"

"Just friends."

"Hmmm." Viveca wasn't sure she believed that, but she let it ride for now. "So you all lived here together, right? Growing up?"

"Yeah," Eric said. "My parents and me, Andrew's parents and him. All here together, just like the Ewings at Southfork. Now my parents spend most of their time in Phoenix. My dad was never involved with the company."

The touch of irony in his voice sparked more of her interest. "Did you want to move? Was that too much family all the time?"

"I don't know. That's just the way it was. We didn't know any different. Andrew and I did pretty much everything together."

"And yet *you* seem so normal."

Her unguarded words bit her in the butt right away, to her immense regret. Grinning with wicked delight, Eric sucked a smudge of cream cheese off the end of his thumb, obviously gearing up for some mischief.

"Is anything going on with you and my dear cousin?"

Eric wiped his thumb on his napkin. "An attraction, maybe? Spare no detail."

"Of course not," she said, wincing. "Why would you ask such a dumb question?"

Eric's grin widened. "I'm just wondering what you did to him. He seems *very,* ah, *interested* in you."

Viveca snorted. "He's very *interested* in anyone with two X chromosomes."

"Hmmm." Eric's laughing mouth disappeared behind his coffee mug and she thought about how much she'd like to smack him upside the head and see the dark brew spill all down the front of his pale green shirt. "So you don't feel the same way?"

"Andrew's an ass," she said flatly.

"Absolutely. And you like him anyway."

Remembering, too late, that her trusty voice recorder was picking up every syllable of this stupid conversation, Viveca snapped it off and shot him a withering look.

"What is this?" she demanded. "Second grade? Are you going to offer to pass him a note for me?"

"No need. He'll be here any second."

This unexpected and unwelcome bit of news started her whole annoying body meltdown process anew—skittering heart, flushed face and overheated skin. If only those symptoms belonged to some other condition, something less dangerous. Anything other than Andrew Warner-itis.

Sneaking a glance at her watch, Viveca wondered if she could disappear before Andrew arrived. But it would be rude to take off when Mrs. Warner was visiting the ladies' room, and Eric's suspicions about the chemistry between Viveca and Andrew would only be confirmed if she left— and God knew she didn't want to give Eric any more fuel for his raging fire. Her heart sank.

If only a bolt of lightning would incinerate her on the spot and spare her from seeing that man again. A tornado. An earthquake. Something. Feeling sullen and trapped, she forked a chunk of fresh pineapple into her mouth and chewed it with a vengeance, tasting nothing.

"He likes to spend Sunday mornings with Nathan," Eric continued.

Viveca glared up at him, wishing she could tell him to shut up about Andrew, but he'd piqued her curiosity. In all her reading, she'd come across nothing about Andrew and any charitable activities, and that was very strange. Most men in Andrew's position gave away millions of dollars per year to various causes. No doubt Andrew did, too, but he apparently kept quiet about it. The question was, *why?* And who'd've thought he'd spend so much of his time with a young child when he could simply write a large check and be done with it?

"Tell me about Nathan," she said. "I've been curious."

"He's an inner-city boy in foster care. His mother was a druggie and his grandmother died about a year ago. Andrew's very involved with him."

"Oh."

"Oh, and you should ask Andrew about his foundation." Eric smirked, as though he knew exactly how Andrew affected her and how much she didn't want to hear nice things about him. "Only, don't tell him I told you."

Foundation? What foundation?

Stunned, Viveca stared at Eric and wished she could eject this harmful information from her brain. She did not want to know that there was anything nice or good about Andrew. If he was a real human being rather than a one-dimensional jerk, it was none of her business. Far, far better for him to remain the hornless devil she believed him to be.

It was easier to hate him that way and keep him at arm's length.

The sound of drumming heels on the floor inside made them both turn around as Mrs. Warner reemerged from the house. Judging by her serene lady-of-the-manor smile, which was now firmly back in place, she'd forgiven Viveca for her earlier insubordinate questions and was willing to overlook the incident.

"Andrew's here," she announced as she sat again. "He brought Nathan."

Oh, God. Frozen with nerves and excitement, Viveca waited.

Chapter 8

Voices, more footsteps…and then Andrew was there in the doorway, looking around, not even bothering to be discreet about it as his intense gaze swept the scene and zeroed in on her. His face softened and warmed, and Viveca's heart skittered.

Andrew walked onto the terrace, one hand atop Nathan's shoulder and the other arm anchoring a basketball against his hip.

Viveca barely registered Nathan. Nor did she remember that she was supposed to avoid Andrew or, failing that, avoid looking at him. As always, if Andrew was there, she was staring.

Today he wore black athletic shorts and a white T-shirt and it was… Nope, no improvement in the sexiness department. She was beginning to realize that nothing would be. If he showed up in tattered coveralls and a straw hat he could still be the centerfold for a farmer's magazine calendar.

Their gazes met, his flickering over the gathered white folds of her peasant top—or maybe it was the bare tops of her shoulders that caught his attention—and his half smile widened fractionally.

For no apparent reason, Andrew's gaze tracked to one side of her and suddenly he was all sharp angles and pending doom, a stick of dynamite who'd found a lit match and was ready to blow. Bewildered, she followed his line of sight and discovered, with surprise, that Eric's chair was a foot or two closer to hers than it had been mere seconds ago.

Another interesting phenomenon had occurred while she'd been distracted. Eric had one of his long arms slung across the back of her chair, a position it had definitely not occupied until this very moment of Andrew's appearance.

Eric, ever the prankster, shot Andrew a politely puzzled whatever-could-be-the-problem? glance.

Andrew looked murderous, Eric smirked and Viveca read between the lines. *Wait a minute.* Wait, wait, *wait...* Was Andrew being *possessive?* Of *her?*

Heat and excitement hit in a thrilling rush, but then she caught herself and horror kicked in. What was she thinking? Determined not to be a pawn in whatever ridiculous, unknowable power game these two clowns were playing at her expense, she scooted her chair forward, out of Eric's reach, and reached for the coffeepot.

Eric chuckled. Andrew made an indecipherable, threatening sound.

After a split second, during which several more subliminal messages were exchanged between the cousins, most involving raised or lowered eyebrows and throbbing jaws, they apparently reached an understanding of some sort.

Leveling a last, silent death threat in Eric's direction, Andrew turned away. "Grandmother." Walking to the head of the table, he pecked Mrs. Warner on the cheek she tilted up for him and indicated his guest. "I brought Nathan with me."

"Hello, young man." Beaming, Mrs. Warner held out a hand and Nathan shook it. "How's Mrs. Sanders this week?"

"Mad." His eager gaze skimmed over the treats on the table.

Mrs. Warner looked bemused. "Why's that?"

Nathan shrugged, grabbed a muffin and sat in the chair between Mrs. Warner and Eric, his skinny bare legs dangling. "I dunno."

Andrew sent another quick glare in Eric's direction and then spoke to Nathan. "Could it be because you left your birthday bike out on the stoop and it got stolen?"

The boy chewed his muffin, head angled to the side, thinking hard and looking unabashed. "Yeah. That's probably why."

Viveca had to laugh. Nathan was adorable, all wide, dark eyes and fun looking for a place to happen. If Eric took him under his wing, there was no telling what worlds of trouble he would introduce the boy to.

Eric laughed, too. "What's up, man?" He held his hand overhead, palm out and the boy gave him a high five. "Playing basketball today?"

"Yeah. And swimming." Nathan grabbed the nearest crystal glass, filled it and loudly gulped orange juice. When a few drops trickled down his chin, he swiped the back of his arm across his face. "I whipped Andrew's ass last time."

Viveca and Eric laughed as Andrew coughed and Mrs. Warner glowered.

"Excuse me, young man." Mrs. Warner regarded him with a tart frown. "Who taught you that language?"

"Andrew."

"Ah," Andrew said quickly, catching Nathan's eye and slashing his finger across his own throat. "You remember Viveca, right?"

"Hi, Nathan." Smiling, Viveca shook his little hand, which was sticky with juice and crumbs. "Nice to see you again. Where's the Game Boy today?"

"At home."

Andrew, who'd moved around the table and now hovered near Eric's shoulder, leaned forward to put the basketball down on the stone floor, out of the way. When he straightened, one of his wide shoulders caught a glass of orange juice and knocked it directly into Eric's lap, making a huge, splattering mess. "Oops," he said.

Eric jumped to his feet, nearly overturning his chair. Muttering, he looked down at himself and surveyed the damage, which was extensive. "I just ironed these clothes."

"Sorry, man." Andrew clapped him, hard, on the back, looking more satisfied than sorry. Upon closer examination, in fact, it seemed to Viveca that he was a hundred percent triumphant and zero percent remorseful.

Grabbing a napkin, Andrew shoved it into Eric's dripping chest, and steered Eric toward the door. "You better get that cleaned up. You don't want any bees to come."

Eric paused on the threshold, his lips twisted into a good-natured, you-got-me-this-time scowl as he looked at his cousin.

Andrew jerked his head toward the house. "Better hurry."

"Your concern is really touching," Eric said. Looking past Andrew, he waved to Mrs. Warner. "Later, Grandmother."

"Try not to drip on the floors, dear," she said.

Eric laughed and turned to Viveca. "I'll call you later." There was a subtle change to his voice. It sounded low and sexy, not at all like the brotherly tone he'd been using with her up until now. Bewildered, Viveca looked around in time to see him give her the kind of heavy-lidded, private look lovers exchanged when making plans to hook up for the night. "We'll talk."

"Great." Viveca smiled brightly and used her professional voice, refusing to play Eric's game, which was, judging by Andrew's now fire-engine-red face, effective enough without her active participation. "We can schedule a formal interview."

Eric's eyes gleamed. With a sidelong look at Andrew, he came back, kissed Viveca on the cheek and said, in a stage whisper, "Think about what I said, okay? About you and—"

"*Yes,*" Viveca said quickly through gritted teeth. "I remember what you said."

"Great. Bye, Nathan."

Startled, Nathan looked up from his bagel-honey-cream-cheese concoction and waved. Eric waved back. Smiling, his morning's quota of troublemaking no doubt filled, he strode out.

Still looking irritated, Andrew wiped a few lingering drops of juice out of Eric's seat and dropped into it. Heat flamed off his body, hiking Viveca's sexual awareness of him up another seventy or eighty notches, and she tried not to shiver.

Furious with Eric and his shenanigans, Andrew and his manipulations, and herself and her weakness for Andrew most of all, she scooted her chair away from Andrew. "Nice," Viveca murmured, knowing he would hear even if no one else did. "With the juice? Subtle."

Andrew snorted as he snatched up a spare napkin, shook it out, laid it across one muscular thigh, and started loading up his plate.

"What do you and your new best friend have to talk about?" His voice radiated quiet annoyance. "What's he doing calling you?"

"That's none of your business."

"Think again."

Pausing in the midst of ladling fruit into a bowl, he gave her an unsmiling, flashing-eyed, possessive glance that awakened something exciting and illicit deep in her belly. Cheeks burning, she managed to keep her chin up and hold his gaze for several excruciating beats.

Unruffled by her silent defiance, he glanced at the half-eaten bagel on her plate. "Eat up. I don't want you getting hungry on our tour."

"Tour?" Viveca wondered if her desire-scrambled brain was now hearing things. "I specifically told you on the phone that I don't need a tour. You should get your memory problems checked out."

This earned her an amazing grin that was as wicked as it was sexy, but he didn't bother to answer. Not for one second did she take it as a sign he'd given up.

Way down at the other end of the table, Mrs. Warner looked up from the bagel she'd been slicing for Nathan, who had a growing pile of food on his plate. "Did you say something, dear?"

"Yeah." Andrew dropped his hands into his lap under the tablecloth. "I was just telling Viveca I'm sorry I was a little late for her tour."

Viveca's jaw dropped with outrage.

Andrew glanced back at Viveca, all wide-eyed innocence, his halo and wings practically glowing. Underneath the table, his actions hidden by the cloth, he trailed a slow finger up the outside of her bare thigh. "Isn't that right, Viveca?"

Viveca jumped.

It was nothing, really. So soft it shouldn't even qualify as a touch, so benign it should've been entirely forgettable. But Andrew's hands on her body could never be nothing. They felt too right for that, too perfect.

Heat shimmered over her skin and all thoughts emptied out of her once-sensible head. Only when he'd begun to inch her skirt higher, nowhere near the red-light district but still well within the danger zone, did she come out from under his bewitchment.

The rules of engagement called for extreme force, and she used it. With a warning growl she pinched the fleshy area between his thumb and forefinger. Hard.

Andrew yelped and snatched his hand back.

Mrs. Warner raised one concerned eyebrow.

"Bee," Viveca told her.

"Oh, no." Mrs. Warner's face fell. "Remind me to have Bishop call the exterminator again."

"Of course."

Andrew, regarding her with new respect but still looking amused, shifted in his seat until one of his hard thighs brushed Viveca's leg and settled against it. "Are you ready, Viveca? I know you want to get away from the *bees*."

"Actually, Andrew—" Viveca infused her voice with syrup, honey and cotton candy as she drew her leg back "—I thought we'd decided against a tour. I've already seen everything and I need to spend some time with your grandmother going through some family photos. So…if you'll excuse me."

"Actually, Viveca—"

Before she could get up and make the speedy exit she had in mind, Andrew caught her hand under the table and held it, making her shudder. His skin was hot and smooth, his grip strong, his touch gentle as his thumb circled her palm. Wild jolts of pleasure radiated out from this central point, expanding like cracks in a windshield and filling her body to overflowing with aching want.

This was bad enough.

But then his thumb strayed farther, skimming over her wrist. Electrifying bursts of sensation echoed through her and pooled in her wet core until she wanted—*needed*—to squirm. Her inner muscles tightened. Clenched and eased, then clenched again, harder. Sending her higher and higher, to a place she couldn't go, not with *him.* She tried to pull free, but he held on as if he knew how he was ruining her.

"—I thought I could show you and Nathan around at the same time. And Grandmother always takes a nap after lunch anyway, don't you, Grandmother?"

"I do," Mrs. Warner said. "I'm not as young as I used to be. And we don't work on the Sabbath around here, Viveca. So she's yours for the day, Andrew."

"Perfect."

Andrew stared at Viveca's mouth with undisguised hunger while she tried not to whimper even as she assimilated the disaster that had just befallen her.

Up until this very moment, Viveca had thought disasters came in the form of tsunamis, hurricanes or tons of snow thundering down a mountainside. She would not have put an afternoon with a handsome man to whom she was violently attracted in that category, but times changed. Now, if she had her choice, she'd rather see a nice funnel cloud headed her way. With a tornado she had a chance of survival intact. With Andrew she had none.

She had to get her hand back before he made her come—right here in her chair, in public—with all his touching and stroking and murmuring.

She tugged her hand, but couldn't get free of his hold.

Her desperation rose. It was so humiliating, learning like
this that she had no control over her own damn body. How
was she supposed to withstand this relentless seduction
when her foolish body wept for him? When she knew a
night—hell, an hour—in bed with him would be the most
fantastic sexual experience of her life?

She couldn't.

Not as long as he touched her. On the verge of open
and outright panic, she did the only thing she could do.
She begged.

"Please," she whispered.

He blinked once and let her go.

Sadness or something like it replaced the naked heat
in his eyes.

"Can we swim in the pool?" Nathan asked.

Andrew blinked again and seemed to come out of a
trance. "Sure."

"I told you I don't play fair." Andrew leaned across
Viveca, reaching for the blackberry jam. His bare arm
brushed hers and reminded her of all the things she didn't
want to remember: he was still there; she couldn't get
away from him; his touch would probably always set her
on fire.

"See the deer, Nathan? Right there… No, there."

Trailing along behind Viveca and Nathan as they walked
down the path toward the greenhouse, Andrew watched her
point to a pair of stags, twins maybe, a hundred feet away,
their small racks of antlers sporting only four points each.

"Deer carry Lyme disease," Nathan said flatly. "Don't
touch them."

"Don't worry. I just think they're beautiful."

They *were* beautiful, Andrew supposed. It'd been so

long since he'd taken the time to walk the grounds and notice them. But Viveca was a Manhattanite and Nathan was also a city kid, and neither of them had much of a chance to see Bambi and the crew. Andrew realized that he wanted to show things like this to them and see them through their fresh eyes.

Especially Viveca's.

She was ignoring him. Again.

For Nathan, meanwhile, she had endless enthusiasm, smiles, laughter and question after question. About Mrs. Sanders, his foster mother, basketball, swimming… No aspect of the boy's life seemed boring or beneath her notice, and Nathan lapped up the attention. He all but glowed, hopping, skipping and orbiting around Viveca as though she was the sun.

Viveca liked children, obviously. This seemed to be a crucial detail about her, something he ought to know and understand. He liked children, too. Loved Nathan.

As they got closer to the enormous greenhouse, Nathan slowed until his little feet were dragging. Viveca reached for the door, but he turned to look at Andrew, his expression doleful. "When can we go swimming?"

A fair question. No self-respecting eight-year-old boy wanted to see orchids when there was a pool to swim in, and goodness knew Nathan had been patient for far longer than Andrew would have at that age.

"Well." Andrew kept an eye on Viveca. "I think Viveca wants to see the greenhouse, so let's—"

"Oh, no." Speaking to Andrew for the first time in what felt like centuries, she looked cautiously hopeful. "Nathan's been very patient, don't you think? Why don't you take him to the pool, and I can see the greenhouse by mys—"

"Wouldn't dream of it." Andrew pulled out his cell phone.

"It's no big d—"

"I insist."

Her face fell, poor thing. She was so desperate to get away from him he wondered if he should have mercy on her and let her go. But then he thought of the way her skin heated and her eyes glazed over when he touched her, and he just couldn't do it. Punching a couple of numbers, he waited.

"This is Bishop."

"Can you meet Nathan at the pool for me?" Andrew asked. "He wants to swim. I'll be up in a few."

There was a pause during which Andrew could feel wheels turning in Bishop's mind, pathways connecting, and conclusions being drawn.

"Aren't you with Miss Viveca?" Bishop's voice was now heavy with suspicion.

"That would be correct."

"What're you planning to do when you get her off alone, Scooter?"

"Nothing to get worried about," Andrew lied. "I'll send Nathan up. Thanks."

He snapped the phone shut on Bishop's outraged spluttering, and when it buzzed again in his hand, he ignored it. "Go on up," he told Nathan, and the kid took off at a dead run, his legs circling like the Road Runner's, leaving Andrew where he wanted to be—alone with Viveca.

Feeling as though he'd just made a killing in the market, he couldn't stop an undignified grin of absolute glee from taking over his face, but then he caught sight of Viveca's stricken expression and all his good cheer evaporated.

She looked irritated, which was fine. That he could deal with. But she also looked suspicious, maybe even scared, a little girl lost and trying to be brave in front of the big bad wolf. Knowing that he did that to her broke what passed for his heart.

"I'm not all that bad," he told her, stung.

Those lips he wanted so much twisted with derision. "*Really?* Which part isn't that bad? The part that traps me into being with you? The part that tries to bribe me—"

"Viveca—"

"—or is it the part that touches me when I don't want to be touched?"

He couldn't let her get away with this last part. His temper and pride wouldn't stand for it. "*Don't want to be touched?* Is this a joke?"

A direct hit, one she didn't bother to deny.

She glowered, her face turning a vivid, near-purple color he was pretty sure he'd never seen on a human being before. He felt a nanosecond's satisfaction to have his point made so clearly—she wanted him to touch her and he was getting damn tired of her denying it every two seconds—but then he thought about what he was doing.

As if she'd really beat a path to his bed with him badgering her like this, plowing over her feelings every chance he got. She was stubborn, proud and independent, and the power of the attraction between them scared her half to death. Hell, it scared him, too, and *he* had an iron stomach, ran a multinational billion-dollar company and parachuted in his spare time. So, yeah, slowing down a little might be good.

"Look," he said quickly. "I, uh… I'm sort of a control freak—"

Those fine eyebrows rose. *"Sort of?"*

"—and I get a little carried away sometimes."

"You don't say."

"When I want something, I get it." He felt the beginnings of frustration that he had to explain himself. Again. "But I don't mean to be overbearing, so if I—"

"This is the sorriest apology I've ever heard."

"I'm not apologizing."

He regretted the words the second they hit his ears because of course he'd meant to apologize. Thought he was, in fact, apologizing. But something about this woman scrambled his thoughts and jammed the circuits in his brain. Maybe it was her arrogance, which matched his. Or maybe it was the strength of her will and the knowledge that he'd have to bend it to his if he wanted to get inside her body, which he desperately did.

Whatever it was, it rubbed him like sandpaper over a sunburn.

Made him crazy because he knew this woman would be his equal in bed—in *everything*—and he had so few equals in his life.

"Of *course* you're not apologizing." Anger radiated from her, waves of red he could practically see. "You don't apologize. How foolish of me."

Turning her back to him, she reached for the greenhouse door and jerked it open with the obvious intent of getting this unpleasantness over with so she could be rid of him as soon as possible. He stared, seeing all her resignation and frustration. And suddenly he couldn't stand the idea of her marching through a tour with him as if he was Hitler and she was Churchill. He just couldn't.

"Wait."

She paused, her shoulders squared and braced, her back still to him.

"I *am* sorry. I'm going to… I'm going up to the pool."

And then he left.

Walking up the path, he congratulated himself on his newfound, though excruciating, spirit of self-sacrifice. So what if the pain in his chest expanded the farther away from Viveca he got? He was doing the right thing and that should count for something. Except…it didn't.

"What's with the sheep's clothing?"

He stopped. When he turned back, he saw open suspicion and grudging curiosity in Viveca's wide baby browns. No hostility, though, and he supposed that was a miracle worth noting.

"Not all wolves are bad," he told her.

"They are if you're a sheep."

"Viveca," he said with utmost sincerity, "you may not know it, but I'm in more danger than you are."

Maybe that was too much for her to hear. God knew it was a lot for him to say. She looked away, her color high, and that thing about her, whatever it was, called to him, telling him to come closer, but he stayed where he was.

Finally she met his gaze again, all raw vulnerability, honesty and bravery, and there went another tiny piece of himself, lost to her forever.

This, he thought unhappily, *is a woman I could love. If I could love.*

"I don't trust you," she said. "Part of me wants to but…I don't."

"Yeah," he said with real sorrow. "I don't trust you, either."

This confession, strangely, seemed to reassure her. Maybe it was knowing that he wasn't in the driver's seat on this thing any more than she was.

She nodded, looking satisfied.

He stood there like an idiot, wondering if they'd reached an accord of some kind, and then she moved into the greenhouse and held the door for him. A soft expression, a distant cousin of a smile, maybe, crossed over her face, stunning and humbling him.

A man like him had no business being anywhere near a woman like this, much less receiving the gift of her almost-smile. It'd all be over for him if she knew what she was really dealing with. A man who was hollow on the inside, who'd slept with and discarded enough women to give Hugh Hefner serious competition. A man who'd never loved, never been loved by a person who truly knew him, and didn't believe in love.

If she knew, she'd run screaming for the hills. But she didn't know, thank God.

And his day was a complete success because he'd managed to make a small chink in her armor. He crept closer, trying to keep that idiotic grin off his face.

"Well." She met his gaze with those bright eyes and he felt himself going under. "What's so great about this greenhouse?"

This is the place where I fell a little harder for you.

"I'll show you," he said.

Chapter 9

They roamed among the tables and planters, walking in relaxed, aimless silence.

He wandered ahead, his hands clasped loosely behind his back, managing to look nonthreatening even though he was the single biggest problem she'd ever encountered. Nothing in her life had ever prepared her for a man like this.

She was out of her depth, entirely overmatched.

And she was glad to be with him. Would even go so far as to say there was nowhere else she'd rather be. If that didn't qualify her for the Nobel Prize for stupidity, she didn't know what would.

"I like Nathan," she said to distract herself from her growing funk.

He grinned over his shoulder. "He's a great kid."

"How long have you been mentoring him?"

"Over a year. I'd been tutoring at his school, and we just hit it off."

Tutoring at inner-city schools. Of course. What wonderful qualities would she discover next about Andrew? Knitting afghans for the elderly? Washing the feet of the homeless?

"Well." Feeling surly, she strove to be gracious. "He's lucky to have you."

Andrew turned away and shrugged, and she could tell she'd made him uncomfortable. "I'm the lucky one."

"You should adopt him."

His head whipped around, eyes wide and astonished. *"What?"*

Yeah, stupid idea. Millionaire playboy CEOs didn't usually go around adopting kids. Kids tended to cramp people's style. "Sorry. I didn't mean—"

"I never…thought about it." His voice was faint, his face bemused.

Viveca clamped her jaws shut, determined not to say anything this far-fetched again, and they resumed their meandering in silence.

"Grandmother likes orchids," he told her after a while.

They were everywhere. On the tables, in huge planters, waiting to be repotted, lining the shelves. In every conceivable color, from hot pink to lilac to shades of white and yellow.

"Me, too," she said.

"But…?"

"They're a little too delicate for me. Sunflowers are better."

"Sunflowers?"

His amusement fired her up, naturally. Feeling insulted, she crossed her arms over her chest and frowned. "What's wrong with sunflowers? Too pedestrian for the great Warner family?"

"No." He winced and she felt bad for breaking the fragile peace. "I was thinking that's the perfect flower for you. Bright, beautiful, strong and unbendable."

"Oh." Her voice was weak with surprise. If she'd ever received a more meaningful compliment in her life, she couldn't think what it was.

"So." He leaned back against the nearest table and crossed his long legs at the ankles. "What do you think of Heather Hill?"

"It's, ah… It's unbelievable. I didn't know real people lived on estates like this. I can't even imagine what it must have been like for you to grow up here."

This seemed to be the wrong answer, judging by his response. "Huh."

He uncrossed his legs and stared down at his feet in their athletic shoes, the sudden picture of discomfort. She waited, but he didn't explain his less-than-glowing commentary on a childhood here in paradise.

"So…?" she said.

"So what?"

"So what was it like growing up here?"

When he looked up, she saw cynicism and, beneath that, an endless sadness in his eyes, the kind that could wrap around the equator twice if you stretched it out.

"Is this Viveca the reporter asking or Viveca the woman?"

The reporter, her self-protective half screamed. *Tell him it's the reporter, the reporter, the rep—*

"The woman."

"Well," he said softly, "to the woman I would say it wasn't exactly Disneyland."

"Why not?"

He waved a hand, dismissing the questions and the

topic. "I don't want to get into this poor-little-rich-kid stuff. I'm not a whiner. I was very fortunate that we had money and food on the—"

"Stop with the disclaimers, okay? Just tell me...when you think of your childhood here, what goes through your mind?"

"All that glitters sure ain't gold. That's what goes through my mind."

That shut her up as effectively as superglue to the lips. If the reporter in her had been in charge, or even present, she would have thought of a good follow-up question. But only the woman was there, and the woman's heart broke and bled for him.

A new challenge flashed in his eyes. "Is this going to be a chapter in your book? 'Andrew Warner's Bitter Childhood Memories'?"

It should be. This was exactly the kind of thing she'd come here to unearth and shine a spotlight on: the dysfunctional Warners and all their various emotional issues.

Except that the idea of going public with something so private about him, when he'd seen fit to share it with her, now seemed unthinkable. Before she could stop herself she opened her mouth and uttered words she knew she'd regret.

"It's...off the record."

A flare of hope crossed over his features and tugged at her, demanding a response she didn't want to give. "Is everything between us going to be off the record, Viveca?"

She paused because it took a long time to force the word out of her mouth. "No."

The reward for this honesty was the withdrawal of whatever light she'd seen in his eyes, the slamming of invisible doors between them, and a sickening knot in her belly.

With a curt nod, he shoved away from the table and wandered off down another row of orchids. There was a slight slump to his shoulders that almost had her thinking she'd hurt him.

"What about you?" he asked. "Did you grow up in Shangri-La?"

"Well…yeah."

His head whipped around, eyes narrowed with interest. "How's that?"

"Well, I mean…don't get me wrong. We were dirt poor, but—"

"In Brownsville, right? Brooklyn?"

"Yeah. In an awful little apartment with rotten plumbing—"

"Brothers and sisters?"

"No. Just me and my mom and dad, but we—"

"What was so great about that?"

His rapid-fire delivery of questions and accompanying intent stare should have unnerved her, but didn't. He seemed so anxious to hear about her life, so interested, that she could forgive his obvious impatience.

"We had a lot of fun together. That's all."

"Fun?" His heavy brows came together over his nose in an uncomprehending frown. "With no money and awful plumbing?"

He stared at her like she was describing life on Mars without oxygen and she had to laugh. "Yeah, *fun.* We took the subway and went to the zoo and to the museums and to Zabar's for bagels one Sunday a month after church. We planted daisies and sunflowers and tomatoes in our window boxes because my father had a green thumb. We drank apple cider in the fall. We—"

"Your parents loved you," he said flatly.

"Of course they did."

This information seemed to startle him as much as the

question had startled her. His questions dried up for a minute. In the silence she began to wonder what had been done to this man as a boy. Not that she cared.

And yet she couldn't help wondering if he had been abused by his awful grandfather. Neglected? Was that it? The idea made her sick to her stomach and, worse than that, made her want to smash something.

There'd been nannies; she knew that much. Maybe his globe-trotting parents hadn't had time for him. Disinterested parents could certainly damage a child. And his father, Charles Warner, had been, by all accounts, a disappointment with a strong interest in scotch and soda.

And there had been recurrent rumors of a pending divorce before they were both killed in a plane crash. She couldn't forget—

His voice, sharp and annoyed now, intruded. "Don't feel sorry for me."

"I don't," she lied automatically, mindful of his pride.

"Right." He snorted. "Do you ever tell the truth?"

That was pretty much a negative, at least as it pertained to him.

God, she hated when he did that. Read her mind as though he had a user's manual to her brain. No one else could do it. Even her own mother hadn't been able to do it. How did *he*—the one person she wanted to hide her thoughts from—manage it?

"It's because of your expression," he said. "Your face gives it all away. So maybe you should try being honest, up front. With me, if not with yourself."

This was too much, even for the over-the-top world she and Andrew inhabited whenever they were together. Annoyed, she headed to the small pond, desperate to get away from him.

His voice followed her. "Are they still in Brooklyn? Your parents?"

Viveca was so surprised at this question she almost stumbled. She had, luckily, reached a wrought-iron bench near the pond and sank into it. "They're dead."

A new stillness fell over him, a rapt concern that made the sudden tightness in her throat worse. "I'm sorry."

He sounded it, and that made it impossible for her to hate him the way she wanted to. Wasn't it his family's fault and, by extension, *his* fault that her father had died one year and her brokenhearted mother the next? Why was it so hard for her to remember that when she was with him?

Approaching slowly, he sat at the other end of her little bench and watched her with sad eyes. For once he was careful to give her space. "You must miss them."

"My father became an alcoholic." She was determined to tell him at least part of what'd happened to her. "In the last years of his life. Then he developed liver cancer when I was in college. My mother died a year later. Her heart gave out."

The recitation of these central facts of her life and the basis of her revenge mission should have hardened her heart against Andrew, but the words didn't have much power when he sat there looking upset on her behalf. "I'm sorry," he said again.

Sorry, she thought bitterly. *Yeah. You should be.*

She just hadn't expected him to be. "Well," she said into the growing silence, "I guess we're both orphans, huh? Just like Nathan."

The funniest thing happened then. His brows flattened, his lips twisted and his midnight-blue eyes flashed black. And she'd bet her last dollar that it was anger, not grief, that did it.

"I was an orphan way before that plane crash killed my parents, Viveca."

A powerful urge rose up in her, as strong as a committed couple's urge to make love and breed or a mother's urge to protect. She wanted to put her hands on the sharp angles of Andrew's throbbing jaw and kiss his cheeks and eyes. She wanted to pull him into her arms, hold him tight, and kill anything that tried to hurt him. She wanted to tell him that he had been loved as a child, even if he hadn't known it then and didn't know it now.

"There you go feeling sorry for me again."

The words were light, but the new flush across his face told her how uncomfortable he was with his own vulnerability and her concern.

She started to deny it, just to save his pride, but thought better of it. "I'm sorry the adults in your life didn't love you the way you deserved to be loved, yeah. But I'm sure they loved you."

He took a sharp breath and looked away, blinking furiously.

Way to go, Viveca. She'd opened her big fat mouth and made things worse, and that was the last thing she'd meant to do. Sitting there like a mute idiot, she wondered what to do now, but then he turned back and there was a disquieting, cynical glow in his eyes as he shifted closer.

"Maybe," he murmured, staring at her mouth, "I should take advantage of all this pity."

She froze.

"What do you say, Vivi?" One of his hands came up to the side of her head and he trailed slow fingers from her temple all the way down the curve of her neck to her collarbone. "Maybe you can kiss me and make it all better."

It was bravado. A primitive defense mechanism. Viveca

knew that as surely as if he'd written up a detailed game plan and e-mailed it to her for review. He'd had a moment of emotional vulnerability and just couldn't stand it.

This was what he did: lash out, distract, and use sex to his advantage. This was Andrew—complex, damaged and human. A unique combination of sexiest man in the world and little boy lost that enthralled and destroyed her.

She wanted every bit of him, and she hated him for it.

Jerking away, she lunged to her feet and tried for a little composure. "Thanks for the tour. I'm guessing we're done…?"

"Not quite."

"Don't tell me." Flustered, she lapsed into her own favorite defense mechanism: sarcasm. "Did we miss the moat? The peasants' cottages? Tower and battlements?"

His dark mood dissipated and he laughed, flashing that astonishing smile at her. It was amazing, really, the way he did it every time as though he were waving a magic wand. He smiled and therefore her belly tightened with need. Maybe she could work out a corresponding mathematical formula or something. Like $E=mc^2$.

He stood, too. "Don't you want to schedule my formal interview? I'm thinking we'll need to spend lots of time together. Work closely."

"Aren't you the team player."

"I try."

Oh, how she would love to pop him right in his amused kisser. He was right, of course. If he was willing to submit, she needed to interview him. This would, alas, entail talking to him. A lot. Probably five hours at least.

"Great." She stretched her lips in a painful smile. "I'll call you."

"Anytime."

The sound of his voice, when he spoke to her with such sexual promise, was soothing and seductive, as irresistible as free money.

She did *not* want to be soothed or seduced. "Is that all?"

"And you'll want to see the office, of course."

She cursed him for using such effective bait to land her on his hook. There was no way she'd pass up the opportunity to see the king in his kingdom, commanding his serfs.

"Of course." But then she had a sudden inspiration, one that wouldn't require her to spend quite so much time with him. "Or maybe it'd be better if Eric—"

A sea change came over him, sucking away the amusement and leaving bad attitude with a healthy dose of pissed off in its place.

"*I'll* show you." His quiet, level voice didn't remotely match the dangerous expression on his face. "You and my cousin seemed awfully chummy, by the way."

Not that caveman stuff again. What was with those two? Did they go through this exercise whenever a woman of childbearing age crossed their paths? "Listen, Cro-Magnon Man—"

His scowl headed south, into glower range.

"—I don't know what kind of territory-marking game the two of you are playing, but I'm not going to—"

Whatever nonsense she'd planned to say after that died a swift death when a crooked, humorless smile inched across his face. He edged closer, a silent panther deep into his hunt. Staring into his glittering eyes, she fought hard for the strength and courage to stand her ground, knowing she could run but never escape.

And in her foolish mind and weak body the question was growing: how much running did she really want to do?

When he got within a foot of her, he stopped. He didn't

touch her and didn't need to. She *felt* him—his heat, his desire, his unshakable determination. In her full, throbbing breasts, pounding pulse and creamy sex…down to the marrow in her bones, she *felt* him.

"There's no game, Vivi." His tone was so serious she had no problems believing him. This thing between them, whatever it was, was a life-and-death matter to him, as crucial as the company he ran and the air he breathed. That being the case, he'd tolerate no gray areas and leave nothing to chance. "You're mine. Whether you know it or not or accept it or not or admit it or not. You just are."

If there was something to say to this pronouncement, Viveca couldn't think of it. He didn't look like he was in a particularly receptive mood anyway. For several long beats he held her gaze, challenging her—*begging her*—to deny it, but she didn't dare for fear he'd put his hands on her and prove, for once and for all, what a liar she was.

She almost wanted him to touch her.

To make the choice for her and put her out of her growing misery.

But he didn't, and she should have known he'd never make things that easy. He wanted her, yeah, but he wanted her to submit of her own free will, something she told herself she would never do. No matter how much she wanted to.

Chapter 10

Another week passed, during which Andrew avoided her. Viveca told herself she didn't care, which was a lie. She began a rough outline of the first few chapters of the book, continued with her interviews of Reynolds Warner's many and varied business associates and friends, and tried to forget that Andrew Warner existed.

First thing Monday morning, Viveca went to the tiny, white-picket-fenced home of Beulah Rivers, the woman who'd been Reynolds Warner's personal secretary for thirty years. With heavy emphasis on *personal*.

This woman, Viveca knew from interviews she'd already conducted with business associates of Reynolds Warner, none of whom had liked or seemed to feel the slightest loyalty toward him, had been Reynolds Warner's mistress for most of her adult life. She'd no doubt seen him at his best and worst, and was a secret keeper for all kinds of information about the man and his family. If Viveca could get her to open up, to tell her side of the story, Viveca's exposé would be halfway written.

That was a big *if,* of course.

Viveca was halfway up the stone path to the small but pretty white house when the door opened and a woman stepped onto the small porch, a delighted smile on her face. "Viveca?"

Viveca hurried forward, trying to hide her surprise that the woman wasn't another cool, willowy beauty like Mrs. Warner. Quite the opposite, actually. Beulah Rivers was short and plump with glasses. She had hair the unfortunate reddish shade of a woman with brown hair who overshot the whole highlights thing. Her light brown face was dimpled, sweet and warm. The overall effect was of a black Mrs. Claus—Viveca had to resist the urge to look around for Santa and a reindeer or two.

"It's so nice to meet you, Mrs. Rivers." Viveca shook the woman's hand.

"Oh, I was never married." This was a fact of which Viveca was well aware. "And you can call me Beulah."

"Thank you for agreeing to the interview."

"You're welcome, honey."

Beulah ushered Viveca through a fussy, frilly living room and settled at the kitchen table with coffee. Viveca turned on her voice recorder and pulled out her notes. "What was Mr. Warner like to work with?"

Beulah laughed. "That's like asking what it's like working with a tiger. Some days he's a pussycat, but you still don't ever forget he's a tiger."

"Ummm," Viveca said, distracted by the woman's use of the present tense for a man who'd been dead for decades. "Before I forget, I have a list of other people to interview. Business associates, mostly. I haven't contacted all of them yet. Roger Davies. Did you know him?"

"Oh, yes. Reynolds's golf partner. You'll want to talk to him."

Viveca made a note and consulted her list. "Great. And I understand that Andrew's mother, Barbara Warner, worked at the company for a while. Did some redecorating or something, and I wanted to ask you about that because she's—"

"I didn't see much of her. One day she decided she wanted to get out of the house for a while, do something other than shop all day, so they hired her to redecorate the office. She didn't last that long."

The sudden clatter of flatware onto china, as well as the icy frigidity in Beulah's warm voice, startled Viveca. She looked up from the papers in her lap to discover that Beulah's face had turned to stone. The woman got up, stacked the empty cups with trembling hands and headed to the sink, her cheeks aflame.

There was a story there, no question. Probably a personality clash because Barbara Warner had been, by all accounts, a spoiled diva. Most likely she and Beulah, who definitely had an old-school work ethic, had gotten along like nitro and glycerin. *Interesting.*

A minute or two at the sink rinsing the dishes seemed to be all Beulah needed to collect herself. She came back, her expression placid as a misty lake at dawn, sat and smiled. "Where were we?"

For two hours, Viveca asked detailed questions about every aspect of Beulah's professional life with Reynolds Warner, and then, finally, it was time to stop circling the eight-hundred-pound gorilla in the room and get to the heart of the matter.

"Beulah," she began, regretting the imminent loss of her blossoming acquaintanceship with the woman, who was a lovely person, "I've noticed you refer to Mr. Warner as if he's still alive."

Beulah started and spoke with a new wariness in her eyes. "Do I?"

"Yes. You miss him very much, don't you?"

"Well, I—" Beulah's face went a vivid shade of red. Flustered, she picked at the edge of her napkin. "I worked with him for many years, so I—"

"You loved him."

"He was a wonderful man. Very kind to me, you know—"

"You were *in love* with him."

"Who told you that?"

"Beulah, please." Viveca tried to be gentle and sympathetic. "Your face lights up when you talk about him. You blush. You talk about him in the present tense. You never married—"

"My mother didn't raise me to have affairs with married men."

"But you did. For years."

The woman deflated right before Viveca's eyes. Keeping her gaze lowered, she smoothed the curls at the base of her neck. "I don't know what I've done to make you think so little of me after I invited you into my house. I think it's time for you to leave."

No way. "I don't understand your blind loyalty to this man, Beulah. I really don't."

"I'm not blind." Anger sparked in the woman's eyes. "Reynolds Warner dipped his pen in a lot of ink pots over the years. Some of them very close to home. I know everything there is to know about him."

Viveca didn't doubt it. The stories this woman could tell, if she ever decided to tell them, would probably uncurl Viveca's hair. Still, she paused for a minute, trying not to push too hard.

Beulah planted her hands on the table and pressed to her feet, her movements now slow and revealing every one of her seventy-plus years. Deep lines that minutes ago had been unnoticeable ran down her face, bracketing her mouth and making her look haggard.

Staring at her, thinking about what she'd just done to this sweet old woman, Viveca hated herself. For the first time ever, she doubted her mission. Wondered if writing a tell-all about Reynolds Warner was the right thing to do, even to get justice for her father. Questioned whether she had the stomach for turning over rocks and seeing what kind of unpleasantness crawled into the open.

But then, in her mind's eye, she saw her father on his deathbed, and she shook off the guilt. Pushed it away and tried to pretend it didn't exist.

She'd come to Columbus to reveal Reynolds Warner for the corrupt, hypocritical bastard he'd been, and she wasn't going to let soft feelings for the man's mistress stop her.

"Beulah." Standing and putting a hand on the woman's arm, Viveca spoke quickly because she knew her time with Beulah was running out. "I'm not trying to make you the bad guy here. I'm not blaming you—"

"Have you ever been in love, Viveca?"

Astonishment snapped Viveca's mouth shut, or maybe it was the new sheen of tears in Beulah's eyes as she raised her gaze and looked Viveca in the face for the first time in several minutes.

"Have you?"

For some ridiculous reason, Andrew's brooding image

came to mind, flustering Viveca even more than the question had. There was no reason on earth for her to think of him, no reason a woman would ever love a man like him unless she wanted to commit emotional suicide. But there he was, taking up all the space in Viveca's brain and insisting that she see him.

"I don't see what that has to do with anything," Viveca said.

"Some men," Beulah said, "you just can't say no to."

Again Viveca thought of Andrew.

"Even if you know something is wrong," Beulah continued, "even if you know it's bad for you…even if you know it could break your heart…sometimes…you just can't help yourself."

There was Andrew again, smiling at Viveca, scowling at her, touching her… Even as Beulah's words were soaking into her brain, she saw Andrew. Not any of the few other men she'd dated. Only Andrew.

"Sometimes…the price is worth it to be with the man you love."

Viveca wanted to clap her hands over her ears because there was no corollary between Beulah and her feelings for Reynolds and Viveca and her growing feelings for Andrew. There couldn't be. *No, no, no.*

"Have you ever loved anyone that way, Viveca?"

Viveca couldn't answer.

Viveca was back at the cottage, working at the desk in the corner of the living room, when Andrew found her that afternoon. Mrs. Warner had gone to one of her ubiquitous committee meetings until dinner, and Bishop and the other staff had the day off, so she hadn't seen another living soul for hours.

She'd been sitting quietly, enjoying the breeze rippling through the open windows and screen door, and the summer fragrances of cut grass and roses from the garden as she sifted through a huge stack of yellowed Warner family photographs: adorable baby Andrew with his parents; Arnetta and Reynolds smiling at a party; Arnetta accepting a kiss from the mayor with Reynolds and Barbara in the background.

At the other end of the desk sat a small blue box filled with a stack of pictures that Viveca never went anywhere without. Her own precious pictures. Daddy, memorialized forever in twelve curled, yellowed photos that told the tale of his abbreviated life and early death, the only tangible things that linked the life she'd lost to the life she had now.

Lost in her thoughts, Viveca stared at picture after picture until, without warning, she felt a prickle of awareness along her bare arms. She knew, without knowing how she knew, that Andrew was there. Raising her head, she looked across the room and there he was, standing on the other side of the screen door, watching her.

A darkness hung over him that had nothing to do with the fine wool of his navy suit and everything to do with his mood. The lowered brows told her of storms brewing and disasters to come. The angle of his jaw, which was sharper than usual, warned that any dodging or hedging on her part would not be tolerated.

He *knew.*

One look at that face revealed a thousand things. One, Beulah had called him at the office, probably right after Viveca left, and told him about Viveca's questions and conclusions. Two, Andrew knew and liked Beulah, probably knew all about her tragic love for his married grandfather, and felt protective of her. And three, he didn't want Viveca bothering Beulah or stirring up all those sleeping dogs.

Feeling edgy and guilty—yeah, she had some explaining to do for badgering a senior citizen—she watched as he came inside and approached with a hard gleam in his eyes. They hadn't seen each other since the interlude in the greenhouse, which felt like two or three millennia ago, and she was dismayed to realize that, his anger notwithstanding, she was almost glad to see him.

He looked amazing in his corporate-titan uniform—white shirt, red power tie, polished oxfords that even her untrained eye could see cost as much as keeping a family of four in groceries for a month, and a king-of-the-world attitude.

Intimidating. Sexy. Breathtaking.

His gaze skimmed over her hair, lips and bare arms in her sleeveless black dress before going back to her eyes, where it lingered. "Hi."

"Hi."

He sat in the chair nearest her desk, leaned his elbows on his knees and stared down at his hands for a minute. When he looked up again, he looked more puzzled and troubled than angry. "What're you doing?"

Playing dumb crossed her mind, but that seemed like a spectacularly bad idea given his dangerous mood. Rather than say something glib—*reviewing photos, what's it look like?*—she decided to be honest.

"Writing a *nonfiction* book. Beulah is a witness with a lot to say."

"She doesn't want to say it."

Viveca shrugged. "I can change her mind. I'm good at getting information out of reluctant people."

Andrew twined his fingers together. His knuckles had

gone white, and she felt his temper strain to run free. "I don't think you understand. Beulah is near eighty with diabetes and colon cancer, and she's never done anything to this family."

Viveca went on the offensive to hide her sudden shame. "Other than have a thirty-year affair with your married grandfather, you mean."

His lips thinned and twisted. "I can't see what good it does to hurt Beulah and my grandmother for no good reason. What's the point of rubbing my grandmother's face in her husband's infidelity?"

"I am writing a book. Not a propaganda pamphlet. Your grandfather was a real person and I am getting to the bottom of—"

He'd had enough. She knew it even before he surged to his feet, threw his arms wide and roared at her, furious in a way he'd never been until now. "For *what?* What is the *point* of this righteous mission you're on, Viveca? To hold a dead man's feet to the fire?"

"Yes!"

"Why? He's *dead!* His widow has a bad heart and his mistress is probably going to die soon of cancer! What good can come of this?"

Viveca reached the end of her own rope and slammed her palms on the desk, scattering pictures. "Someone has to hold him accountable. Do you understand that? He cannot get away with—"

Too late, she realized what she was about to say and stopped herself. Running a shaky hand through her hair, she focused every particle of her being on straightening the photos so she wouldn't have to look at Andrew.

"Get away with *what,* Viveca?"

Hearing the new sharpness in his voice and knowing

he'd scented her blood and was now circling for the kill, Viveca cursed her own impulsivity.

"Nothing." Keeping her head bent low, she stacked the nearest pile. "I'm tired of hearing about the glories of the great Reynolds Warner. That's all."

"Really?"

"Yeah, *really.*" Looking up at last, feeling braver, she picked up a glossy black-and-white of the old man and flapped it in Andrew's face. "I'm not going to pretend he wasn't a real man with a real man's failings."

"He was a ruthless bastard. That make you feel better? That he cheated on his wife and was borderline abusive to most people he met? That he was a piss-poor father and grandfather? That what you want to hear?"

"It's a start."

"Well, let's keep going, shall we? Lay it all out there for you. Save you from having to do all that research."

"Andrew—"

He screwed up his face. "My father was a raging alcoholic who never worked hard a day in his life."

Viveca stared at him with growing alarm. Something inside him had ripped or burst, she realized, and was now oozing enough damage and poison into his system to kill him. "No."

"My mother was a shrew who shopped her life away. They hated each other and me by extension."

This was too much. It was one thing to put Reynolds Warner under the spotlight, but the last thing Viveca wanted to do was make Andrew bare his wounded soul like this. *His* pain had a way of becoming *her* pain, and she just couldn't stand it. *"Don't."*

"I drink too much sometimes and sleep with a lot of women. Eric's jealous of me, but that's okay because I don't give a damn what anyone thinks. Oh, and Grandmother likes him best. Always has. Let me think…let me think…"

Frowning, he cocked his head to one side, tapped an index finger to his lips and stared up at the ceiling in an exaggerated pose of absolute concentration. "Yeah. That about covers it. Does that give you enough material for your vendetta?"

She jerked as though he'd thrown bleach in her face.

Was she that obvious? Had she given everything away, or was it just that he could read her that well?

"Vendetta?" Forcing back the panic, she tossed her head and tried to look annoyed and scornful rather than worried. "I have no idea what you're talking about."

"You don't?"

"No. Just because I want to paint a balanced picture of this family doesn't mean I have a *vendetta*."

Andrew stared at her with shrewd, narrowed eyes, weighing and analyzing what she said with the precision and accuracy of a NASA analyst working with a multi-million-dollar computer. Finally he delivered his conclusion. "Bullshit."

Caught, Viveca told herself she would not blink, flush or show any other sign of weakness. Keeping her voice level, she tipped her chin up and didn't give an inch. "It doesn't matter whether you believe—"

"Yeah, actually, it does." Planting his hands on the desk, he leaned down in her face, two-hundred-plus pounds of unforgiving determination. "I'm not sure you understand that I can make one phone call and have an investigator on your tail in an hour—"

That simmering panic low in her belly rolled to a full boil.

"—and by the end of the day I'll know everything

about *you,* from your best friend in second grade to what size bra you wear—"

Viveca felt her defiant gaze waver.

"—and I can discover all the little skeletons in *your* family's closet that you'd rather not have anyone know about. How would *that* be, do you think?"

Three beats passed, and then she said the two stupidest words of her life: "Do it."

In the echoing silence, she felt instantaneous regret over her impulsivity. What the hell was she doing? Losing her temper and taunting him? How self-destructive was she going to get? Ten minutes with him and she became an unthinking kamikaze who couldn't blow herself up fast enough. She had to pull it together.

After a moment's awful pause during which they both glared and she wondered how it was possible that they didn't kill each other with all the toxic chemistry between them, he cursed, straightened and wheeled away to pace in front of the windows.

Too soon he came right back. To her astonishment, he came around the desk, dropped to his knees in front of her chair and trapped her by putting his hands on the arms and giving her nowhere to go.

Gasping and alarmed, she rose halfway and tried without success to roll back, far enough away so she couldn't feel his heat or smell the spices on his skin.

He held tight to her chair and to her gaze, showing not one ounce of mercy. "I don't want things to be like this with us." His husky, urgent voice had panic tightening her throat and warm honey flowing between her legs. "We don't have to do this."

"There's no *us,*" she said automatically.

A killing fury flashed in those blue eyes, terrifying her,

but in no way preparing her for the ruthlessness of what he said next. "So if I reached under your dress and touched you—right now, Vivi, right this very second—I wouldn't find you soaking wet for me?"

Stunned and enraged, humiliated by her own body's obvious weakness for this one man, the worst possible man, she tried again to roll her chair away. *"Go to hell."*

He must have sensed some of her despair because his expression softened immediately. "I'm sorry... I don't mean to hurt you. Don't mean to...don't..."

Reaching behind her, he planted his hands on her butt and slid her forward in the chair. She stiffened but it didn't make one bit of difference to those unyielding arms. Despite all her best intentions to never let him touch her, somehow he was between her legs doing something unthinkable. In a gesture of stunning tenderness, he laid his cheek against her breasts.

"No," she whimpered.

"Vivi."

The reverence in his hoarse voice ripped her heart to shreds. His arms came around her, binding her to him physically in a way that was almost nothing compared to the way she was beginning to feel about him emotionally.

There was no way to get free.

She couldn't even remember why she wanted to.

"Let's not do this." He buried his lips between her breasts and murmured to her, his breath hot against her sensitive skin. "Let's work this out."

Yes... She wanted that, too... Desperately wanted...

For one second she let go and touched him. Ran her hands up his broad back, cursed the suit jacket that kept his skin from hers, and speared her fingers through his curly hair. He groaned and shuddered, pulling her closer until her sex was pressed against his raging arousal. The exquisite rightness of it nearly killed her.

In a desperate effort to get near enough, she arched her back, mewling and rubbing against him like a shameless cat. He whispered her name, and that was when she really lost her mind.

She tightened her legs around him, ignoring the way her dress rode up around her bare thighs. Fisted her hands in his hair so he couldn't get away. For one second let herself imagine how it could be with him moving inside her.

That would have been the end of it.

Her intention was to push him away, pull her hem down, and resume hostilities. It really was. But she was no longer in control of her body, and probably hadn't been since the second she laid eyes on Andrew Warner. From up out of her throat came one agonized, unstoppable word, a word that changed everything: *"Andrew."*

Silence, for one second. And then everything made a cataclysmic shift.

Even as he pulled far enough back to look into her face, his trembling arms tightened around her, hurting with a delicious pain and telling her his control was gone.

So was hers.

"Tell me no," he demanded.

The savagery in his voice should have scared her, but didn't. If anything, it freed her and simplified everything. He needed this. She needed this. There would be no *no*s between them. Not today.

He waited while she held his gaze and said nothing.

When she could have stopped him, she didn't.

"Vivi," he said, reading the surrender in her eyes.

As he lunged for her, she tried to ignore the triumph in his voice and that in her heart.

Chapter 11

Neither of them could move fast enough.

He pressed her thighs to his waist, solidifying their grips on each other, and hissed out a "Yesss" when she clamped her thighs tight and linked her fingers behind his nape. Then he put his hands on her butt again, surged to his feet and swung her around as though she weighed nothing.

There was a crash and a clatter, and she realized, with her dazed brain, that he'd swiped all those photos to the floor, making space on the desk.

Laying her down on Mrs. Warner's cool, polished mahogany, he let her go long enough to rip his jacket off and toss it away. She helped him as much as she could, loosening his tie with her shaking hands and trying to undo the top couple of buttons on his starchy shirt. When that got her nowhere fast, she gave up and worked at the shirt from the bottom, pulling the tails and his undershirt out of his waistband. When she finally reached the hot satin of his skin, she crooned, making sounds she'd never heard come out of her mouth before.

Unzipping the back of her dress, he pushed the straps down over her shoulders, ripping something in the process. Seeing her black strapless bra, he gasped and jerked it down, freeing her breasts with a bounce. They puckered under the heat of his gaze, aching for his hands, his mouth, his chest.

"Oh." Panting, he stared at her with absolute absorption, a slight crease between his brows. "Beautiful… Brown… Small."

"What?"

"Your nipples. They've been on my mind." A rough stroke of his palm sent swells of exquisite sensation directly to her sex and had her arching backward until she almost lay flat on the desk.

He jerked her upright and there was no gentleness in him, which was good because she didn't want gentle. She wanted fast and hard.

"Didn't I tell you that the next time I touched you, it would be like this?"

She was incapable of answering. His hot breath feathered over one breast and she waited…waited…but nothing happened until, with a frustrated, incomprehensible sound, he put one hand in her hair and tugged, hard, to catch her attention.

Crying out, she tried—*tried*—to focus.

Lips poised half an inch from one pointed nipple, he watched her, his eyes glittering like sapphires in the sun.

"Answer me. I'm talking to you."

Viveca tried to think. What had he said? *What?*

Shuddering with the effort to hold himself back, he repeated his question. "Didn't I tell you it'd be like this?"

"Y-yes."

Another sound of triumph erupted from deep in his throat. His hot, wet mouth closed in, suckling hard, and the first rippling mini-orgasms spasmed through her. Surprise caught in her throat, choking off his name, which was right on the tip of her tongue.

He would kill her before this was over, she thought, stunned.

This was something she couldn't possibly survive.

Raising his head, he stared at her and, even in her dazed state, she could read the victory in his eyes. "You like that, don't you, Vivi?"

"Yes."

Half a smile, ruthless and intent, crossed over his face. Leaning closer, he licked her. Stroked his tongue right across her lips and then took her mouth deeply and relentlessly, the way she knew he was about to take her. Raw instinct took over and had her sucking his mouth, biting hard but not enough to hurt.

With a growl—there was no other word for it—he wrenched free and stared at her with wide-eyed awe. "You little tiger. I knew it. *Knew it.*"

He reached down and shoved her dress up her thighs, his huge body shuddering with excitement, but then his movements slowed and she had the feeling he wanted to savor her.

With extreme focus, he pulled her lacy black panties down over her hips and off her legs. Watching her, he put the scrap of material to his nose and breathed deeply. Rapture softened his face and his eyes drifted shut. The sight rocked her deep to her throbbing belly and sharpened her desperate need.

"Touch me," she said helplessly. "I need you."

Those dark eyes snapped open. Without hesitation he tossed her panties away and fumbled with his belt.

It took too long…too long…and her overheated, starving body couldn't wait. Spreading her legs, inviting him, she urged him on. He cursed, struggling with his zipper. Frenzied now, she palmed her breasts, rubbing and circling her aching nipples.

His eyes bulged.

"I knew it," he said again. "I *knew* it would be like this with you."

"Hurry. Stop talking."

He laughed. "You want more, don't you, Vivi?"

"Yes."

Beyond uninhibited, she groaned and squirmed for him, panted. The slide of his zipper was the most thrilling sound she'd ever heard and she almost wept with relief.

"You want me, don't you?"

"Yes."

Instead of entering her then, as she needed him to, he slipped his hand between her thighs and stroked her. Again she cried out. A look of dazed ecstasy crossed his face, but then his head fell back and his eyes rolled closed. Over and over again he stroked her and she rode his fingers, climbing higher than she'd ever been before.

After a while he opened his eyes and stared at her with undisguised reverence. "This is for me, isn't it?" She knew he was referring to the hot river that flowed between her legs. *"All for me."*

"You know it is."

Another half smile, and then he rubbed one of his wet fingers across her lips and gave her another deep, endless kiss. The primitive, broken sounds he made as he tasted her told her exactly what she did to him.

Finally he pulled away and reached for the wallet in his back pocket. Shaking it open, scattering bills and credit cards on the floor, he pulled out a foil package, ripped it open with his teeth and put a condom on.

"Hurry," Viveca said. "Hurry…hurry…*hurry.*"

Something about her chanting seemed to amuse him. A flash of merciless humor crossed over his face, and he took his hard length and stroked it between her swollen lips, driving her out of what little was left of her mind.

"You're a liar, aren't you, Vivi?"

"Hurry."

"Answer me." Unsmiling now, he stroked again, causing another agonized whimper to escape her mouth and another wave of contractions to ripple through her belly. "When you tell me there's no *us,* and say you don't want me, you're *lying,* aren't you?"

Helpless to do otherwise, knowing he wouldn't make love to her unless she answered, even if it took all day and all night, she told the truth: "Yes."

"Every time you say it, it's a lie, isn't it?"

"*Yes.* Please, Andrew. Now. *Please.*"

That was enough. His body's trembling told her he'd reached the end of his rope and couldn't wait another second any more than she could.

His hips surged and with that one stroke he was deep inside her, seated to the base, every considerable inch of him stretching her past endurance.

The afternoon's quiet was filled with their astonished cries and whimpers. Tightening their arms around each other, they moved together as if their mating had been choreographed by Balanchine.

"You feel so good, baby," he whispered. "So good, *so good…* You're killing me. I can't… I *can't*—"

His hips surged and flowed and hers met him stroke for deep stroke. Pleasure dimmed her vision, making her blind and incoherent until all she could do was *feel,* hold on and try not to lose consciousness.

Hampered as she was by her dress and his shirt, she couldn't get close enough, but she clung, digging her nails into the clenching and unclenching muscles of his round butt.

Andrew...Andrew...Andrew...

The world began and ended with him. With the rough scratch of his suit pants against her thighs. With his taste in her mouth. With his body inside hers.

Possessing her as he'd been born to do. As no other man ever had, or ever would.

The orgasm surged through her, choking off the breath in her throat and leaving her mouth open in wordless surprise. The violent pulse of her inner muscles drove him over the edge, and he came with a hoarse cry and a fury of pumping hips. His entire body went rigid and then he jerked, over and over and over again, as though a million volts of lightning reverberated through his body. *"Vivi."*

Burying his fingers in her hair, anchoring her to him, he rocked and kissed her. His lips touched every part of her face—lips, cheeks, eyes and temples, over and over again—and the love words poured out.

"Vivi. Vivi. Beautiful girl... I knew it would be like this... I knew it... You're mine. You know that, don't you? Mine...beautiful Vivi..."

Yes was on the tip of her tongue. A thousand times *yes.* Of course she was his.

Then her vision slowly cleared and everything changed.

Over his shoulder, down on the floor, she saw Reynolds Warner's shrewd, vivid gaze staring up at her from an eight-by-ten glossy, mocking and condemning, even in death.

The rest of the world slammed back to her with the force of ten nuclear weapons.

Her dead father. The book.

The Warner family's closet full of skeletons and secrets.

"Oh, no." She could barely get the words out. *"Oh, no."*

Andrew looked down at her, the happiness leaching from his face bit by bit. *"Vivi?"*

Answering was impossible. Shaking her head, she looked around the room, beyond horrified at what she'd just done. Every object she saw seemed to accuse her:

Mrs. Warner's expensive antique desk, on which she'd just had sex with a man she hardly knew, didn't trust and was probably in love with.

Her rumpled dress, which was bunched around her waist.

Andrew's jacket on the floor and the rest of his clothes, which were still on.

Her thighs, which remained wrapped around his hips.

The screen door, through which daylight streamed and through which any passerby could have peeked.

"Oh, my God." She looked around the room again with growing humiliation. "What did I *do?*"

"No, Viveca," Andrew said sharply, his arms tightening. *"Don't."*

He was still inside her, buried deep. Worse, she wanted to make love with him again.

Actually, it was screwing, wasn't it? When you had sex with a known enemy in broad daylight in a semiprivate place with most of your clothes still on, that was *screwing,* right? No need to glamorize it by calling it *making love.* As if Andrew Warner had ever *made love* in his life, or was even capable of *making love.*

Andrew Warner had just…screwed her.

And she wanted him to do it again. Repeatedly. Endlessly.

Even knowing he had an agenda and she had a mission and had just betrayed her father, she still wanted him with the kind of desperation that drove people to commit violent acts. How stupid did that make her?

Criminally, sickeningly, unforgivably stupid.

Just to add insult to injury, she'd given herself willfully. Gleefully. Wantonly. Worse, she'd admitted how much she wanted him and then, if that hadn't been clear enough, she'd demonstrated it. She couldn't very well go back to issuing cool denials about her feelings after *this,* could she?

"*Viveca.*"

The plea in his voice somehow made it all worse.

"Let go of me."

Behind his eyes, a light went out. Something disappeared or died; she couldn't tell which. Moving slowly, he dropped his hands and slid free of her body, leaving behind a glorious ache that would be her reminder and her punishment for her colossal stupidity.

As soon as he let go, she hopped down from the desk, a mistake since her knees were loose and blood flow to the northern parts of her body hadn't quite returned to normal. To her everlasting embarrassment, she wobbled. He, as surefooted and strong as ever—naturally—shot out a hand and steadied her.

The second she was sure she wouldn't fall flat on her face, she hurried away, out of his reach, grabbed her panties from the floor, turned her back to him and slid them on. Pulling her dress back down, she smoothed it and her rumpled hair and tried to look dignified, even though she knew her lips were swollen and she probably had telltale marks on her breasts and neck from where he'd kissed her.

He went to the bathroom and came back. When she looked around again, every stitch of his clothing was back in its place. Even his credit cards and wallet were put away. He looked perfectly normal as long as she ignored his high color, the slight sheen of perspiration across his forehead and the insistent bulge in the front of his pants. Seeing it, she felt a responsive pull in the pit of her belly, even *now.*

Furious with herself, she looked away.

"Congratulations." Her pulse thundered in her dry throat. "You won."

"Won?"

"Well, you said you have sex with every woman you meet, right? And you wanted to prove that I wanted you. So you killed two birds with one stone over there on that desk, didn't you? That's a pretty good day."

He stared at her, looking murderous. He seemed incapable of speech, and that felt oddly satisfying. Enough so that she kept talking when a wiser woman would have shut up.

"But don't get too excited, okay? Just because I'm stupid enough to have sex with you doesn't mean I'm stupid enough to drop the book. I'm still going to write it. Just so we're clear."

Several beats passed, and then, for the second time that day, he lunged for her. One second he was ten feet away, watching her, and the next he was in her face, roaring with rage and catching her by the arms.

Panic took over and, like a coward, she tried to break away and run.

He dragged her back, up against him. "Yeah." He palmed her butt with both hands and ground her into his erection. "By all means, let's be clear."

"Let me go."

He smacked her butt, hard. She cried out with unexpected pleasure, not pain, and he smoothed the ache by kneading the tender flesh. Bringing her as close as he could with their clothes still on, he circled his hips, unerringly rubbing his hard length against the sweet spot between her legs until the room swayed around her.

"First things first." He spoke against her ear, sending the words directly to her overwrought brain. "What just happened here had nothing to do with anything other than us wanting each other."

"No."

Another hard smack silenced her, and he continued.

"It had nothing to do with your book, your vendetta or my grandfather. It had nothing to do with me wanting to kill the book. It had nothing to do with me and women in general. It was about *you* and *me,* period. Okay?"

Viveca clung to his arms and didn't dare answer.

"Second." He licked and nipped at her ear until her knees liquefied and his grip was the only thing keeping her upright. "What just happened is going to happen again. And again and again."

"No, it's not."

Those hands on her butt turned into claws, digging in and bringing her even closer to the part of him that strained for her. Another orgasm appeared on the horizon, hovering just out of her reach.

"Do you see that desk, Vivi?" He pointed, as if she needed any reminders. "One of these days, I'm going to bend you over it and take you from behind. I can get deeper that way."

Her heart skittered to a stop.

"See that sofa?" Another point. "I'm going to lay you

on it and ride you, hard, and we're both going to have a tough time walking by the time we're finished. See that rug over in front of the fireplace? Guess what I'm going to do to you there? Well…I'll let you wonder about that."

Viveca gaped, too aroused to think, much less speak.

Backing her into the nearest wall, he ground into her. His concrete length, her soft, wet, overstimulated sex, and the promise of illicit things to come, led to one inevitable result.

The orgasm tore through her, a force of nature as uncontrollable as the sun's daily rise. Throwing her head back, she stopped struggling and let it wash over her, crying out because all that pleasure had to escape from her body one way or another. He watched, eyes glittering, as she came for what seemed like five minutes.

Finally it was over and she was limp and devastated.

Taking advantage of her momentary helplessness, he stroked her, touching everything as though he absolutely couldn't help himself. Her arms…her shoulders… breasts…hips…butt…breasts again. When he was done with that, he palmed her face, again kissing her cheeks and eyes, and the unspeakable tenderness made her want to sob and beg him never to let her go.

"We're together now, Viveca," he told her the next time his lips passed her ear. "We're going to be together for a long time. The sooner you get that through your thick skull, the happier we'll both be."

The reverberations were still rippling through her when he let go and gave her a last hot, possessive look that, unbelievably, sent heat skittering over her skin.

"Just so we're clear." He walked off.

Light-headed, dazed, she slumped against the wall and waited for the bones in her legs to solidify. When she reached up a hand to brush her hair back from her over-heated forehead, she saw something on the floor.

Another photograph. Her father this time, not Reynolds Warner. Squatting gingerly, she picked up Daddy's last picture, taken in the hospital on his fortieth birthday, the month before he died.

He was hooked up to untold tubes and wires, dressed in an undignified baby-blue patterned gown, his stub wrapped in white bandages, and his skin gray from the cancer and the cancer treatments, none of which had bought him an extra day. He'd lost his will to live when he lost his arm, then died a gruesome death, and here she was having sex with a member of the family that had killed him.

Andrew had made it across the room and opened the screen door before she recovered enough to get angry. White-hot fury surged, and she directed it all at Andrew, the man whose touch she craved and who made it so easy for her to forget her life's mission.

For fifteen years, fully half her life, she'd sworn she'd get justice. Sworn that the Warners would pay for what they'd done to her father. This had been her sole mission. If she didn't have her mission, what did she have?

If she wasn't her father's avenger, who was she? *What* was she?

Andrew Warner's sexual plaything until another Brenda came along?

Not in this lifetime.

She'd been weak this once, true, but she wouldn't be weak again.

"You do whatever you have to do." Pushing away from the wall, she stood on her own two feet and squared her shoulders for the fight to come. "And I'll do the same."

Andrew looked around in disbelief, his mouth open.

Deadlocked, they stared at each other with the battle-field between them and no visible middle ground. For a minute she thought he seemed angry enough to hit her, but then he did something far worse.

"Keep talking." Rubbing the enormous bulge in the front of his pants, making her nipples tighten with the bottomless lust she had for him, he smiled, and it was crooked and humorless. "Everything you say makes me want you more. Every fighting word that comes out of your pretty little mouth only proves that you're the only woman for me and I'm the only man who can handle you."

Eyes hard and glittering, he wheeled around and stalked out, banging the door hard enough to shake the rafters.

Chapter 12

Andrew went up to the main house rather than back to work, partly because he didn't want to be that far away from Viveca, and partly because his emotions were running so high he didn't trust himself behind the wheel of a car.

After a few minutes' relentless pacing in the foyer, he headed up the curved staircase, taking the steps three at a time, and turned into the back wing. Inexorably drawn, he crept down the hall toward his inevitable destination, his parents' old room. The situation with Viveca made him miserable, so why not wallow in it in the perfect place for misery?

Outside the door he stopped, just like he always did, when all the usual sensations hit him. The knotted stomach, the clammy skin, the phantom smells of vanilla, scotch and cigarettes.

Most of all he felt *devastation,* made worse because of Viveca's ongoing rejection when he needed her like he needed protein, oxygen and sunshine.

He stood there, rooted to the floor by indecision.

This was the point where he would normally turn around, retrace his footsteps and get the hell out of here. This was the line he would not cross, the step he would not take. Ever. But sudden fury took over.

What the hell had he let happen to him?

He, who prided himself on the control he maintained over every aspect of his life and, whenever possible, the lives of those around him, had lost control. Viveca, a woman who didn't like him even if she wanted him, had control.

He marched to her drumbeat. Came to her on her terms, when she let him, smiled when she smiled. Wanted her to the point of insanity. Had let protecting his inheritance and his family become a distant second in importance to being with Viveca. Was prepared to go to great lengths to get her to accept him in her life on a long-term basis.

Possibly even…a permanent basis. Had even begun thinking that maybe he was in love with her.

So, yeah, it didn't look like he was in control of any part of his life.

And if he needed further proof of this painful fact, he had only to look at his reactions to this room, the one that defeated him every time he darkened its threshold and catapulted him back to the unhappiest moment of his painful childhood.

A question came to him, burning through his anger— was he a man, or not?

Hell yeah.

Maybe he couldn't control the Viveca situation, but he could damn well control his reactions to this room.

Taking a deep breath, he lifted a foot and crossed from the polished wood of the hallway onto the plush cream of the carpet.

One step…two steps…three. He was inside.

Everything rushed back to him, as he'd known it would.

It was dark and late.

He was supposed to be in bed, and his parents were supposed to be at Grandmother's big party downstairs. Normally they were out of town, in Europe or somewhere, letting him have the run of the house and live his own life with a nanny or two, but they reappeared two or three times a year for the important events, like parties for the mayor.

If it occurred to them, they'd act like they thought parents should act and take him out shopping or something, as though throwing a little money at him was enough to fool him into thinking they gave a damn.

Tonight they'd gotten the brilliant idea of tucking him into bed, which only showed how stupid they were. Half the time they didn't seem to know how old he was—ten— and most of the time they didn't care.

Andrew endured the tucking, grateful they hadn't decided to also read him a Dr. Seuss book. After waiting a decent interval for the party to get into full swing, he snuck into their room to spend a little quality time with his father's stash of Playboy *magazines, which he'd recently discovered while snooping.*

He'd just gotten settled into the chair by the window and opened up to the centerfold when angry footsteps drowned out the faint music from the jazz band. With only enough time to click off the overhead light, he dove under the bed, taking the magazine with him.

The door flew open and Dad came in, frog-marching Mom ahead of him, his hand around her upper arm tight

*enough to leave finger marks on her fair skin. Slamming
the door, he turned her loose, catapulting her onto the bed.*

The mattress creaked ominously and she cried out.

*Alarmed, Andrew scooted around on his belly until he
could peek out from under the bed's skirt and see his
parents' reflection in the cheval mirror in the corner.*

What he saw terrified him.

*Dad lighting a cigarette with shaking hands. Mom
struggling to her feet, her defiant face burning with red
patches over her cheeks.*

*Andrew had seen her earlier, looking like a movie star
before she went down to the party, and she didn't look
anything like that now. Her honey-brown hair was down,
swinging around her shoulders—but it'd been up before,
in one of those fancy styles with lots of swirls. And her silky
blue dress was wrinkled from the waist to the floor. Her
lips were a swollen smear of lipstick, and across the top
of her bosom was a flaming red mark, almost like she'd
been scratched, or bitten.*

*Andrew didn't know what any of this meant, except that
it was nothing good.*

*After a long time, Dad snuffed out his cigarette and
looked at her.*

*"So this is what you do now? Screw people in bath-
rooms during parties?"*

Andrew's heart stopped.

*He waited for Mom to slap Dad, deny it, or do anything
other than what she did. Tossing that thick hair, she made
an ugly sound that may have been a laugh. "Like you
care."*

"You stupid bitch."

*That was when Andrew, who never cried, started crying.
Silent, fat, scared tears rolled down his cheeks, humili-*

ating him even though he knew no one could see them and wouldn't care if they could. Mom laughed again, almost like she was glad Dad was so mad.

"I don't care who you spread your legs for." *Dad could barely spit the words out. He had his fists clenched at his sides, and Andrew was half-afraid he would punch Mom across her smiling, puffy mouth.* "Hell, you've already done every man in the tri-state area at least once—"

Smirking, Mom sauntered over to the mirror above the dresser, leaned in, grabbed a tissue and wiped the lipstick smears.

"—but if you think I'm going to stand by while you do it right under my nose during my mother's party—"

Dad, roaring again and totally out of control in a way Andrew had never seen him, broke off, swiped the back of one hand across his spittle-dotted mouth, and took a shuddering breath before he continued.

"—or pass another one of your bastards off as my child, then you'd better think again."

This, finally, wiped the smile off Mom's face.

Andrew was still replaying the words through his frantic brain, trying to think of an interpretation—any possible interpretation—that meant something other than that his father wasn't his father, when Mom marched up to stand in Dad's face.

"Well." *Sneering, Mom flung out the sentences that ended Andrew's childhood, ruined his fragile identity and destroyed life as he'd known it.* "Since *you* couldn't get me pregnant, you should be glad I did it with someone who looked like you. Now no one will ever know Andrew isn't yours, will they?"

There was more before they left, but Andrew didn't hear it because he was too busy thinking of all the dots in his life that now had been connected. Why his parents didn't want him. Why they didn't love him. Why they couldn't stand to be in the same city as Andrew for more than a week at a time.

Why his father—yeah, right—never looked him in the face. It all made sense. They didn't love him. Couldn't love him. And he would never love them—or anyone—ever again. Loving hurt too much, and look how it turned out.

It wasn't worth the risk.

After what seemed like hours but was probably only a minute or two, the door banged open again. "Scooter." Bishop, looking panicked, appeared. "Scooter. I know you hear me. Jesus, Lord." Bishop saw him, ran around the bed, dropped to his knees and studied his face. "Help this boy, please."

Maybe Bishop had heard his parents shouting, or maybe he just knew in the way people know when they love a child. No household could keep secrets from a man with eyes as sharp as Bishop's.

Gathering Andrew close, he rocked him. "It's okay, Scooter. None-a this is your fault. They love you. They just don't know how to show it 'cause they got their own problems. It's not your fault."

Andrew didn't believe him.

That was the day he had decided women were good for sex and nothing else. The day part of his soul—a large part—shut itself off, hid in the dark and avoided emotional pain of any kind. The day he stopped caring about much of anything.

Until now. Until Viveca forced him to care.

"Scooter?"

Blinking, Andrew came slowly out of his thoughts and

glanced around to discover Bishop looking down at him with concern, a feather duster in his hand. Somehow Andrew had sat in that same chair by the window without even knowing it and hadn't heard Bishop's approach.

"Viveca's barking up the wrong tree, Bishop. She knows about Miss Beulah. She thinks the big secret has to do with Granddad and his affairs."

"Well, the Warners got a lot of secrets, Scooter," Bishop said reasonably. "Pretty much any tree will turn up something."

This was true.

"You gonna let her bark?"

"No." Andrew knew what he had to do even if he didn't want to do it. "I have something else in mind." He'd go back to the office, call one of his best investigators and have him put together a little information on the mysterious Viveca Jackson. He should've done it sooner. And then he'd go to New York to talk to people who'd known her. People were always happy to talk for the right price.

He couldn't shake the feeling that if he knew what drove her, he could stop her. Possibly even help her. As much as he hated to admit it, he was worried about her because he didn't think her revenge mission would make her happy, even if she achieved it. If anything, he feared it would make her even more bitter than she already was. His stomach knotted at the thought because he absolutely could not stand to think of Viveca in any sort of pain. It killed him.

"You in love, Scooter?"

Possibly. Probably. Andrew decided to own it, to himself, if not to Bishop. "Don't call me Scooter," he said, not meeting the old man's gaze.

With a kind, enigmatic smile, Bishop patted Andrew

on the shoulder and left. Andrew wasn't sure he wanted
to be alone with his thoughts, which were spinning out
of control.

He'd made love to Viveca, and he just couldn't believe it.

She'd damn near blown the top of his head off, his little
Vivi, she of the don't-touch-me disdain. What an aggres-
sive, demanding, uninhibited tiger she was with him. Just
as he'd known she would be.

She was his, finally. Well… No. She wasn't.

He'd been so desperate to get inside her body, he hadn't
thought about the obvious problem, which was that she'd
regret it afterward, for a variety of reasons. First, she didn't
like him. Second was the whole book thing. Third was the
fact that doing it quick and hard on the desk opened the
door for her to form exactly the wrong conclusion, namely
that he just wanted her for sex.

So how was he going to get out of the sewer-sized hole
he'd dug for himself? Because he had to get out of it. Had
to get with Vivi. He needed her. No matter how much he
didn't want to, he just did. She made him laugh, she drove
him crazy, and she excited him to the point of heart attack.
Was he just supposed to ignore all that?

Maybe, but he wasn't about to. He couldn't.

Everything rode on his plan: gather as much information as he could about Viveca. And then pray that he could
figure out what to do with the information once he had it.

They were there in the cottage later that night when
Viveca got back from dinner at the main house. Sunflowers.

Great, giant sunflowers in shades of yellow and orange
with heads the size of dinner plates. In an enormous silver
bucket sitting just in front of the dormant fireplace. In a
wicker basket atop the coffee table. In a silver pitcher in

the middle of the small kitchen table, crowding each other, their faces jockeying for space among other greenery.

The most beautiful flowers she'd ever seen.

Joy, as light and free as a hummingbird, flew through her chest, and for thirty of the best seconds of her life, as she leaned in and touched her precious sunflowers with gentle fingers, she was happy.

But then, with dread, Viveca read the inscription on the envelope, which was scrawled in bold blue handwriting: *To My Beautiful Sunflower*.

Shaking now, totally ruined, she made it to the nearest chair and sank into it. After another several deep breaths, she worked up the nerve to look at the note.

Opening the flap, she pulled out the card of Andrew's personal stationary with A.R.W., *Andrew Reynolds Warner,* at the top, and read it:

Think about me tonight, because I'll be thinking about you. A.

Hot tears burned the backs of her eyes and she swiped at them, helpless to understand her emotions or even what kind of tears they were.

Well, no. She knew. They were angry tears because she'd let him do this to her. Frustrated tears because she had no idea what to do now. Scared tears because he was a world-class schemer and player who would inevitably break her heart. Desperate tears because she wanted him and knew they would never find a way to trust each other.

She knew she should just leave. Except that then she wouldn't get the justice she'd come for. And the idea of never seeing him again *hurt.* Actually stabbed through her chest like a white-hot pitchfork. And if push came to shove, she doubted she could do it. Foolish to the bitter end, she would probably stay here and wait for her inevitable destruction at his hands, like a lamb skipping off to slaughter.

What should she do?

In answer, the phone rang.

Startled, it took three more rings for her to answer. "Hello?"

There was a long silence, and she was going to hang up when she heard a deep breath. "I, ah… I told myself I wasn't going to call you."

Andrew.

Chapter 13

Viveca's foolish heart leaped like a child on a trampoline. "Hi."

Pressing her precious card to her chest, she collapsed on the nearest sofa and wished she were a better woman, one strong enough to slam the phone down and tell him not to bother her again.

There was another long pause, another deep breath, and then he said, "I can't stop thinking about you. I miss you, Vivi."

Ever stupid, she wanted to weep with gratitude and jump for joy. He, on the other hand, sounded miserable, as though missing her was the worst fate he could endure this side of hell.

The responsive words—*I miss you, too... God, I miss you*—were right there on her tongue. She choked them back in an act that felt as unnatural as breathing water, and cleared her throat. "Where are you?"

"I, ah...have important business in New York."

Wow, she thought, stunned. Andrew had sex with her and then left town.

It figured.

"Oh," she said, trying not to sound as glum as she felt. "Thank you for my beautiful flowers. They're incredible."

"It's nothing," he said gruffly. "I've got some good news for you."

He didn't sound like the bearer of anything good. He sounded unhappy, as though he brought news of a death in the family. "What's that?"

"I'm backing off a little. Giving you some space."

It *should* have been good news. She knew that. In theory, his backing off was the solution to most of her problems, but in practice it sounded as appetizing as a mud pie.

"Is that so?" She wondered if this was the same kind of kiss-off he'd given Brenda, the patented Andrew Warner kick-to-the-curb.

"Yeah. Maybe if I'm not pressing so hard, you'll come to me on your own. I don't want you to regret what happens between us."

"Oh." Staring at the nearest sunflower arrangement, she felt surly and had the unaccountable urge to smash it to the floor.

"Don't get me wrong, though. I can feel your wheels turning—"

No, you can't.

"—and you're wondering if I've decided I don't want you."

There he went again, reading her mind with utter precision, as though he had a Viveca Jackson Rosetta Stone to translate her every syllable, mutter and sigh. It was so damn irritating.

She paused, working up her nerve so that when she spoke her voice would be stammer free. "It really doesn't matter."

There was a stony silence. When he spoke again it was with the purring, ruthless tone she'd come to know and dread, liberally laced with sensual knowledge.

"I'm so glad we used this afternoon to establish—*on the record*—what a liar you are, Vivi. Otherwise my feelings would be really hurt right now."

He was using pillow talk against her?

Outraged and mortified, her cheeks burned white hot. The snappy retort she needed to put Mr. Arrogant in his place didn't come, so she sputtered, defenseless.

"Since you're so big on us being *clear* with each other," he continued and, if possible, her face got even hotter at this further reference to their wild interlude in the library, "I want to make sure you understand. I still want you. I'm beginning to think I'll *always* want you. I am going to figure out a way for us be together, or die trying. Are we clear?"

Crystal. Perverse as it was, she felt a fierce, secret joy that his feelings hadn't changed and this wasn't the end of whatever they had between them. Where that left them, she had no idea.

All she knew was that her insides had gone tingly and her face wasn't the only place in her body where her blood ran thick and hot. If only he knew how truly *bad* she had it for him, he'd laugh until he wet his pants.

"You know," she said, hiding her turmoil behind a thick layer of indignation, "you have a way of saying the most romantic things and making them sound like a drill sergeant barking out orders to climb a hill."

To her complete astonishment, he laughed. And she felt ridiculously pleased.

"God, I l—" he began, and then caught himself.

In the abrupt silence, she heard the echo of what he'd

started to say, or maybe it was only her projection of what she wished he'd say. *God, I love you.*

It wasn't possible, of course. A man like Andrew wasn't capable of love and, if he was, she was hardly the most likely candidate. Knowing this didn't stop her from wanting him to say it, though. Her yearning for him ached and grew, a virus that slowly spread through her body and would no doubt lead to her ultimate destruction.

He cleared his throat. "You really make me laugh, Vivi. You know that?"

"Is that right?"

"Yeah."

"Well." She tried to sound upbeat and unconcerned, but couldn't keep the bitterness out of her voice. "So I've got some space. Great. *Perfect.*"

He said nothing, letting her twist in the wind.

She twisted, hating him for it. She wished she could just hang up, but that was impossible because, if she didn't know when she would see him again, she would die.

"What about my book?" Feeling desperate and ridiculous, she plowed ahead. "You promised me an interview. When are you going to sit for that?"

"You and your mixed signals," he muttered.

She ignored this unhelpful commentary. "When?"

More nothing.

It was the longest silence of the night, and the most painful. Was he silently mocking her for being so transparent? The waiting and agonized wondering went on and on, and when he finally spoke, his answer did nothing to put her out of her misery.

If anything, he made things worse, which was probably his point.

"I'll check my calendar and let you know."

* * *

A few agonizing days later, Andrew invited her to the office and waited while she rode up the elevator. It took forever for the doors to slide open and then, suddenly, there she was. She froze a little as their gazes locked. So did he. A pretty flush bloomed over her cheeks, heightening her color until she seemed to glow with an inner energy he really hoped had something to do with him.

Those sweet brown eyes brightened and, in a gift sent to him directly from above, she gave him the beginnings of a smile, as though she was glad to see him and had made some sort of peace with their relationship.

Illumination flashed through his brain, shining light in dark corners, showing him the obvious and clarifying the complex. This woman was special. She was funny and strong, smart and determined, wounded, fascinating and sexy. More than that, she was special to *him*. When he was within range of her brightness and beauty, he wanted to do the right thing, to be *worthy*. Wanted to know that she didn't think he was a complete waste of tissue and bones.

Most of all, he wanted to protect her and make sure she had everything she needed to be happy and secure. If she needed to talk, he would listen. If she wanted to laugh, he would be Bozo the Clown. If she had to cry, he had shoulders. If she wanted to rule a country, he would buy one for her.

It took a moment for the complete picture to emerge. When it finally did, he was left stunned and speechless, but resolved and unflinching.

This woman belonged to him. He already knew that. Had told her that. He just hadn't considered the corollary:

He belonged to her. Always had, always would. Stunned, he held her gaze while his world shifted.

Andrew had fallen in love with his enemy.

"The office is really something." Viveca fought back a smile, obviously trying not to gush lest her praise go straight to his already overinflated ego. "I had no idea how…I don't know…how vast the company was."

"You should see the New York building."

His nickel tour had taken about an hour, and they'd circled back around to the reception area outside his office. He'd shown her the glittering, soaring atrium with its huge fountain trickling down most of one wall; the employee café; gym and day care; the research, marketing, advertising and legal floors; the roof with its helicopter pad; and everything else he could think of. She'd taken copious notes and absorbed it all like the curious sponge that she was.

He, on the other hand, had stared at her every possible opportunity while simultaneously trying to repress his idiotic grin from the thrill of being in her presence.

It came as no surprise that she'd been most impressed by the day care, which he'd added years ago in one of his first acts as CEO. With Viveca it was all about family and making the world a better place.

She gave him a bemused look. "You sound jaded. Are you used to all this?"

"Sick of it, more like," he muttered without thinking.

"What do you mean?" Viveca's gaze sharpened, but, unless he was much mistaken, it was with concern, not generalized nosiness.

"Just that…I'm a little…burned out."

"Who wouldn't be?"

Again with the concern shining in those brown eyes. He

really could get addicted to it. "The work is too much...*work*. It used to be fun, but now it's a job. Too many meetings, too much infighting, constant fires to put out." He shrugged. "The nature of the beast, I guess."

He'd long ago resigned himself to his fate, which he likened to that of a reluctant crown prince. Maybe you didn't want to be king, but that was what you were born to do, so you did it. Period. So he was totally unprepared for what Viveca said next.

"Why don't you do something else?"

He gaped at her. *"Something else?"*

"Yeah." She laughed. *"Something else.* What is it about what you used to do that made it so much fun?"

"Well...I spent more time with the rank and file. Getting ideas from them. Investigating some of the newer technologies that are more environmentally sound."

"The green stuff?"

"Yeah."

"Why can't you do that again?"

"I don't have another company, for one thing."

"Find one."

His jaw flapped like a door on a hinge. "Who would run this one?"

"Someone else."

Andrew stared at her, beyond speechless.

This was an idea as revolutionary to him as democracy in czarist Russia, and here she was throwing it out there like it was nothing. Unbelievable. What was there to say to that? It took him a minute of frowning and stammering to think of something.

"I prefer to think of myself as much too important to quit. The company would collapse immediately without me."

She laughed again. "I'm sure you like to think so."

"What would I do for investors under this little scenario, Pollyanna?" he mused. "What about income until the new company is up and running? Huh? Did you think about that?"

"Andrew." She spoke slowly and with exaggerated patience. "You have an Ivy League education and you're worth about ninety million. I'm sure you'll think of something."

Aghast, he blinked, opened his mouth, shut his mouth, and blinked again. She looked amused, as though she knew exactly how much she'd just blown his mind.

It sounded so simple when she said it, like a true possibility. Well, it was *possible,* of course…

And Viveca said it like she had absolute faith in him. Like she thought he could accomplish whatever monumental task he set his mind to. Like she trusted him to spin straw to gold. That she believed in him, even some miniscule, negligible amount, was stunning. Humbling.

If only she knew how much he wanted to be worthy of her faith.

Rational thought was impossible with her smiling up at him like this, but he tried. He couldn't just quit his job on Viveca's say-so. Obviously she had no real idea what she was talking about. No business acumen, no concept of how hard he'd worked to get the company, and himself, to this point.

And of course she didn't know that being Andrew Warner, heir and CEO, was his entire identity. She probably gave him credit for having more of a life than that, poor misguided thing.

Taking business career advice from a reporter. Not a good idea.

And yet…it was as though she'd planted a little seed in

his mind and watered it. He could almost feel it growing, stretching and sending out roots.

Yeah, he had a little money. Yeah, he knew a few people. Yeah, he knew of a couple of little companies that were underperforming.

But right now all he wanted to do was to wallow in all things Viveca. To be with her. As for the career thing, he'd file it away to think about later. "Are you hungry?"

"Yeah, actually." She waved a hand toward the elevator and took a step in that direction. "Should we go back to the café?"

Right. Like he'd spend what precious little time he had with her in public, with employees interrupting every thirty seconds to kiss his ass.

"Ah," he said quickly, "let's order something up."

Viveca looked doubtful. "I don't want to put you to any trouble."

"Don't worry."

He walked over to June, the receptionist who'd been sitting out of earshot behind her counter and watching them with avid eyes and open amusement.

"Ah, June." Narrowing his eyes, he gave her a warning look. "Could you arrange for the café to—"

"Why, sure, Andrew." Grinning and overplaying it, she sounded as if she was reading from a script as she reached for the phone. "Let me see what I can do."

Shooting her a repressive glance that Viveca thankfully didn't seem to notice, he put his hand to the small of Viveca's back, steered her into his office and closed the door. *Alone at last.*

She went straight to the windows and admired the view of the city below. After a minute or two, she turned to the far wall, where he kept his collection of Japanese art, including his three sets of samurai swords in their display cases. Double-taking, she leaned in closer, gasped, and then swung back around to look at him with astonishment in her eyes.

"These are real."

He laughed. "Of course they're real. Did you think I ordered them from an infomercial on TV?"

She raised her eyebrows. "What kind of message are you trying to send to the competition?"

Intensely satisfied that she understood him so well, he laughed again. "I think you can figure it out."

Muttering, she shook her head and turned back to the Japanese art, which she touched gently. "How was New York? You never said."

Ah, New York. Another wrinkle in his relationship with Viveca. "Very productive. I learned almost everything I needed to know."

Not for one second did he think she'd let him get away with such a cryptic statement. Sure enough, she opened her mouth, but before she could question him further, there was a knock at the door.

June poked her head in and grinned. "Food's here."

Three servers wearing starched white shirts, aprons and dark pants streamed in with a small table, a cart loaded with food, and two chairs. While he and Viveca watched, June directed them. Within thirty seconds they'd set up the table in front of the windows, thrown a white cloth on it, and loaded it down with slices of rare beef tenderloin, breads, cheeses, pasta salads and a tray of cookies and pastries.

Trying to keep his face blank and innocent, he glanced at Viveca, who now had her hands on her hips, her lips pursed, and a disbelieving expression on her face. When one of the servers produced two crystal goblets and popped open a bottle of chardonnay, Viveca snorted.

"Excuse me?" June looked around, brimming with solicitous concern and the desire to please. "Did you say something, Ms. Jackson? Can I get you something?"

Viveca hastily shook her head. "No, no. This is wonderful. Thank you."

June beamed and turned back to the servers. Viveca shot Andrew a death glare and he tried not to laugh while everyone finished and left. Once they'd gone, he didn't have to wait long for her reaction.

"'Send something up from the café,' did you say?"

"Uh-huh." Trying to look unconcerned, he reached for the bottle of wine, which was now chilling in a stand on the floor, and poured some into both goblets.

"Andrew, when people ask for something to be sent up from the café, they generally get a soggy grilled cheese and cold tomato soup."

"Well, you know." He offered her one of the goblets. "Perk of the job and all."

"So do you have standing orders with the kitchen?" She stared at him with open suspicion, although her voice was soft, shaky and vulnerable, and both her hands remained firmly in place on her hips. "It's Thursday, so the CEO must be serving lunch to yet another one of his lovers in his office? Is that how it works? Brenda last week, me this week, someone else next week?"

Andrew flinched, feeling as though he'd absorbed a swing to his ribs from Barry Bonds's bat. The woman knew how to hit where it hurt, didn't she? Not that he didn't deserve such a question. He'd lived exactly the kind of life she suspected, the kind that should earn any thinking woman's suspicions. Until now.

So, yeah, she had every right to doubt his intentions, but it still hurt that she did. Coming from the woman he loved, it hurt.

Replacing the goblet on the table, he swiped the back of his hand across his mouth and tried to tamp down some of the bitter taste on his tongue.

"You're the first woman I've ever done this for." There was an embarrassing new hoarseness in his voice. "So, no, I don't have a standing order from the kitchen."

Viveca blinked once, her defiance wavering.

"You're the only woman I want. I haven't thought of Brenda once since I saw her the last time. And there won't be another woman next week." *Or ever,* not that she was ready to hear that now.

He told himself to shut up before he gave away the whole farm, but the words, damaging as they were, kept coming. "And if you had the slightest idea how much you mean to me, you'd sit down, have some wine and give this a chance."

Chapter 14

Something soft and hopeful appeared in her face, magically easing the pain in his chest and letting his lungs fill to capacity again. After a moment's hesitation, she moved to the table, sat and sipped her wine.

With insane, irrational gratitude, he sank into the other chair and neither of them said anything for a long time.

Reaching for the nearest serving spoon, she made a quavery sound that may have been a laugh. "I want you to know that I'm normally a very sane person."

"I know you are."

"It's just that with you…"

She trailed off, maybe running out of steam or, more likely, lacking the words to explain this thing they did to each other. It didn't really matter. At least she'd come this far and was willing to go a little further.

And here he was, about to rock their leaky boat. Again.

But…in a minute.

"Let's eat," he told her, and they filled their plates in complete silence except for the occasional clink of silver and china.

Viveca ate a bite of bread, wiped her mouth and replaced the napkin in her lap. "I've really been impressed with the company's social conscience, by the way."

"The nursery, you mean?"

"The nursery, the health care, the retirement plans, the green plans."

As always, praise made him twitchy, mainly because he could never quite believe he'd earned it. Praise from Viveca made him feel downright manic. Better to deflect it and send the conversation off into a safer direction. "Are you a tree hugger, Vivi?"

"And," she said, ignoring the teasing, "I want you to tell me about your foundation."

That stopped him dead. Left him stammering and idiotic because he'd gone to great pains to keep his name out of the foundation's work. After a lengthy and embarrassing silence, he came up with a pathetic reply. "What are you talking about?"

"The Educated and Free Foundation." She smiled warmly, ratcheting up his discomfiture. "Based on that quote by Epictetus, I think. 'Only the educated are free.' I'm sure you've heard of it."

"I've heard of it." His voice was sharp. "How have you?"

"A good reporter never—"

"Reveals her sources," he finished, but then a lightbulb flashed in his brain. His nosy cousin had never yet kept his mouth shut when it counted. *"Eric."*

Viveca watched him over the rim of her goblet as she

sipped her wine, not bothering to hide her amusement. He didn't squirm often, but he caught himself sliding a finger under the starched collar of his shirt, which suddenly felt like a tightening noose.

"Is it that hard for you to take credit for doing something good?"

It was, actually, but he didn't like admitting it.

"Tell me, Vivi." He dropped his fork because it didn't look like she'd let him eat in peace anytime soon. "Am I talking to the reporter or the woman?"

She scowled. "I hate it when you do that. I'm a reporter *and* a woman. Stop trying to weasel out of my questions."

"Fine, Lois Lane." Suddenly in dire need of a little fortification, he grabbed his goblet and gulped it dry. "Send a formal request to my assistant, and she'll get in touch with my personal publicist, and he'll send you a press release about Educated and Free in the next week or so. How's that?"

Just like that, the power between them shifted again. She glowered, her eyes flashing brown fire, and he tried not to laugh. It was funny how much of their limited time together they spent jockeying for position. All the negotiating, all the power struggles and all the fun.

No other woman had ever challenged or fascinated him like this. Every second with Viveca was a mystery, an experiment for which he couldn't wait to see the results.

She didn't concede right away, and he hadn't expected her to. Taking her sweet time about it, she scooped up a bite of beef tenderloin, heavy on the horseradish. Trying to look bored, he slapped together a little sandwich and hummed absently.

"I can…take off my reporter's hat." The words came slowly, as if she was being fined ten thousand dollars for each one. "For a while, anyway," she added sullenly.

Well, that was one round for him. He felt extreme satisfaction, and it had nothing to do with besting Vivi and
everything to do with a sudden and unexpected need to tell
her how he'd improved his company and why.

Looking down at his lap, he smoothed the white napkin
and tried to decide where to begin. "Since we're off the
record again… I think we've already established that my
grandfather was an SOB."

"Yes," she said impatiently.

"If he ever did anything for the good of his employees—
which I don't think he did—it was by accident."

Viveca went very still.

Looking up, he discovered that she'd squared her shoulders. Her lips were tight, her jaw tense. "Are you okay?"

She blinked once and nodded.

Andrew wasn't quite sure he believed her—she looked
a little pale, too—but he continued anyway. "When I took
over the company, it was in bad shape. Factory conditions,
worker satisfaction, morale, it was…terrible."

"But the company has always been profitable—"

"Of course it was *profitable*." The word irritated him
because, as far as he was concerned, it was only a single
part of the bigger picture. "Anyone can make a *profit* if he
doesn't pay his workers a living wage or cover their health
insurance. But what's the cost in terms of your people?
Your reputation? The long-term health of the company?"

The conversation seemed to be affecting Viveca
strangely. "You… You almost say it like you were ashamed
of the company."

"I *was* ashamed."

She stared at him with a vaguely glazed look in her eyes.
No doubt she was trying to hide her disgust for all things
Warner. Hell, maybe he should tell her he wasn't one of

them. That'd raise her opinion of him up into the low negative digits at least.

"So you…made changes," she prompted. "You started the foundation. Now you help all those employees' kids with college tuition if they keep their grades up. I read it on the foundation's Web site. And you funded it with your own money. I know you did."

He shrugged. "It needed to be done."

To his surprise, she looked downright miserable. He thought he saw the gleam of tears right before she dipped her head and swiped her nose with the napkin.

"Are you sure you're okay?" She'd worried him. "I can take you home if you're not feeling—"

An unrecognizable sound came out of her. Fifty percent sob, fifty percent reluctant laugh, a hundred percent confusing. When she looked up, her eyes were wet, but not horrified. In fact, they almost looked…warm. Admiring.

"I'm not sure what to make of you, Andrew." Her voice was faint, as though she'd forcibly extracted this confession from the depths of her soul. "You're not the man I thought you were."

He was afraid to ask. "Is that good or bad?"

It looked good, but he didn't want to trust his eyes lest they play nasty little tricks on him. Sure enough, when she spoke, it was to dash his hopes a little.

"I'm not sure."

Where did that leave him?

In a better place, he supposed. At least she wasn't regarding him with open horror, and he could build on that. Staring at her, feeling profound gratitude that she hadn't written him off, he lost his head a little.

"If I told you how I feel about you, would you believe me?"

A ripple went through her, a shudder of awareness that told him she did, on some level, know what he wanted to tell her even if she wasn't ready to either hear him say it or believe it. When she spoke, it was with obvious regret. "No."

So there it was. They were right back where they started, where they always were, with him reaching out and her pushing him away. It hurt, every single time.

Not that his love was worth much anyway, but he'd never given it before and he'd hoped—really *hoped*—it might mean something to her. As long as she was pushing him away, he may as well give her a good reason.

"I hired that investigator." He fought a losing battle to keep the raw ache out of his voice. "I went to New York to talk to some people and find out more about you. Old teachers and neighbors and coworkers. It's amazing what you can find out when you wave some money around."

The words hung in the air while she stared, disbelieving, for several beats, and then her face twisted into a snarl. "You talk about *trust* and *feelings,* and then you go out and hire someone to spy on me?"

"You're spying on my family."

"I'm writing a book."

"You're extracting your pound of flesh. Don't deny it."

Shaking her head, furious, she threw her napkin on the table, backed her chair away, and started to get up. "I'm leav—"

Moving on instinct, he grabbed her wrist. "You're not going anywhere." Even if he had to rip the tablecloth in strips and use it to tie her to the chair, she wasn't leaving. "We're working some things out."

Enraged didn't begin to describe how she looked as she snatched her arm away and sank back into her chair. "By all means," she spat, "tell me what you found out. Let's see if your investigator got my bra size right."

He hadn't expected her to be happy, but he hadn't expected her to be murderous, either. Keeping her away from the samurai swords suddenly became a big priority. "I didn't want to do it, Viveca—"

She made an outraged sound.

"—but I am the head of this family, and I have to protect it."

"Of course you do."

"I'm not capable of sitting by quietly while someone— even you—tries to destroy the Warner name."

"Does it occur to you that you're talking out of both sides of your mouth?"

That shut him right up. It *had* occurred to him, many times, but he hadn't expected anyone else to ever see his hypocrisy. Why couldn't he keep anything from Viveca? Why did she see all the things he wished would stay hidden in the dark?

"On the one hand, you were ashamed of the Warner name," she said. "On the other hand, you're going to protect it at all costs. Why don't you make up your mind?"

The taunting pushed him over the edge, until something deep inside became unglued. Ran free and wild when it should have been locked in its cage where it could never hurt anyone.

"I am Andrew *Warner.*" Roaring, he slammed his palms on the table and made the china jump and clatter. "The name may not mean much, but it's all I have and *I will fight for it.*"

"Well, what've you got on me, *Andrew Warner?*"

This was not the way he wanted things. Hurting her was the last thing he wanted to do, ever. "Your father was Ryan Jackson."

"Oh, God." Her hand went to her heaving chest.

"He lost his arm in one of our factories. The company gave him a pitiful settlement, patted him on the head and sent him on his way. He drank himself to death."

She didn't say anything and didn't need to. The astonishment and horror she radiated were so palpable that satellites orbiting the earth could probably pick up on them.

Andrew went on, hating himself more with every syllable he uttered. "Your mother died right after that. You…had a meltdown in college—"

"A *meltdown?*" She laughed bitterly, a sound so ugly he wondered if it would make his ears bleed. "I had a nervous breakdown. I was in the hospital for three weeks. I thought about *suicide*—"

Lord God. The thought of Viveca harming herself was enough to knock him to his knees in a howling panic. *"Don't."*

"—and the only thing that kept me going when the rest of my family was dead was the thought of making you Warners answer for what you did to my father and the way you forgot about him as if he never existed."

Looking at her with those unshed tears glittering in her eyes, all naked pain and raw anguish, Andrew died a thousand agonizing deaths. This was so much worse than he'd anticipated. If only she would let him touch her now. Comfort her. He'd happily sacrifice his right arm for the privilege.

Desperate for her not to cry, he said the first thing he could think of—the truth. "I'm sorry, Vivi."

"Don't you *dare* talk about him to me."

This time she was too quick for him. Lunging to her feet, she was halfway to the door before he caught her arm and reeled her back. Though she stiffened, he held on tight and wrapped around her in a pitiful attempt to ease her pain.

"I am sorry." He whispered in her ear and rubbed her shoulders. "I know that won't bring him back, but I—"

"Let me go."

"—am so sorry for what happened to him."

After a minute, she stopped struggling and collapsed against him, submitting to his touch because he didn't give her a choice. When she spoke again, her voice was detached and mechanical. "I'm fine. Let me go."

He did, with dread, afraid of what he would see in her face.

She took a step back and met his gaze with dry, dispassionate eyes. "Just so we're clear. You're Andrew Warner. I'm the daughter of a dead father. It's my responsibility to hold someone accountable for his death."

"No, Vivi. This vendetta book won't make you happy. You're not that kind of person."

"Maybe not." She shrugged as if the point was irrelevant. "But I promised myself that I would do this because I owe it to his memory. I have to do it. I'm Ryan Jackson's daughter. That's all I am. It's all I have."

Again he lost his head a little. Maybe it was because she was so flat and emotionless now, so far away. Maybe it was the fear that he wouldn't be able to pull her back, or maybe it was just that he needed so desperately to say it. Before he could think, or stop himself, the words bubbled up.

"That's not true, Vivi. You're the woman I l—"

"Don't." She held her hands up and backed away as though she needed to take immediate defensive measures against the word. "We had amazing sex one time. Don't make this something it's not."

In the silence that followed, Andrew told himself she was only minimizing their relationship because it was so overpowering. Because she felt vulnerable and confused.

It really didn't matter. What she said still sliced through

him like a guillotine through Jell-O. Staring at that scared, stubborn face, feeling the pain of her rejection, Andrew decided she'd do less damage if she just pulled out a 9 mm and shot him point blank.

Suddenly exhausted, drained of every life force that'd ever flowed through his veins, he ran a shaky hand through his hair. He turned away, walked to his desk, braced his palms on it, and tried to decide what the hell he should do now.

His desk phone beeped, breaking the tension.

"Andrew?" June's voice chirped. "There's, ah, someone here to see you—"

"I'm busy."

He regretted barking, especially when Viveca shot him a reproachful look, but it was too late by then. He'd apologize to June later.

June, meanwhile, sounded unaccountably worried and her voice was now muffled. "Hey! Wait! You can't just—"

Abrupt silence followed.

Andrew and Viveca had just enough time to exchange quizzical glances before the office door flew open and Andrew's day got exponentially worse.

Appearing out of nowhere, the only person on earth who could make his goal of getting close to Viveca harder than it already was burst into the room.

Brenda.

Muttering a curse, Andrew wished the ground would swallow him up.

Whatever turmoil Viveca had been feeling about her father died a swift death the second she looked around and saw Brenda standing there with her pissed-off-supermodel attitude, a perfect cross between Naomi Campbell and the Terminator.

Like magic, Viveca's angst, sorrow and confusion over her ongoing mission and evolving feelings for Andrew disappeared, to be replaced by a single mega-emotion that was a billion times more powerful than the ones she'd felt before—fierce, primitive, murderous jealousy.

It took over her body, making her skin simultaneously hot and clammy, her throat tight and her vision dim. But not dim enough that she couldn't see the woman, with her sleek bob, low-slung, size-four skinny pants that barely cleared her hip bones, and breasts jammed into the cups of some lacy purple bra that was clearly visible under her sheer, flowered tunic. Brenda had, obviously, come dressed to impress.

Viveca's self-esteem had never suffered before. Men thought she was pretty, and she had turned Andrew's head, after all. But in the same room with Brenda's movie-star-caliber perfection, Viveca may as well have been a troll with blue Don King hair.

Viveca wanted to grab the gleaming brass letter opener from Andrew's desk and jab the woman's perfectly lined brown eyes out.

So much for Andrew's claims that there was no one else. So much for all his heartfelt talk about wanting Viveca, and their *relationship,* and his so-called feelings for her. What a freaking joke. Maybe he should install a revolving door to ease the transitions of women into and out of his office. Make life easier for all concerned.

Andrew seemed to know some of what Viveca was thinking. Shooting her a worried glance, he sidled closer until he was in front of her, almost like he wanted to protect her.

"Brenda." In his voice Viveca heard a rough, uncivilized edge that made her wonder how strong a hold he had on his temper. "What are you doing here?"

"I wanted to bring you *this.*" Brenda glared at Viveca

as she slapped a white envelope into his hand. Her little-girl voice, it turned out, got a little shrill when she was upset, reminding Viveca of an irate Minnie Mouse. "It's the bill for the photo shoot I missed because I was spending so much time with you."

"Great." Andrew tossed the envelope on his desk. "Anything else?"

Brenda's pouty lips tightened. Her narrowed gaze flicked between Andrew, the food and wine on the table and Viveca. "Can I talk to you for a minute? In private?"

Viveca had to hand it to Brenda. Even though her eyes flashed brown poison and she obviously wanted to rip a big strip off of Andrew's hide, she managed to sound pleasant.

Viveca, on the other hand, wasn't feeling pleasant at all. She was feeling violent and unstable. Maybe she could hold Andrew down while Brenda ripped that strip. The thought was strangely cheering for about one second, and then her remaining half ounce of common sense took over.

She should leave and she knew it. This whole scene was beneath her dignity. Jealous women, confrontations and a man trying to weasel out of a hot spot—who needed it? Not her. The best thing for her to do would be to extract herself, go back to the cottage and leave Andrew and Brenda to their own devices, whatever they were. It wasn't like she had any claim to Andrew anyway.

Except…the thought of leaving these two alone to-gether made her want to reach for the nearest samurai sword and do something illegal with it. And she really wanted to hear what Andrew told Brenda, to watch him weasel and worm, to see a master player at work.

"No." Andrew's voice was sharp, his tone absolute. "I said everything I had to say the last time I saw you."

Brenda gaped at him. So did Viveca.

This didn't sound like a player operating. It sounded like a man who wanted a woman to get the hell out of his office but was too polite to say so outright. Like a man who was slamming doors and burning bridges with impunity.

Brenda didn't look too happy. Huffing, she stretched up to her full, spindly height and jammed a fist on her hip.

"So this is how you're gonna play me?"

Ah, there it was, Viveca thought. The end of the civility, and the first shot fired in the Nasty Wars. Andrew made a growling sound.

"You're screwing *her?*" Brenda's emphasis on *her* made it sound as though she'd interrupted an intimate moment between Andrew and a farm animal. "Is that why you kicked me to—"

A shudder rippled through Andrew, like he was trying to hold himself back. He exuded danger. Violence barely repressed. That being the case, Viveca was totally unprepared for what happened next.

He reached back, grabbed Viveca's hand and tugged it until she stood next to him. Keeping their hands together, he gripped her hip, brought her flush against his side and held her within the iron protection of his arm.

It was an act of possession and of warning, an open declaration of their relationship, and it left Viveca stunned.

"You remember Viveca Jackson, don't you?" he asked Brenda.

The woman's mouth flapped open and closed and open again.

"I expect Viveca to be treated with respect. Since you're not doing that, I want you to leave and don't come back. *Do you understand me?*"

Both women stared at him. If Viveca hadn't been so surprised, so gratified, so inappropriately thrilled, she might almost have felt sorry for Brenda, who experienced the full might of Andrew's icy temper and disdain.

The poor woman's face had gone purple and her eyes swam in angry tears. She didn't seem to know what to do, and since she probably didn't get rejected by men on a regular basis, Viveca could understand her humiliation.

Finally, Brenda smoothed her tunic, squared her shoulders and raised her chin. With a final withering look at Viveca, she pivoted on her stilettos and swept out, slamming the door behind her.

The second she was gone, Andrew turned Viveca loose, shoving her away a little as he did so, as though contact with her ate away at his flesh. Stalking to the window, he shoved his hands in his pockets and stared out.

"Andrew." She had no idea what to say.

He swung back around, and the anger in his flashing eyes hit her like a spray of water from a fire hose. This time it was directed solely at her and she almost wished she had Brenda back to act as a buffer.

"I have three things to say to you, Vivi." In the back of his jaw, a muscle pulsed so insistently he had a tough time getting the words out. "One, I'm sorry about your father. Two, I hope that one day you'll let me tell you how I feel about you—"

Viveca couldn't speak.

"—and three, I really hope you decide what you want to do about our relationship sometime soon. While I still have some sanity left."

Viveca couldn't sleep that night.

At two, when Andrew's image flashed again through her mind's eye, she gave up trying to sleep. Settling onto the sofa with only the light of one small corner lamp to keep her from the absolute darkness and only her beloved sun-flowers to keep her company, she curled into a fetal position under Mrs. Warner's baby-blue cashmere throw, tossed caution to the wind and faced the obvious and inevitable truth that had been glaring her in the face since she left him this afternoon—she was in love with Andrew Warner.

Learning about his social conscience and all the reforms he'd made to the company cinched it. His good deeds weren't news to her, of course. She'd done her research and knew he'd been a proactive CEO. But seeing his passion and personal commitment to the well-being of his employees, well…that had done her in.

Not to mention his compassion and apology about her father.

And, of course, his handling of Brenda.

She tried to talk herself out of it by enumerating his many irritating qualities. He was arrogant, complicated and had hidden motives. He probably wasn't capable of love, or, if he was capable of love, didn't love her, or—and this was the worst possibility—if he was capable of love and thought he loved Viveca, would soon come to his senses and go back to Brenda or someone like her.

To say nothing of their competing interests on this book project and their differing backgrounds. They were opposites—oil and water to the nth power, fire and ice, Gloria Steinem and Cinderella trying to find some middle ground. They had as much business being in a relationship together as a dolphin and a vole.

They were, in short, hopeless, futile and doomed.

Her foolish heart didn't care.

She pulled the throw tighter around her shoulders, growing chilled in her tank top and shorts, and wondered if she had any chance of seeing him before Arnetta's birthday extravaganza. And then the phone rang.

It was *him*. She knew it.

Sitting up straight, manic with excitement, she lunged for the phone and answered it midway through that first ring. "Hello?"

A pause, and then, "Open the door for me."

His voice sounded rough with sleep, as though he'd just rolled out of bed. Moving automatically, never thinking of arguing, Viveca hung up, flung the throw away and hurried in her bare feet through the shadowy living room and foyer to the front door.

She opened it, and there he was.

One quick look confirmed her initial impression that he'd been in bed. He had rumpled hair, bleary eyes, scruffy chin and cheeks, and was wearing only a white T-shirt, knit shorts and flip-flops.

He loomed in the doorway, one hand gripping his cell phone. His night, she realized instinctively, had passed pretty much like hers—trying to sleep, to not think about her, tossing and turning and, finally, giving up and coming here.

They stared at each other.

She saw a thousand contradictions in his expression as he watched her. He looked moody and dangerous, but also vulnerable. Angry but needy.

Most of all she felt the power of his overwhelming desire for her in his huge, vibrating body, and that was before she looked down and saw the size of the erection straining against his shorts.

Her belly tightened reflexively and her breasts peaked and ached. She had the vague thought that she shouldn't stare, but making such an effort just seemed idiotic and unnecessary.

Seeing the direction of her gaze, he ran a shaky hand through his hair and she felt him reining something in with difficulty.

He took a ragged breath. "You've had enough time to decide."

"Yeah, I have," she said without hesitation. "I know what I want."

He went absolutely still, waiting. When he spoke again, his voice was so faint she could hardly hear him. "What's that?"

Watching him, she acknowledged the decision she'd already made. The one that had, most likely, been made the second their gazes locked that first time.

Maybe tomorrow she'd regret it. Maybe tomorrow she'd look back on this night as the single worst choice she'd ever made in her life, her one most self-destructive act, ever. But that was tomorrow. This was tonight.

Reaching down, she stroked his hard length and cupped him, wringing a groan from deep in his throat even as his head fell back and his eyes rolled closed.

"You," she said, stepping into his arms. "I want y—"

Chapter 15

Andrew's phone clattered to the floor. He didn't give her time to finish her sentence before he slammed the door with one hand, lashed her body to his with the other, and kissed her with so much pent-up passion it nearly knocked her flat on her butt. They wrapped around each other, clinging, and his big hands crisscrossed her body in a continuous loop as though he needed to reassure himself that she was really there in his arms and not a figment of his imagination.

Viveca, totally outside herself, wept with the pleasure.

Standing on her tiptoes, she opened her mouth and took his as deeply and greedily as he took hers, sucking and biting, tasting the faint mint of his toothpaste and the delicious flavor that was just him.

Getting him close enough turned out to be impossible although she tried desperately. She raked her fingernails across his back and shoulders and tugged at his T-shirt. Finally, frantic now, she broke the kiss, jerked the thing over his head and threw it to the floor.

Though she needed to taste his silky-hot skin, she never got the chance because he recaptured her lips the second he could.

That mouth.

The things it did to Viveca were nearly unbearable. Licking, nuzzling, panting and, best of all, chanting her name as though he couldn't shut himself up even if he'd wanted to. "Viveca… Viveca… *Viveca…*"

Then they were moving, and she realized he was backing her through the foyer and living room toward some destination he had in mind. At last her calves hit something… *What was it?* The sofa? *Who cared?*

She started to sit, thinking that was what he wanted, but at the last minute he swung her around, sat and pulled her between his strong muscular thighs.

In another of his stunning acts of tenderness, he rested his face between her breasts, breathing her in with great, shuddering gulps. Her feverish body couldn't keep still and she writhed against him, seeking the relief he could give her if only he'd get around to it before she collapsed with need. He didn't get around to it.

In no particular hurry, he ran his hands up the backs of her legs, under her shorts and panties, to her butt. Murmuring love words that she couldn't quite hear or understand, he held her like that for a long time, rubbing his face against her breasts and belly while she fisted her hands in his silky curls and tried not to pass out.

At last he looked up into her face, showing her so many raw emotions she wondered if this was all a wonderful, impossible dream from which she would soon wake up.

Adoration was there. So was a fierce, glittering need almost frightening in its intensity, as though his life hung in the balance and only she could save him.

Most of all, she saw absolute focus and she knew down to every atom in every cell inside her body that he was determined to give her more pleasure tonight than many women experienced in a lifetime.

Viveca trembled with anticipation.

The fingers gripping her butt dipped lower, into the hot slick cleft between her legs, and stroked with consummate skill. Need ratcheted higher inside her body, sending spasms of pleasure streaking low through her belly. She whimpered and moaned without shame, a porn star in the making with Andrew's hands on her body.

"One of these days, Vivi," he said, "we're going to make it to a bed."

"But not today." There was no chance in hell, not with the way her knees were weakening by the second.

"Not today."

With sudden impatience, he grabbed the bottoms of her shorts and panties and ripped them down. She tried to kick them off, but he wouldn't let her get that far away. His hands went right back to the globes of her butt, fingers digging in with their short, sharp nails, driving her wild. In one swift motion, he slid to his knees on the floor, pulled her forward and ground his face against the triangle of her sex.

Dazed, already overwhelmed, and knowing what was coming, she cried out, squirmed and, when that failed, tried to back away.

"*Please.*" Whether she meant *please hurry* or *please stop,* she had no idea.

A rumbling growl, a clear warning if ever she'd heard

one, rose up out of Andrew's throat. He glanced up long enough to flash a glittering, narrow-eyed frown, and Viveca clamped her jaws tight shut.

Scared to be so vulnerable but, above all, unable to deny him anything, she took a deep breath and stilled except for the slight trembling she couldn't possibly control.

"Good girl."

With a faint smile now curving his kiss-swollen lips, he lowered his head, used his thumb and forefinger to open her wide and touched his tongue to her.

Viveca moaned and her heavy head fell back.

She wasn't going to make it. No woman could endure such an excruciating and thorough assault. It was all too much…the licking…the kissing…the sucking and the swirling. She swayed dangerously, but he held her up and relentlessly drove her higher.

How did he do it?

Slowing when she needed him to slow, speeding up when she needed that, and unerringly showing her that her body could do things she'd never dreamed.

She panted and cried as the pleasure grew, clinging to him as the only thing that kept her earthbound amongst all the seething sensations. The tension expanded, coiling in her belly, and then the rippling spasms started, rolling over and over, siphoning off some of the ache and filling her with bright pleasure.

Boneless and relieved, she sagged against him, thinking she'd just had the best orgasm of her life, but then the strangest thing happened.

Andrew said, "Come for me, baby," and his mouth moved and he did *something* with his lips and tongue, something *else,* something *more,* and sudden, violent ecstasy slammed through her, so strong that the ripples in her belly turned to contractions that racked her body, so piercing that for a long moment the world went dark and silent.

She made a loud, strangled sound of astonishment and joy, and then Andrew, moving jerkily and giving her no time to recover, swung her around and swept her feet out from under her. She tumbled, flat onto her back, on the sofa.

There was a two-second delay during which she thought he pulled off his shorts and jerked a condom on, and then, with a single surge, he was inside, stretching her to the limit and far beyond.

Starting the delicious pleasure all over again.

Though she would have sworn she was too exhausted to move, she found herself arching her hips for him, lifting so he could go deeper and wrapping her arms tight around his trembling body to hold on for what was sure to be a hard, wild ride.

Only he didn't ride. He rocked.

To her agonized dismay and torment, he propped himself on his elbows, cupped her face, stared down at her with gleaming, worshipful eyes even as he moved against her in slow circles that had ecstasy returning for another visit, and he started to speak.

She knew what was coming and wasn't ready. Panicked now, already far too vulnerable, she shook her head. *"Don't."*

"Don't *what?*" He rocked again and she squirmed, desperately needing to escape the sensations and emotions trying to erupt inside her. "Tell you I love you?"

Tears gathered in the corners of her eyes, not the hot, involuntary tears of passion, but real, heartfelt tears of fear and unwanted hope. "You don't really—"

"Don't tell me what I feel." Anger now laced his raspy voice. "You don't know what you're talking about."

"Please don't. I'm begging you."

Another well-placed pivot of his strong hips had her whimpering even as she wrapped her legs tight around his waist to take him deeper.

"Are you a coward, Vivi?" After nuzzling against her lips for a minute or two, he pulled back enough to look into her face with that dark, implacable gaze. "Is that it?"

"No."

This was a lie. When it came to emotions, with him, she was as lily-livered as they came. She could handle almost everything he threw at her—the sultry looks, the slow seduction and the dominating sex.

But there were three things she absolutely could not endure—his tenderness, the possibility that a man like him really could love a woman like her; and the depths of her feelings for him. The thought of him loving her and her loving him broke her into a million tiny pieces.

She'd loved her father and mother, and what had that ever gotten her? They were dead and gone and she was here, all alone.

And now she was supposed to love someone else and accept his love? The worst possible person? No. She couldn't do that. More tears came, shaming her, but she couldn't stop them.

Still moving gently, he wiped her wet cheek and then sucked his thumb into his mouth, savoring another part of her. "Listen to me, Vivi."

This was really too much. Looking into those eyes, taking him so deeply into her body, exposing herself like this. In a childish act, so silly it was embarrassing, she shook her head and covered her eyes, as though that would ever stop him.

It didn't.

Tugging her hand away and staying in the absolute center of her line of sight, where she couldn't see anything but *him*, he kissed her fingers. "I love you." He sucked her forefinger into his mouth, pulling hard and almost sending her over the edge. "*Love you.* You need to know." Lowering his head, he kissed her, sweetly and deeply, tearing her apart.

The armored defenses around her heart ruined, Viveca stopped fighting and surrendered this one time. Arching, she wrapped her hands in that thick curly hair and flowed up to meet him until, with three more strokes, Andrew shuddered and cried his release against her mouth. She followed, soaring through the dark night with him.

When she thought he'd dozed off, Viveca pulled out of his arms, being careful not to ruffle the linens and wake him. Scooting to the edge of the bed, she managed to stick one foot out before his hoarse, lazy voice stopped her.

"Where're you going?"

Caught, Viveca clutched the sheet to her breasts, twisted to look at him over her shoulder and braced herself for the amazing sight she just couldn't get used to.

Andrew sprawled across the middle of the enormous bed, taking up most of it. He lay propped against a stack of pillows with his arms stretched overhead and the sheet slung low over his square, notched hips, barely covering his assets, which were considerable, even at rest. The ridged slabs of his chest, belly and shoulders gleamed warm in the light of the candles they'd lit earlier, inviting her mouth to taste even though her mouth, by rights, should have done quite enough tasting by now.

"I, ah, just thought I'd get a T-shirt."

She smoothed her hair, which must look like a fright

wig at this point in the proceedings, and started to plant her other foot on the floor. Andrew reached out and caught her wrist, a slow smile of immense male satisfaction and, let's face it, smugness on his face. "Why do you need a T-shirt?"

"To sleep in. So I don't get cold."

Those dark brows lowered in mock concern. "You're cold, Vivi?" His hot gaze swept over her body, lingering at key spots, like the small of her back and her butt, igniting goose bumps across her skin. "Looks like I'm falling down on the job."

She flushed and shivered, unable to completely repress her grin. "You're not falling down on the job and you know it. Stop fishing for compliments. It's beneath you."

He laughed, but then his roving gaze snagged on the hand she used to anchor the sheet to her breast. When he looked back at her face, there was a tinge of annoyance in his eyes.

"You don't need a T-shirt. When we're in bed together, we're not going to need any clothes. *Ever.* So you can just throw away all your little shorts and T-shirts right now. You can keep one robe to wear around the house at bedtime, but you won't need the rest."

Gaping and speechless, she struggled to find just the right comeback for this ridiculous directive. "You are so overbearing it just boggles my mind. Does this routine really work for you? If I want to wear a T-shirt, I will wear a T-shirt."

His mouth twisted. "It's not about the T-shirt, Vivi. It's about you hiding from me every chance you get."

He was right.

It would always be like this with him—his need to be close, to possess, her need to get away and shield herself from his absolute mastery over her and her obsession with him. He would never back off, never allow her to draw away and protect herself a little, never let her emotional bull—and she *knew* it was bull—keep her from him. He wanted it all, every single part of her down to the darkest corners of her soul, and he wouldn't stop until he got it.

But could she accept these terms for being with him?

Some of the trepidation must have shown on her face because his grip on her wrist softened, and so did his face. "It kills me. You know that? To see that you're still this afraid of me? *Kills me.*"

Yeah, it was pretty much killing her, too. "I don't know what to do," she told him helplessly. "I wish I did."

"Come here."

He let her go, opened his arms and threw back the covers for her, wrenching her end of the sheet out of her hands in the process. Enthralled, she did as she was told and crawled back across the bed.

Immediately gathering her up in the linens, creating an inner world where it was just the two of them, the dark and the things they did to each other, he covered her breasts with his hands, squeezing and loving them with no finesse whatsoever.

His thumbs rubbed over her tight, aching nipples, driving her right to the brink of orgasm with that caress alone. Squeezing her breasts together, he ducked his head, stuck his tongue out and licked them both, back and forth, back and forth. Viveca writhed and mewled, nothing but a wild animal when he touched her like this.

"Please." Desperation rose in his voice. "Is it the way I say it? Is that it? Do you want me to ask nicely?"

"Andrew…"

Rolling on top of her, he wedged one of his thighs between hers, opening her wide. Viveca's sex throbbed and wept for him and she waited for him to enter. But he merely settled in the cradle of her hips and ground his erection against her sweet spot.

"*Please* don't cover this body, Vivi. Don't hide from me, okay?"

"Okay."

Fears momentarily forgotten, she tightened her legs around his waist, crossing her ankles at the small of his back to keep him from ever, ever, leaving and taking her heart with him. His lips went to the curve of her neck and shoulder, nuzzling and nipping. "We belong together, just like this. Don't we?"

A moment of sanity intruded because she knew this was a point of no return. They'd been passing them all night, true, but this one was different. If she conceded this point now, he would consider it a promise and hold her to it, use it against her the next time she tried to put some space between them as she inevitably would.

"Don't we?" he demanded again.

He raised his head and stared at her with that piercing, determined, unrelenting gaze, daring her to argue with him. Frozen with indecision, Viveca opened and closed her mouth, mute.

That was when Andrew decided to play dirty.

Reaching between them, eyes flashing, he stroked the head of his swollen penis against her wet lips, taunting her with the reward she could have as soon as she uttered those three letters he wanted to hear.

She knew what his intent was, knew it was extortion, but her feverish body didn't. Whimpering, she angled her hips, inviting him, hoping his own need would force him to drop his demands, but she should have known better.

Should have known his will was a million times stronger than hers.

"Andrew, *please.*"

There was no verbal answer, only another stroke of his length against her, another little rub that drove her ten steps closer to insanity.

"Please." She scraped her nails up his back.

Only the slight tremble in his heavy arms and sheen of sweat across his forehead told her he was having difficulty controlling himself. The expression on his face was almost bored, but she knew better.

Still, she didn't think she could outwait him.

"I've got all night," he said.

"What's the question again?" She only asked because it would irritate him and she needed to win one little point in the ongoing struggle between them.

The punishment was swift. "You little smart-ass." Lowering his head again, he nipped that curve of her neck with sharp teeth. She cried out, utterly lost, as he stroked her again. "The question is whether you agree we belong together like this. You do agree, don't you?"

"Yes." Her vision grew dimmer by the second. *"Yes."*

A lopsided smile curved his lips and the trembling in his arms got more pronounced. "I have another question for you."

"What? No. Please, no."

"You shouldn't have gotten smart with me." The wicked gleam in his eyes intensified and his voice dropped. "We belong together, like this…and you belong to me. This—" he rubbed his thumb in a slow, agonizing circle around her hard nub "—belongs to me. Isn't that right?"

Though she was at the absolute limits of her endurance and felt like her entire body may explode at any time, her fighting instincts just could not let her concede this point to him, the most arrogant man in the universe. No matter how she felt about him.

"For tonight."

"No." The amusement vanished from his face, and suddenly the playing was over and all bets were off. His entire body went rigid and his expression turned to stone. Viveca realized he would extract the truth from her even if he killed them both in the process. "No."

Without warning, he entered her, surging with a force that sent her several feet up the bed.

Viveca gasped and tried to hold on, tried to match the relentless pumping of his hips as he rode and she came in one shuddering wave after another. Even more desperately, she tried to retain a part of herself and keep something hidden in case he ever walked out on her.

He didn't let her do any of that.

The second she'd finished convulsing, he flipped her onto her belly, pulled her up until she was on all fours, and drove into her from behind. With one hand he braced himself on the bed and with the other he cupped her swinging breasts, rubbing them roughly, hurting her with the sweetest pain.

He surrounded her on all sides and commandeered her senses until there was nothing else in the universe but him. Nothing but the way his heavy body felt slapping against hers, the scent of the spices on his skin and the sound of his harsh, labored breathing.

Nothing but his complete possession of her, and she reveled in it.

"You belong to me, don't you, Vivi?"

"Yes."

"For tonight?"

"Yes."

"And tomorrow?"

"Yes."

Each question was punctuated by another powerful thrust, another pass of his palm across her exquisitely sensitive nipples.

"And always?"

"*Yes.*"

He laughed, the sound one of raw male triumph, but she was too sated and exhausted to work up any outrage. He kissed her right between her shoulder blades, a wet, licking kiss, and she mewled with pleasure.

"Good girl. *Good girl.* We're done with the questions. For now."

"Thank goodness." She sagged face-first against the pillows.

He went very still, pausing, even though she knew he hadn't come yet. Sensing the change in him, feeling that it was a big one, she lifted her heavy head and turned to look at him over her shoulder. "What is it?"

He rested his forehead against her cheek, whispering now, tender again. The hand against her breasts gentled, stroking with the barest of touches, as though she were a newborn chick that couldn't handle harsh treatment of any kind.

Viveca crooned.

"I have another question for you, when I think you're ready. When I ask you...*please, please say yes.* Okay?"

The craziest thought crossed her mind. He sounded so solemn, so intense, but...no. He couldn't possibly mean... No. Of course not. She would not let her girlish thoughts cloud her already foggy brain.

"I'll do anything for you. You know that."

Against her back she felt his muscles relax. Gathering

her in his arms, rubbing his lips against her nape, he made two easy circles of his hips and came with a muffled cry. Viveca tightened her inner muscles around him, absorbing him and this moment.

The most beautiful of her life.

Chapter 16

They were still joined, their limbs twined around each other. He'd arranged himself so that he was half-leaning, half-propped on the pillows, not crushing her, and had one arm free to stroke her cheek.

Of all the things they'd done together tonight, sleep wasn't one of them. Sleep was, in fact, pretty much off the table as an option for now.

Weak morning light streaked around the edges of the lowered Roman shades at Viveca's windows and fell upon her beautiful sunflowers. She couldn't imagine a more wonderful, peaceful scene. The warmth of Andrew's skin against hers, the comfort of the cloud of linens surrounding them, her deliciously sore, satiated body smelling of his intoxicating musk.

If ever in her life she'd had a perfect moment, this was it.

This, naturally, caused a vague knot of panic in her belly.

She tried to ease his weight off of her. Not because she wanted to, but because she had already become far too used to it. "You should go."

It was the wrong thing to say, of course. The absolute absorption with which he'd been studying her features morphed into a scowl that twisted his face and returned him to the fearsome man who'd tried to bribe her the day they met.

"I just meant your grandmother will be up soon, and Bishop—"

"Skip the explanations. I understand better than you think."

"No, you d—"

"You're so predictable." His muscles tensed and solidified, and all the peaceful relaxation that had filled the room ten seconds ago vanished as he jerked his body free and pulled away. "You should work on a new routine. This one's really getting old."

"Sorry I'm such a disappointment," she muttered, thinking that her ongoing doubts, even after the night they'd spent together, were as much a thorn in her side as they were in his.

His movements rough from anger, he flapped the covers up to his waist and smoothed them out. "How can we get past this trust thing, Viveca? Because I know what's running through your mind. You're still—*even now*—wondering if I'm only manipulating you to stop you from writing the book. You still think I'm running an agenda here. *Don't you?*"

The suppressed rage in his voice wasn't helping matters any. She'd expected it, maybe even deserved it, but that didn't make it any easier to deal with.

"Well," she said, "you don't want me to write the book.

I want to write it. Nothing's changed with that, but I'm guessing you're going to play on my feelings for you to see if you can change my mind."

"Your feelings for me?" His gaze sharpened to laser focus and his voice dropped down into that low, ruthless range that struck terror in her heart every time she heard it. "That sounds like a topic worth pursuing. Care to elaborate?"

Heat licked at her face, flames of embarrassment and fear strong enough to singe her eyebrows. "No."

The ticking muscle in his tight jaw told her they were going from bad to much worse. "Of course you wouldn't."

Levering himself upright against the pillows, he scraped his hands through his hair, watching her the whole time. "Let's get one thing clear. I know how your mind works. It's the cold light of day now, and all the doubts are starting to percolate in your brain, and you're wondering if you made a huge mistake—"

She looked away and tried to keep her features even. How would she ever learn to deal with his unerring vision into her fractured psyche and all her worries and fears?

"—and wondering if I was serious and if I'm going to hold you to everything you said to me last night." He lashed out, grabbed her chin and turned her head back around to face him and his blazing eyes. "And I want to make sure you understand that I heard what you said and I'm not going to do the gentlemanly thing and pretend I didn't. I don't have any problems with you admitting your feelings to me in the heat of the moment. I consider everything you said as binding as if you'd testified in open court. Maybe more so. Are we clear?"

"Perfectly." She swallowed hard against the enormous lump in her throat. "I wouldn't expect anything less from you."

He studied her with suspicious eyes, obviously trying to decide whether she was serious or just blowing him off. Satisfied at last, he nodded. "Let's get some more things straight. I don't want you to write the book—"

"Of course you don't."

"—and I don't think you will, but not because I'm going to pressure you about it. I'm not. You're one of the most decent people I've ever met, and I'm hoping that when you stop to think about it, you'll realize that writing this exposé listing all the numerous failings of my grandfather will hurt lots of innocent people, like my grandmother, and you won't do it. And I told you before—writing this book won't make you feel any better about your father's death."

"*This* is you not pressuring me?"

"Yeah. Because here's my bottom line—if it's a matter of me choosing between getting you to trust me and stopping that book, there's no choice to be made. So go ahead and crucify my grandfather's memory. Have at it. Knock yourself out."

"Wha—?"

"Screw it. Write a thousand books. I don't give a damn."

Those three sentences brought her up short and scrambled her brain. If he'd told her he was descended from a long line of royal Transylvanian vampires, she couldn't have been more surprised.

"You're all about uncovering secrets, aren't you, Vivi? Well, you should like this one. You want to know why I offered you all that money to leave town and drop the book?"

"No," she said, and she didn't.

Not when he had that strange light in his eyes and that fierce, almost feral energy shimmering around him and making him almost unrecognizable. Dread crept up on her, squeezing the air off in her throat. A secret that could do that to him was something she didn't want any part of.

His lip curled in a humorless smile that scared her even worse. "Too late. Here it is."

He opened his mouth, looking like he was going to spit out whatever it was, but then sudden emotion seemed to overcome him and he floundered. Color rose high over his cheeks and his nostrils flared. Pausing, he stared at her and she had the feeling he was shoring up his courage.

"No." She shook her head and touched his arm because her overwhelming instinct to protect and comfort this man made her do it. "You don't have to—"

Jerking away, he drew a harsh breath.

"Charles Warner isn't my father, Vivi. I don't know who the hell my father is."

The horror on Viveca's face was just about right. Just about what he'd expected. So was the pity in her shimmering eyes, and that really pissed him off because he hated pity. Especially hers.

"I don't… I don't understand," she stammered.

He slid out of bed because he couldn't sit still while he confessed his darkest secret to the woman he loved but wasn't sure he could trust. The woman who wanted him but apparently still didn't love or trust him.

Life, it turned out, was a real bitch sometimes.

He paced back and forth at the foot of the bed, unmindful of his nakedness. "It's really simple, Vivi. One day when I was about ten, there was a huge party up at the big house. While everyone was downstairs, I snuck into my parents' room to look at my father's stash of porn magazines. The last thing I expected was for my loving father to drag my loving mother in by her arm and throw her around."

"Oh, my God." Viveca gaped at him, pressing a hand over her heart.

"Oh, don't worry. I had time to hide under the bed. Had a great view of the fireworks. Turns out he'd caught her screwing some guy in the bathroom—"

"Oh, *God.*"

"And during the course of the ensuing, ah…*discussion,* he told her he wouldn't pass off another man's kid as his for a *second time*—"

Viveca cried out.

"—and my wonderful mother taunted him by saying that at least she'd been considerate enough to get knocked up by someone who looked like my father so no one would ever have to know the truth. And you know what, Vivi? No one does know the truth. Well, other than me and Bishop, that is. Hell, I never even found out who my real father is. Not sure I want to know." He laughed bitterly. "Not real sure my mother knew. There seemed to be lots of potential candidates."

"I don't understand this." Her voice had degenerated into a panicked wail, a screech. Taking a ragged breath, she swiped a hand under her eyes and nose. "This whole time I've been thinking you look like your father. This doesn't make any sense."

"Vivi," he said tiredly, "I've been trying to make sense of this mess for most of my life."

Back and forth he stalked, bed…window…pivot…bed again. Adrenaline spiked through him, making it hard to think even though all kinds of thoughts and fragmented memories flowed through his mind. To his astonishment he felt…lighter. Free, almost. As though telling his secret, after holding it so close for so long, was the right thing to do. The first step on the road toward gaining control of his life.

In the resounding silence, he heard a muffled sniffle and, turning, discovered Viveca with one end of the sheet pressed to her mouth, her shoulders shaking.

Quite a show of emotion from the woman who'd told him to leave after he'd spent the night showing her in every possible way how much he loved her. Hell, he'd almost asked her to marry him, and she could barely even admit that she wanted him. How funny was that?

Taking a shuddering breath, she wiped her face and blinked up at him, her eyes still wet. "I'm sorry you had to go through—"

"*I don't want your pity.*" Roaring at her like a maniac, he threw his arms wide and put it all on the line for her. "When will you wake the hell up? I want you to *trust* me. I want you to *know* me. I want you to *love* me even though I'm a bastard whose own parents didn't love me. I want us to get past this book nonsense."

"Andrew."

Getting out of bed, she came around, making like she wanted to touch him, but he was maxed out on the touching. He really was. No one was more surprised than he was at the discovery he'd made in the last few hours, but the simple fact was that sex with Viveca without emotions wasn't enough. Not even close.

She reached out a hand, but he held his arm up to ward her off. She froze, respecting his new boundary, but he could tell she didn't like it because she crossed her arms over her chest and looked like she was struggling not to cry again.

"Here's what I want from you, Viveca. I want you to stop wallowing in your bitterness and your fears and your suspicions and look around long enough to see that I have just taken a huge calculated risk."

Viveca looked away, a frown creasing her brow.

"Do you get that? You're so afraid of my agendas and what I want and what I'm going to do to you. Well, now I've given you all the power. All the power. It's all in your hands."

"What am I supposed to do?" she asked miserably. "I feel like I've betrayed my father and everything I stand for by being with you. I'm afraid you'll cheat on me. I'm afraid you only think you love me."

"First off, do you really think it'll honor your father to refuse to be with me when I can make you happy?"

"I just don't know—" she began again, but one impatient shake of his head had her shutting up as fast as she could.

"Second, I do really love you. Third, I'm not going to cheat on you."

"But you *might*—"

"For God's sake," he roared, his lifetime's supply of patience used up in this one discussion with her. "I really hope this is the last time I have to say this. I want you to take a minute or two and decide whether you want to be with me. Whether you can trust me. And I'm not talking about this half-assed stuff from last night, either." He flapped a hand at the bed. "You're either in, or you're out. And this has *nothing* to do with that damn book."

He headed toward the bedroom door because he needed to get the hell away from her before he said or did something even crazier than what he'd just done.

Before he stripped any more of his flesh raw.

At the threshold, though, he discovered it wasn't as easy to walk out as he'd thought. Stopping, he looked at her over his shoulder and remembered the beauty of last night even though it hadn't been beautiful *enough*. He didn't want to walk away, but he would. He had to have her love, had to have it all. Having nothing was better than half, but…God, he didn't want nothing.

A new thought occurred to him. "Are you on the Pill?"

Something soft but guarded crossed over her features. "No."

Good, he thought with savage satisfaction.

Let her think about the beautiful child they may have created. Let her think about the life they could have together if and when the glorious day ever came that she decided to overcome her fears. Let her think and, please God, come to the right decision.

"Well." More scared than he'd ever been in his entire life—and it had *nothing* to do with the potential loss of his godforsaken inheritance—Andrew prayed for the strength to hide it. "I guess I'll see you tomorrow at Grandmother's party."

He strode into the living room to find his clothes and left his entire life, financial and emotional, in Viveca's hands. She did not stop him.

Arnetta Warner's eightieth birthday party was an extravaganza the likes of which Viveca had never seen except in *InStyle* magazine.

It was also one of the lousiest nights of Viveca's life.

In her black gown, which she'd bought at a highfalutin consignment store and *still* paid too much for, she arrived early and snagged a crystal champagne flute from the tray of the nearest uniformed server.

Roaming from room to room and feeling comically out of place, like a fly in the caviar bowl, she miserably noted all the lavish decorations and all the people she knew only from their pictures in the papers, locally and nationally.

There was the ice sculpture of leaping dolphins, and

there was U.S. Senator Jacobson and his trophy wife. Over in that corner of the living room sat Mrs. Warner in a tall, straight upholstered chair, holding court in her beaded ice-blue gown and diamonds like Elizabeth I, and in the other corner a group of Bengals players clustered around a fountain the decorators had installed this afternoon.

She couldn't stop staring at Andrew. She'd heard nothing from him since last night's explosive conclusion, except for one brief, electric moment when their gazes caught across the room and he raised his champagne flute to her in a silent, mocking toast.

He was, obviously, still angry with her.

No brightly colored bow tie for him, no trendy tuxedo. He wore the blackest double-breasted with black tie and the whitest shirt. Anyone else would have looked like an undertaker, but he looked like a god.

Ignoring her was, apparently, part of the punishment he'd devised. Damn effective, too. Being banished from the addictive intensity of his attention, especially after wallowing in it last night, was the worst possible torture, a stint of the rack followed by a nice drawing and quartering.

"It's not that bad, is it?"

She turned to see Eric grinning at her, his date by his side. Unlike Andrew, he'd gone the nontraditional route and wore a black suit with black dress shirt. Though he could never be as handsome as Andrew, he still managed to look like he'd just stepped off the runway at a Paris fashion show.

"Wow. You look great," she told him.

"Thanks." He drew his date closer. "This is Izzy. Well, Isabella Stevens. Izzy, this is Viveca Jackson."

"Oh, *Izzy*."

Viveca took a good look as she held out her hand, very curious about Eric's so-called best friend from college. What kind of single woman of childbearing age could be just friends with Eric Warner, one of the best-looking men on the planet? Viveca had seen them together earlier, from a distance, and they'd had their heads together, laughing and chattering.

Viveca's first impression had been of a girl-next-door type, because Isabella seemed cute and a little bohemian in a fluttery multicolored halter dress that was beautiful on her but definitely *not* on the cutting edge of couture. This had been a surprise because she expected anyone with Eric to look like…well, Brenda. A model or an actress, someone who specialized in making regular women look like crones with hairy chins and warts.

But now, staring into Isabella's smiling face, Viveca had to rethink her assessment because the woman was stunning. All warm, dimple-cheeked fun, with wide brown eyes and the kind of natural magnetism that put people right at ease.

Sure enough, Isabella ignored Viveca's hand and pulled her in for a rib-splitting hug. She smelled summery fresh, as inviting as a day at the beach and Viveca knew she would like her. "It's so nice to meet you, Viveca. Eric says you've got Andrew's nose wide open. So I said *this* is a woman I've got to meet."

"I don't know about that." Viveca pulled back and shot Eric a quick frown for gossiping about her. "But I've heard a lot about you, too. I don't know why you hang around *this* guy."

"He's not so bad." Smiling up at Eric, Isabella patted his face and then stood on her tiptoes to kiss his cheek. "And he's pitiful without me."

Judging by the way Eric stared at Isabella, as though he just couldn't get his mouth to grin wide enough at her, Viveca thought this was probably true.

Isabella winked at Viveca. "I'll catch up with you later. Right now I'm going to get some champagne."

With that she was off, weaving through the crowd and leaving Eric to call after her. "Don't worry about me. I didn't need any champagne or anything." Muttering, he shot an apologetic glance at Viveca and followed Isabella.

Alone again. Wonderful. Viveca tried not to look as pitiful as she felt.

Right about then a server marched by with a tray of stuffed mushrooms or some such. Determined to do something other than gape at Andrew all night, Viveca reflexively snatched one, put it in her mouth and chewed, tasting nothing.

"Mushrooms are fungi. Not fruits or vegetables. And you have to make sure they're not poisonous. Some of them are, you know."

Viveca looked around and saw Nathan standing there, wearing a tuxedo and a bow tie decorated with— She squinted, leaning in closer for a better look. Yes, it was, in fact, a SpongeBob SquarePants and Patrick design. One corner of his mouth was smudged with something white and, no doubt, sticky.

If she'd ever seen a cuter kid before, she couldn't think when.

In one hand he held his Game Boy. In the other, he held a crystal tumbler filled with some sparkling pink liquid, about thirteen maraschino cherries and a paper umbrella perched on top. A Shirley Temple, probably.

"Hey, Nathan." The night looked a little better suddenly. "How are you?"

"Good. I'm spending the night." Using his tongue, he tried to push the umbrella out of the way so he could sip his drink.

She watched him, bemused. "What's the best food so far?"

He frowned, thinking hard. "I think it'd have to be the cinnamon rolls. But I only had three because they're pretty unhealthy. Lots of sugar and fat."

"Cinnamon rolls?" Cream cheese icing would certainly explain the white stuff on his mouth.

"Yeah. Bishop let Mrs. Warner have some since it's her birthday." Trying to point, he sloshed his drink all over his hand.

Viveca glanced across the room to see Mrs. Warner holding a small plate loaded with the largest cinnamon roll Viveca had ever seen. The old woman scooped up a bite with her fork, slid it into her mouth and closed her eyes, looking rapturous.

Viveca laughed. "Remind me to get one of those before they're all gone."

"Okay." Nathan looked up at her with wide-eyed enthusiasm. "I planted some stuff in the greenhouse with Bishop."

"Oh, yeah?"

"Yeah. Tomatoes, which are *fruits,* and carrots and some ugly flower I didn't want to grow but Bishop said I should try."

"Orchids?"

"Yeah. Orchids." He made a face. "So will you come see what I planted?"

"I'd love to," she said, thinking of all the time she and her father had spent with their window boxes and tomatoes.

"Good." He regarded her solemnly for a minute and then nodded. "I like you."

Trying to match his serious tone, Viveca gave him a grave look. "I like you, too."

Nathan beamed as though a genie had erupted out of his bottle, but then he saw something that ripped the smile right off his face. "Uh-oh. Hide me."

With no further warning, he ducked behind Viveca.

"Um…Nathan." She looked over her shoulder at him. "Are you running from the law, or—"

"It's Bishop." Nathan crouched lower. "He wants me to go to bed."

"Oh, no." Viveca stifled a laugh. "Not bed."

"Cover for me."

He took off. Moving like a special operative for the CIA, he made his way across the room, hiding first behind a pillar, then a huge potted palm, and then a laughing crowd of people. Finally he disappeared through the doorway into the music room, casting a last, furtive glance in Bishop's direction.

Bishop marched up to Viveca, looking harried. "You seen Nathan?"

"Yeah." Thinking fast, Viveca pointed toward the hall. "He went that way."

"That boy." Scowling, Bishop headed off in the wrong direction.

Left alone with no distractions, Viveca gave herself a stern warning not to look at Andrew, but two seconds of ignoring him was, alas, all she could manage.

Turning back in his direction, she discovered that a woman had appeared at his side and was rubbing a good thirty inches of her size thirty-eights against his arm. Shifting a little, Viveca got a better look…long auburn hair…a negligible purple dress that plunged forever, revealing the line of an ivory back and the curve of a shapely hip… It was the senator's trophy wife, *a married woman*.

And then another woman came and stood on his other side. Viveca watched the scene unfold and read the body language while her stomach tied itself in knot after sickening knot. The two women on either side of Andrew, exchanging strained smiles and narrowed, catty glances. Jockeying for position. Doing everything but reaching under their expensive dresses, shimmying their panties down their toned legs and off, and tucking them into Andrew's breast pocket.

"Your claws are showing."

The low voice in her ear jarred her out of her jealous stupor. Blinking, she turned and discovered that Eric was back, watching her with unmitigated amusement as he raised his champagne flute to his lips.

"I have no idea what you're talking about," she lied.

"I'm talking about you staring daggers at my cousin and his groupies." Giving her a mock frown of deep concern, he put a hand to the small of her back and steered her into a corner so they could talk privately.

She wasn't at all sure a quiet moment with Eric was a good idea, especially given the current subject matter. He did not move away, but stayed close to her side so he did not have to raise his voice against the music.

"Again," she said, "no idea what you're talking about."

"If you say so." His gaze, respectful but still unmistakably that of a man who was aware of her as a woman, skimmed her from head to toe. "You look great. I can see why Andrew is so bent out of shape about you. Poor guy."

"*Okay.*" Flushing furiously and embarrassed by his uncanny ability to pick up on the signals between her and Andrew, she tried to hide it with a little bluster. "First of all, Andrew doesn't get bent—"

"Did I hear my name?"

Chapter 17

From out of nowhere, Andrew materialized between them. Startled, Viveca looked up to see him looming with something dangerous glittering in his dark eyes, something possessive that she didn't want to test. Not tonight.

Shouldering past Eric, he deftly pulled her away from his cousin and into his arms, exuding both sex and a powerful warning. "You look beautiful."

Andrew's gaze, unlike Eric's, was not subtle, nor was his husky bedroom murmur. They were red-hot brands, marking her as his and no one else's. His gaze lingered on her cleavage, her hips and her bare thigh where it showed through the slit in her dress.

Sliding a hand up her arm to the side of her neck, he reached under her curls to her nape, to the spot he very well knew drove her right out of her mind. Caressing there, ignoring her slight sputter, he angled her head and pressed a lingering kiss to another of her pleasure spots, the juncture of her jawline and neck.

Viveca melted to jelly.

When he was done with that, Andrew slipped the same hand down her back and, pulling her tight against his side, rested it low on her hip.

Well…sixty percent hip, forty percent butt.

More than a little dazed, clinging to Andrew for support, her face so hot it felt iridescent, Viveca looked around at their rapt audience and tried to think of something to say. Eric looked amused and triumphant. Just past him, near the fireplace where he'd left them, Andrew's two groupies looked murderous. Mrs. Warner, still in her throne, looked wide-eyed and arrested, a forkful of cinnamon roll hovering near her lips.

Andrew, however, was his usual cool-cucumber self.

"What's up?" Andrew extended his free hand and Eric shook it. "What'd I miss?"

"Viveca was just telling me there's nothing going on between the two of you."

Andrew looked down at her, and she could read, even if no one else could, the irritation on his face. "Vivi likes to be discreet. A little too discreet, considering…"

"Considering what?" Eric asked.

Andrew didn't answer, instead giving Viveca one of those screaming, potent looks that said it all—*considering he'd spent all night with Viveca, buried as deep inside her as a man could get.*

Viveca couldn't breathe.

Andrew's gaze never left Viveca's face. "You're pretty smart, Eric. I think you can figure it out."

"Oh, *I've* got it," Eric said cheerfully, "but I think you and—what did you call her? *Vivi?*—may have a little miscommunication going."

"We'll work it out," Andrew said.

"I'm sure you will."

Viveca had finally had enough. Her wobbly legs were gaining strength and she was feeling the beginnings of resentment over all this male posturing. Elbowing her way out of Andrew's grip, she divided her glare between the two of them.

"If you two are finished with all your chest-thumping for now," she said tartly, taking a step toward the hall, "I'm going to the ladies' room."

"Don't go too far. I've called a little family meeting when the party wraps up. In the library." Andrew looked to Eric. "You, too. I want to end the night with a bang."

Shooting a last significant look at Viveca, he wheeled around and disappeared into the crowd.

By the time the last guest had trickled out of the never-ending gala, it was nearly four in the morning. Viveca followed a couple of scurrying caterers down the hall to the library and turned inside. The room, she saw at a glance, was back to normal except for a couple of enormous arrangements of orchids, candles still flickering on the mantelpiece, and a tray of fruits and cheeses on one of the coffee tables. Through the French doors, the lighted pool glittered and dozens of white Japanese lanterns bobbed in the breeze.

The scene would have been beautiful and serene except for two things—the enormous, oppressive portrait of Reynolds Warner glaring down at everyone from above the mantel, disapproving of them all from beyond the grave, and the ominous silence that enveloped the room the second Viveca walked in.

Viveca wished she was anywhere but there. She waited,

but no one said anything to her. Apparently they couldn't talk and stare at her at the same time, so they all elected to stare.

Andrew leaned against the bookshelf, ankles crossed, looking unconcerned.

Eric, amused as always, sprawled over most of one of the sofas.

Mrs. Warner, perched on the end of one of her tall chairs, her shoulders squared and back straight enough to please Emily Post, accepted a cup of tea from Bishop.

Viveca wished she could turn right around and run away. But Bishop caught her eye and gave her a tiny, fortifying wink, telling her she had at least one friend in the room. Immediately she felt better. Braver.

"Good evening." Knowing better than to ever show a weakness to anyone in this crowd of sharks and piranhas, she kept her chin high, plastered a smile on her face and tried to look as though she belonged in a middle-of-the-night meeting with this clan. "Am I late?" Protocol required her to go straight to Mrs. Warner and give the queen her due by pecking her on the cheek. Mrs. Warner obligingly tilted her cheek even as she frowned.

"No, dear." Mrs. Warner took a sip from her cup and replaced it on its saucer, which she held in her lap. "We were just talking about your new, ah, relationship with Andrew."

Viveca, who'd been hovering over a chair kitty-corner to Mrs. Warner's, about to sit, paused. Gripping the chair's arms, she lowered herself, crossed her legs and arranged her skirt to cover her bare legs as best she could. "Is that so?" She shot a glance at Andrew, who stared back, his face placid and unreadable.

Mrs. Warner nodded. "Yes. We've already discussed it with Andrew. Maybe you'd like to give us your version…?"

The question mark tacked on the end of Mrs. Warner's sentence did not for one second fool Viveca into thinking it was a request rather than a command.

With commands, as always, her hackles rose and her obstinate gene kicked into turbo drive. She was not a doormat. She would not lie down and be walked upon.

Viveca looked the old woman square in the eye, laced her voice with steel and prepared for a fight. "I'm sure he told you that any relationship we may have is personal and doesn't concern—"

"Actually," Mrs. Warner said, "Andrew says he wants to marry you."

Viveca gaped at her, looking and half hoping for some sign of joking, misunderstanding or confusion, but no... Mrs. Warner looked as sharp as ever.

It wasn't possible. Of course it wasn't.

Andrew Warner did not want to marry anyone, much less *her,* no matter what strange vibes he'd given off last night. That being the case, she couldn't understand why he would say such a thing to his grandmother. It wasn't that he was impetuous; she knew enough about him to understand that he never did anything, from buying a toothbrush to buying a company, without a thorough analysis.

But...why would he say he wanted to marry her?

And why did she feel the craziest glimmer of joy deep inside?

From a great distance Viveca was aware of Eric's soft chuckle. Over near the fireplace, Andrew checked his watch, looking bored, two patches of vivid color high over his cheeks.

"Mrs. Warner." Viveca had to stop and clear her dry throat. "I'm sure you misunderstood—"

"I never misunderstand." Mrs. Warner focused her

piercing gaze on Viveca and pursed her lips, all pretense of polite conversation gone now. "And I'm sure you understand that I have seen all manner of women trying to entice and trap my grandsons—"

"*What?*" Outrage replaced Viveca's surprise.

"Grandmother," Andrew said.

"—and I will not stand for it. There will, of course, be an ironclad prenuptial whenever Andrew *does* marry—"

"*Grandmother,*" Andrew said again.

"—and you'd better not even *think* about turning up pregnant, because I will not put up with any baby mama drama, so you—"

"*That is enough,*" Andrew roared.

Mrs. Warner trailed off and looked around with surprise, her brows shooting toward her hairline. No doubt it had been fifty years or more since anyone had dared to raise his or her voice to her. "Excuse me?"

"You will not talk to Viveca that way, now or ever." Andrew, all but levitating with fury, glared down at his grandmother. "You will show her the respect that my wife deserves, and you will welcome her to this *family,* such as it is, with open—"

Mrs. Warner, looking aghast, threw a hand over her heart. "You will not dictate manners to me in my own—"

Viveca, furious now, belatedly found her tongue. She wasn't quite sure when she'd fallen through the rabbit hole and slipped into Wonderland here, but enough was enough. She didn't need Andrew as a spokesperson and she certainly didn't need these two discussing her as if she wasn't there.

"Excuse me." She shot Andrew a repressive frown. "I can speak for myself." Turning to Mrs. Warner, she strove hard for a respectful tone. "I am not a gold digger and I am certainly not trying to entice Andrew, so you can rest your mind about that."

Mrs. Warner opened her mouth and spluttered, but Viveca didn't pause long enough to let her get a full head of steam going.

"That's the first thing. The second thing is that if and when Andrew and I discuss marriage, that will be a matter between the two of us, not something for a committee. I hope you can respect that."

Silence fell. Even Eric didn't dare laugh now.

Viveca and Mrs. Warner studied each other, neither blinking, while the echo of Viveca's little speech vibrated through the air for several beats. Just about the time Viveca began to imagine that Mrs. Warner was regarding her with newfound—though grudging—respect, the words sank into Viveca's own brain and she realized, with horror, what she had just done. *What? What* had she just said?

If and when Andrew and I discuss marriage?

Those words had *not* just come out of her mouth, had they?

A glance at Andrew confirmed that they had, that she'd made an admission and he intended to hold her to it. He stared at her, an intent, focused look on his face, a quarter smile turning up one corner of his mouth. Beneath his anger, which was still there, she saw other things—respect. Admiration. Love. All of that and more.

"Do you suppose," he said, speaking to the room at large but still looking at Viveca, "that we can get to the agenda? It's late."

"Yeah, man." Yawning hugely, Eric stretched his arms overhead. "Let's wrap this up. Izzy's waiting for me. We're going for breakfast."

"Great." Andrew paused and looked to Mrs. Warner

when he spoke again. "I'm resigning as CEO of Warner-Brands, effective as soon as I inform the board. I'm calling a special meeting for first thing Monday morning. Eric can replace me."

Pandemonium erupted. Everyone but Andrew gasped and glanced around at each other to make sure they'd heard right. Andrew, unruffled as ever, raised a hand for silence and continued.

"I want my severance package, and I'll exercise my stock options. But I'm going to renounce my inheritance. Eric can have that, too."

More gasps. Mrs. Warner and Bishop exchanged a dark look, but Eric was on his feet, throwing his arms wide. "What the hell's going on?"

Andrew shrugged. "Don't look a gift horse in the mouth."

"I want to know why you'd give up everything you've worked for. Your birthright—"

"It's not my birthright."

Andrew's voice was calm, his expression resolute, but Viveca felt devastated and guilty. She'd been an unintentional catalyst for this monumental decision, and the knowledge hurt. The last thing she wanted was to be in any way responsible for Andrew giving up what he loved, what he *deserved,* by rights if not by birth.

"Andrew, *don't,*" she said. "Think about this. Take some time to—"

"I *have* thought about it, Vivi." A quick, sad smile crossed over his face. "I've had twenty-five years to think about it."

"Think some more, Scooter." Standing by Mrs. Warner's chair, Bishop looked older suddenly, his shoulders stooped, the lines bracketing his mouth more pronounced.

"I don't need to, Bishop. I told Viveca last night, and it felt like I was finally taking control." Andrew hesitated. "I want to be all the way in control. No more lies. No more secrets. Enough's enough."

Eric rounded on Andrew. "What the hell is going on?"

Now that the moment was here, Andrew seemed to have a tough time getting it out, and Viveca couldn't blame him. This was only the second time he'd ever said his secret aloud, and it wasn't the sort of thing that would roll right off the tongue.

Twice he opened his mouth and started to say something; twice he shut it again. Finally he ran a hand over the top of his head, ruffling his hair. "Grandmother, I—"

The weight of the confession seemed to press down upon him, and it took him a minute to continue, to sever the ties that had bound him all his life.

"I'm not a Warner. Charles isn't my father. I don't know who is. I…heard my parents arguing about it when I was ten."

Absolute silence.

Everyone seemed paralyzed. Eric gaped at his cousin, obviously trying to make sense of the words. Andrew just stood there. Viveca sat frozen, desperately wanting to go to Andrew but knowing he had to do this his own way.

Finally Eric spoke. "You… You can't be sure."

"Yeah," Andrew said, "I can."

More silence, except that Viveca noticed movement out of the corner of her eye. Something seemed to be going on between Mrs. Warner and Bishop, who jerked his head toward Andrew. Mrs. Warner frowned and shook her head, and this seemed to be more than Bishop could take. "This ain't right. You know it. You can't let this boy—"

"Bishop." Mrs. Warner pressed a shaky hand to her head and massaged her temple with thin, manicured fingers. "I think we all need a moment to let this soak in. And I think Andrew is a grown man who knows what he wants and doesn't want."

"No." Bishop stood up. His slight body quivered, but he suddenly looked bigger, a force to be reckoned with as he loomed over Mrs. Warner in her chair. "Andrew doesn't know—"

"Bishop," Mrs. Warner hissed, "that is *enough*."

Bishop snapped his jaw shut and wheeled away to one of the far corners of the room, muttering all the way. "This ain't right... This ain't right. Lord, help us now."

"Well." Mrs. Warner stood and smoothed her skirt. Turning to Andrew, she looked hard and unforgiving. Merciless. Not at all like a woman who'd just lost a grandson should look. "I can't say I'm surprised. Your mother always was a slut."

Galvanized by a rage so powerful she could have lifted a car with it, Viveca sprang to her feet and launched herself between Andrew and his so-called grandmother, wanting to protect him from this woman who obviously lacked any maternal genes whatsoever.

"Don't you dare talk to him like that." Viveca's voice shook with fury. "What kind of a woman are you?"

"Don't worry, Viveca." Turning, Viveca saw, to her dismay, that Andrew wore a cynical, bitter smile, the kind that was symptomatic of a decaying soul and a loss of faith in people that might well be permanent. "*Grandmother* isn't telling me... Oh, wait. I guess I shouldn't call her that now, should I?"

Viveca and Mrs. Warner both flinched.

"Correction," Andrew continued. "*Arnetta* isn't telling me anything about my mother that I didn't already know."

With that, he wheeled around and stalked out.

Chapter 18

After a minute's hesitation, during which Viveca debated whether to stay in the library and let Arnetta Warner have it with both barrels or follow Andrew, she decided to follow Andrew out into the night. His car was just screeching down the driveway out of sight, but she jumped into her rental car and followed it, praying all the while that neither of them got pulled over for speeding on the narrow, winding, hilly roads.

Within five minutes Andrew turned onto a private, tree-lined drive marked only by a bricked mailbox. She trailed behind, furious at him for driving like a maniac and making snap decisions, at Arnetta for being a witch, and at herself for being unable to pick a path and stick to it. Her thoughts in a jumble, she was unprepared for the sight that greeted her when the trees suddenly gave way.

A house appeared at the end of the long circular drive,

looking warm and inviting with landscape spotlights shining on it. Stunned, she slowed down and took a minute to gape, vaguely aware of Andrew parking and getting out.

It was an enormous stone farmhouse with dormer windows, black shutters and white trim. Very old by the looks of it, at least a hundred years, but well-loved and tended. The house was breathtaking. Beautiful. Exactly the kind of house a man in Andrew's position should live in. It was also a hundred times too big for a man to live in alone.

Hopping out, she marched up to the front door where he glared down at her, a tuxedoed wall of menace and bad attitude. He'd gotten rid of his jacket and loosened his tie, which dangled on either side of his collar. "Not now, Viveca. It's late. I'm tired. We're both pissed off."

"Get out of my way." She shouldered past him.

Taking a few steps into the foyer, she stopped dead, feeling as though someone had switched houses on her. Several rooms spun off the central hallway, some of which were lit. The kitchen, through there. Over there, a dining room. Library, living room, powder room. She spun in a slow circle, seeing it all but not believing any of it.

Other than a leather sofa and wall-mounted flat-screen TV in the living room and a chair in the foyer, there was no furniture. None.

An echoing emptiness filled the house, yawning and sucking the energy out of the air, ridding the house of any soul. Andrew *couldn't* live here. She'd been in warehouses that were more inviting than this.

Too dismayed to hide it, she decided to address it head-on. "You don't… You don't have any furniture."

"I'd noticed." Shutting the door, he swung around to face her.

"How long have you lived here?"

His smile was hard and crooked. "Five years. What do you want, Viveca?"

So they weren't going to do this the nice way and speak politely to each other. They weren't going to sit and have a rational discussion. Well, fine. But he was going to listen to her. Come hell or high water, he was going to hear what she had to say.

"Why did you renounce your inheritance like that?"

"Why not?" He shrugged and looked bored, as though he'd only given away a paperback and couldn't understand the need for hoopla.

"Because." She strove for calm and patience. "Being a Warner means everything to you. The company means everything to you. You said so."

A wave of dangerous feeling crossed over his features. "You want to talk about what means everything to me? Is that why you're here?"

"I'm trying to understand you."

Another shrug, and then he leaned back against the nearest wall, crossed his ankles and shoved his hands in his pockets. "I'm tired of living a lie. Tired of killing myself for a company that isn't even mine and a grandmother who doesn't like me. Does that make sense, or should I speak slower for you?"

She ignored that. "I think something's going on with your grandmother and Bishop. I don't think your parentage was news to them. They didn't seem all that surprised… I think they know more than they're telling."

"Bishop already knew Charles wasn't my father. As for what my grandmother knows or doesn't know, I don't really care."

"Don't care? I can't believe that."

He stared at her, his gaze flat. "You should."

"I plan to investigate a little. Just so you know."

"Whatever floats your boat. Is there anything else?"

"Why haven't you ever tried to find out who your real father is? With your resources, you could—"

"I don't have the stomach for it. I'm not sure I want to know if my mother didn't know who he was, or didn't know his last name, or if he was the pool boy or something. Anything else?"

"Yes." Feeling vulnerable and exposed, as though she stood on tiptoe on the edge of a cliff, she ran a hand through her hair. Her cheeks flamed. She cleared her throat. She shifted on her feet. Catching herself fidgeting, she told herself to just get on with it. "You told your grandmother you want to marry me?"

He didn't answer.

"Quite a proposal."

"That wasn't a proposal. Just a statement of intent. The proposal will come when I'm a little more sure you'll say yes."

"Do you always discuss marriage with your grandmother first?"

"I've never discussed marriage in my life. I never thought I'd get married." If his jaw went any tighter it would snap in two and sprinkle his teeth all over the floor. "But then I met you, and once I knew what I wanted there didn't seem to be any point to waiting. Just because it was fast doesn't mean it's not real."

Viveca just couldn't figure out what to make of him. He was so decisive. Nothing slowed him down, ever. And when had *she* known? *Did* she know, even now?

"You move so fast, Andrew. I'm not sure I can keep up with you."

"You kept up with me pretty well last night."

For emphasis, or maybe for shock value, he looked her up and down in a sensual assessment that would have been a leer had anyone else done it. When he did it—looked at her breasts and thighs, lowered his lids to half-mast and openly wanted her—it singed her skin and turned her knees to mush.

Even so, she would not let him get her off topic. "There's a little more to marriage than great sex."

"Astonishing sex."

"Don't you think we should talk about it?"

"The sex?"

"Marriage."

"Why?" He gave her a wide-eyed look, all puzzled confusion. "I'm clear on what I want."

"Humor me. I'm a little tetchy since I spent a large portion of the evening watching women hit on you."

"Jealous, were you?"

"Yeah, actually."

The admission seemed to surprise him, and to take some of the wind out of his sails.

Taking advantage of his momentary silence, she plowed ahead, determined to get some of these issues straight. "Where do you stand on the whole fidelity thing?"

"I've already told you. I don't make promises I can't keep."

His apparent sincerity had the perverse effect of irritating her. She should never have asked such a stupid question, anyway. What did she expect him to say?

"How reassuring," she said sourly. "Isn't infidelity sort of a tradition with the Warner family? Your parents and grandparents sure did believe in it, did they?"

He stared at her with glittering eyes and barely moved his lips. "Try to keep up. Haven't we already established I'm not a Warner?"

Now she felt like a royal bitch for even bringing his

family into the discussion. "Yeah. It's just that I know women will always throw themselves at you, exactly like they did tonight."

"Did you bother to notice that I didn't encourage them?"

"Yeah, but did you discourage them?"

"Sure." He had the wicked, satisfied look of a man about to make his point in a big way. "I discouraged them as much as you discouraged Eric when he was sniffing after you."

Viveca winced. "He only does that to get a rise out of you."

"Really?" Even Andrew's heavy brows seemed to mock her, shooting to his hairline to give her a look of utmost derision. "Thanks for the clarification. Now I feel bad for wanting to run him through with the fireplace poker."

God, she hated this. How could they discuss a future when things were so raw right now, so unsettled? "Please. Can't we do this without the anger?"

"Yeah, sure." He shoved away from the door and stalked closer to her, his voice low and rough. "Why not? Where should I start? Hmmm."

He tilted his head to the side with mock concentration and she resisted the strong urge to smack him. Only he would get sarcastic about something as serious as marriage. Only he would try to make her think she was the crazy one for wanting to discuss it.

"How about this. I love you. No, wait. I told you that last night already. Sorry. I hate to repeat myself."

Yeah. Smacking him right now would feel *really* good.

"I want to laugh with you. I want to talk with you. I want to help you get over what happened to your parents so you don't have to fight so hard all the time."

Viveca's annoyance evaporated, leaving her scared and vulnerable.

"I want to tell you my ideas about a new company, and see what you think. I want you with me when I build the new company because I know it'll be hard and you're strong and I know I can do it if I have you to come home to at night."

"Oh," she said.

"I want you to be pregnant, right now—"

Viveca shivered.

"—and if you're not, I want to get you that way as soon as possible because I'm ready to be a father and I know you'll be a hell of a mother. I want us to adopt Nathan together because he deserves a great family, and we would be one as long as we're together."

"Andrew." Tears collected, clogging the back of her throat and clouding her vision.

His voice dropped even lower and he came closer, bringing enough body heat with him to warm this entire empty house. "I want to be in your bed at night, and I want to belong there in the morning so you won't ever tell me I need to leave."

They stared at each other. For a second she thought she saw the gleam of tears in his eyes, but he blinked and they were gone. Another beat passed.

He swallowed, hard, and then the softness and vulnerability receded and the anger came back, along with the mockery and bravado. "I want you to get rid of your revenge bullshit and all your baggage so we can be together. I want you to *love* me, but…if you won't do that—"

Raising a hand, he ran a finger under the crisscrossing black straps at the front of her gown and into the cup, stroking over one of her peaked nipples. She moaned, helpless to withhold a response from him, no matter how much she wanted to.

"—I'd like to peel you out of this dress because I'm up for another round of the astonishing sex."

Viveca went rigid. Throwing her arms up, she jerked his hand away from her bodice and backed up a couple of steps. "You jackass."

"Is that a no, then? On the sex?"

"I must be crazy," she said with a semi-hysterical laugh that more or less proved her point. "I don't know why I'd ever even *think* about marrying you."

"You'll think about it. I may not be the greatest guy in the world, but I'm the only one for you, and you know it."

Oh, how she would have loved to deny it, if only to get rid of that knowing look on his face and knock him down to size. Issuing a credible denial was impossible, though. She'd never manage it. Luckily he moved away just then, sparing her from having to think of a comeback.

The loss of his body heat felt acute and painful.

Opening the door wide in a not-so-subtle attempt to throw her out, he faced her. "Let me know when you're ready to stop fighting me."

Lobbying one last glare in his direction, she left, thinking that fighting was exactly what she was going to do.

Viveca went back to the cottage, as sick of herself as Andrew was of her. Sicker, actually. When had she ever shied away from a challenge? When had she become such an unmitigated coward? When was she going to stop living in the past, walk away from the bitterness and embrace the unexpected chance at happiness that was staring her right in the face?

Enough with the emotional blackness and the endless

wallowing in what she'd lost. It was over. Done. Nothing she ever did could bring her parents back, and she was sprinting down the path to self-destruction if she kept trying.

Had she really thought writing a book would help her? It seemed hard to believe now that she'd ever been that deluded. The only good thing the book project had done was lead her to Andrew, the man she loved. Yeah, the man she *loved.*

She flipped on a couple of lights in the dark cottage, made a big pot of strong coffee, and, without bothering to change out of her gown, sat down at her desk to bury her demons and honor her father.

Gathering up the twelve photos of Daddy, she sifted through them one last time, remembering and letting go. As always, her heart tightened and she felt the loneliness and emptiness, but for the first time the emptiness didn't seem so empty. It was manageable, not bottomless. Because of Andrew she'd made the crucial discovery that her heart wasn't dead and buried with her parents. It had only been dormant.

There was one picture she couldn't put back in the blue box. The one of her father smiling a true smile, not a fake say-cheese smile, on an unimportant, unremarkable day that she couldn't now remember. This one she would mount, frame and place on her nightstand.

By the time she was done with the pictures, the first glimmers of light were visible outside her window, telling her that dawn was coming and it was almost time for her new life to begin.

Booting up her laptop, she brainstormed about an idea that had come to her last night when she saw how excited Nathan was about spending time in the greenhouse with Bishop.

Andrew had used the word *honor.* Daddy had loved

gardening. He'd always found a way to make things grow, even in the city, and had passed that love of green things down to her.

A foundation would be a good way to *honor* him.

A foundation for poor kids at Daddy's old elementary school in Brownsville, to help them grow their own veggies and green things. Not like Andrew's monstrously well-funded foundation. She planned to start small. She could already think of a few people who might want to donate. A foundation to benefit underprivileged children was a far better way to honor Daddy than a book criticizing the Warner family.

Next, feeling lighter by the second, she typed up a letter to her publisher and editor, officially withdrawing from the book project. She would return the advance, which she had, luckily, deposited and not spent. There was no way she could write a credible book about a family she planned to marry into. Talk about your conflicts of interest. After about an hour, it was all over and Viveca slumped in her chair. All her old business finished, just like that.

The sun was up now. Sunshine streaked through the windows, brightening the cottage with something that seemed more profound than mere light. Maybe it was hope, or joy.

Standing, meaning to stretch and work a couple of the kinks out of her back, she bumped the edge of her overloaded desk and knocked a file to the floor, showering pictures everywhere. Not her pictures this time, but ones of the Warners.

Dropping to her knees, she maneuvered the pictures into a loose pile, and that was when she saw it. A single picture that she'd already seen and studied but that now screamed at her like a megaphone pointed directly in her ear.

Frozen with astonishment, she tried to make sense of the incredible while random voices ran through her head and pointed to one inescapable conclusion. A conclusion that was so unexpected and painful she wished she could ignore it.

Everything came into sharp focus, and suddenly Viveca knew what she had to do.

Chapter 19

Exhausted and running on adrenaline, yet feeling strangely peaceful about his plans, Andrew went into the office at sunrise Monday morning. He always got there early because he liked that quiet period before the day's bustle really began, but today the halls seemed more crowded than usual. More than that, there was a hum of electricity in the air that told him rumors of his pending resignation had already hit the grapevine.

It figured. The head of a Fortune 500 company couldn't blow his nose without creating a ripple effect. No doubt the company's stock value would fluctuate a little when the market opened.

Just one more thing he should be worried about but wasn't.

The whole thing with Viveca had an amazing way of clarifying all the other issues in his life. When another person held your future happiness or lack thereof in her hands, you really didn't give a damn about anything else.

Especially a company and family that had already bled him dry.

Andrew turned into his office and saw, to his surprise, that Eric was there, staring moodily out the window at the faint morning sunlight. Andrew flicked on the overhead lights, tossed his briefcase on the nearest sofa and headed for his desk chair.

He couldn't resist a little needling. "Not ready for the majors?"

Eric made a rude gesture.

Andrew grinned. "It's not that bad, man. And I'll be around if you get in a jam." He sniggered. "For a small consulting fee."

Eric grinned, shoved his hands in his pants pockets and leaned one shoulder against the window. "What's up with you and Viveca? Do I hear church bells ringing?"

Andrew snorted with all the bitterness and uncertainty he'd been battling the last few days. "I'll have to get back to you on that."

"She's a good one. You don't want to let her get away."

"I don't plan to."

Eric laughed and opened his mouth to say something else, but just then June, looking harried, appeared at the door. "Viveca's here, Andrew. She wants to see all the family right now, before the meeting. She says it's an emergency."

Andrew couldn't imagine what was going on, or why Viveca wanted to see everyone rather than just him.

Bishop and Arnetta filed into his office, looking as bewildered as he felt. Andrew and Eric jumped up to murmur their pleasantries, and Andrew waited for the snub he felt certain was coming.

Sure enough, Arnetta gave Eric a kiss and hug but

allowed Andrew only a begrudging nod, no doubt as a reflection of his new, diminished status. Good thing he hadn't expected any comfort from her, any reassurances that she loved him just as much as she ever had. There wasn't much difference in warmth between how she treated him now and how she'd treated him when she'd thought he was her grandson. Cool disdain was all he got either way.

"How you doing, Scooter?" Bishop shook his hand and gave him one of those patented, searching looks that always made Andrew feel like he was twelve years old again. "Holding up okay?"

"Never better. And don't call me Scooter."

Andrew and Eric resumed leaning against their respective windows. Arnetta and Bishop sat on a sofa and exchanged long, meaningful looks. The clock on Andrew's desk ticked. The uncomfortable silence grew. With everyone present, settled and greeted, there was nothing else to say and no one made any effort to think of anything.

Luckily they didn't have to wait long before Viveca appeared in the doorway. Andrew's entire body jerked to attention and he drank up the sight of her. Her face seemed a little drawn and she had dark smudges under her eyes, but to him she looked like heaven.

Her unsmiling gaze went right to him, connected and held. Something in those dark, concerned eyes and the tight line of her jaw scared him a little. He realized then that she was on a mission that would hurt him. And while she regretted that painful fact, she would not abort the mission.

"Good morning," she said to the room at large, stepping through the door and gesturing to someone behind her. "I'm sorry to barge in like—"

There was a sharp gasp from the sofa and, startled, Andrew looked around to discover that Arnetta looked pale suddenly, as though she'd just witnessed an ax murder. Her hand clawed at the choker around her neck, gnarled and spotted next to the pristine sheen of the pearls. "What's *she* doing here?"

The *she* in question hesitated. Helping her along, Viveca reached out, took the woman's hand and drew her in. When the woman came into view, Andrew started unpleasantly and wondered what kind of hornet's nest Viveca was stirring up and why.

"Hello, Arnetta." It was Beulah Rivers, Reynolds Warner's mistress.

Dressed in a smart blue suit that hung on her frame, she didn't look any happier to be here than the rest of them were to see her. Her shoulders sagged and she crept inside, as though she didn't want to come into the office and hoped to prolong that eventuality for as long as possible.

Though Andrew had talked to her when she'd called after Viveca's visit, he hadn't seen her in years and was startled to see how she'd changed. She was still plump, but now she had the loose-skinned look of a person who'd lost a lot of weight in a short period of time. Maybe the cancer treatments were going more poorly than she'd let on.

Beulah's gaze caught Andrew's and she studied him with the same kind of loving concern he'd seen from Viveca just now, making his feeling of dread a whole lot worse.

Why would Viveca bring Arnetta and Beulah together?

It'd been an unspoken policy over the years never to bring Grandfather's wife and his longtime mistress together in the same room. A simple act of giving the respect due to a long-suffering wife.

Andrew had always wondered whether Arnetta knew she was long-suffering, but now he had his answer, clear as a bell. Arnetta knew *exactly* what Beulah had been to Reynolds. She knew only too well.

"Miss Beulah has some…information she wants to share with us," Viveca said.

Arnetta's face went purple and her voice vibrated with fury. "I am leaving."

Andrew stared. Never in his life had he seen Arnetta lose her composure like this. He expected Bishop to whisk her out of the office but, to his surprise, Bishop stayed where he was and made no effort to comfort or assist Arnetta.

"Don't you move one inch." Viveca turned a cold gaze on Arnetta and spoke with absolute authority, as though she had the power to lock the doors and physically prevent anyone from leaving if she wanted to.

The women glared at each other. Andrew was tempted to tell Arnetta she was wasting her time trying to intimidate Viveca, but after a second or two she seemed to realize it on her own.

"How dare you?" Arnetta spoke in that hushed, deeply disappointed voice that normally made people cower before her, but Viveca ignored the outburst, turned back to Beulah and squeezed the woman's hand between both of hers.

"Miss Beulah?" she said gently.

Beulah's tired, ruined gaze met Viveca's strong, unwavering one, almost as though Beulah was drawing strength and courage from Viveca. Finally Beulah nodded, let go of Viveca and turned to Andrew. Her pitying expression, clear-eyed despite her illness, worked on that dread in his belly, making it grow. He tensed, knowing that the bad thing, whatever it was, was about to blow up his life.

Beulah came over and took his hand between her cold, gnarled ones. Instinct made him want to snatch away, but Andrew Warner didn't run and hide even if he was no longer Andrew Warner. Worse than this woman's touch right now was the feeling that everyone but him knew what was coming.

"Andrew," Beulah said, "I hope you can forgive me."

Stunned—what on earth would he ever need to forgive this old woman for?—he answered automatically. "Of course I can."

"I'm old now. Sick." She rubbed the back of his hand, offering the kind of comfort his own mother never had. "You think about things when you're sick. Things you did or didn't do. Things you should have done." A weighty pause followed, and Andrew felt the tension level in the room ratchet up another few notches. "Times you kept quiet when you should have spoken up."

"I understand," Andrew told her, but he didn't.

Beulah looked over her shoulder at Viveca, who gave her an encouraging nod and smile, then turned back to Andrew. "Viveca talked to me. She's a good girl, you know. Loves you very much."

Andrew wanted this to be true so much he couldn't work up any answer. Risking a glance at Viveca, he saw that she was watching him intently, a faint smile on her face, almost like she was confirming what Miss Beulah said.

Bewildered as he was right now, he felt his heartbeat stutter.

"Andrew." Beulah spoke gently, drawing his attention back to her. "I need to tell you who your father is."

Andrew gaped, thinking that Beulah was old…confused…sick… The poor woman was misguided, didn't know what she was saying, couldn't be taken seriously. And yet…in a distant corner of his mind, another part of him had somehow known this was coming.

He sensed he did not want to hear this. And neither, apparently, did Arnetta. Over on the sofa she looked apoplectic, her face the kind of splotchy purple that usually preceded a heart attack. She glanced wildly around the room, as though she couldn't understand why all these other people were standing by as silent witnesses to this travesty.

"This is *ridiculous*." Her genteel Southern voice, never raised even in her angriest moments, degenerated into a rough growl, and she waved her arm. "I will not sit by while this…this…*woman* tries to—"

"Hush up now." Bishop, grim and resigned, reached out and lowered Arnetta's arm. Arnetta wrenched away, looking ready to smash the nearest lamp, but Bishop held firm. "Let this boy hear the truth, Arnetta. It's past time."

This simple exchange scared Andrew worse than anything else had or could.

"How could you—" he said to Miss Beulah, then had to stop and clear his dry throat. "How could you know who my father was?"

Miss Beulah took a deep breath. "Because he told me."

"*No.*" Suddenly the old woman's soothing touch on his hand was too much. An annoyance, an abomination. Snatching free, Andrew wheeled around and walked away. Back and forth in front of the windows he paced, trying to think what to do…what to do…what to do.

The office shrank; the walls closed in. There was nowhere safe to look. On their sofa, Arnetta sniffled into one of her white lacy handkerchiefs, and Bishop murmured to her. From his position against a window, Eric stared at

Andrew with an astonished, pitying look, as though he'd put two and two together and come up with something repugnant rather than the number four.

Even Viveca, sweet, strong, Viveca, watched him with damp eyes and hovered just out of reach, as though she wanted to be close but knew that her touch at this moment was the one thing that would send him right into babbling idiothood.

He looked back to Miss Beulah, the source of all his turmoil. This time he didn't see a sick old woman, or the sweet woman he'd known all his life. He saw only a liar, and he hated liars. Walking back to her, he worked up a shrug and a laugh, and tried to put this nonsense into perspective as the colossal joke it was.

"All right. I'll bite." His voice was hard and ugly, even to his own ears, but he couldn't worry about that now because this woman was stirring the pot and didn't care what kind of lies she told to do so. "Solve the big mystery for us, Miss Beulah. Who's my father?"

Miss Beulah gave him a kindly look, as if she saw through his bravado, and spoke in the sort of gentle voice meant to comfort in situations where attempts at comfort were a clear waste of time.

"Reynolds."

Chapter 20

"Sorry. Try again." Andrew's brain felt like it was about to blow. "Reynolds was my *grand*father."

"He was your *father*," Miss Beulah said.

The room blurred around him, and for a minute there was nothing. Not a sound, not a thought, not a feeling. Just the absolute emptiness and complete silence of shock. Then, from the sofa, came Arnetta's low, moaning sob, and that was when he *knew*.

Images came to him, not caring that he didn't want to see them. His powerful, magnetic, handsome grandfather and his string of mistresses. His beautiful, seductive mother, into whose bed countless men had no doubt been welcomed. Wasn't it inevitable and predictable that the two most oversexed people he'd ever known would have had sex with each other?

Trying to fight this conclusion, grasping for another

answer, a better one, he worked his brain for clues. He'd seen them together, of course. He'd never picked up on any currents between them, but when had a young boy ever been a good reader of interpersonal signals? *It couldn't be true…couldn't be true…*

He opened his mouth and forced the words out. "Are you saying…that my mother had sex with her father-in-law?"

"Yes," said Beulah.

Something deep within him, something vital, tore open and bled. There was no way he could deal with this *crap,* and he shouldn't be expected to. He roared at Miss Beulah, losing the last of his composure. *"How do you know?"*

"Andrew." Viveca stepped forward and had the nerve to put a light, restraining hand on his arm, like he was the one with the problem, the one telling lies, and the one who needed to be silenced.

He jerked his arm away, all his focus on Miss Beulah. "Talk. *Now.*"

The old woman's eyes lost focus, and her papery cheeks tightened at some unpleasant memory. It took a moment to gather her thoughts.

"Your mother was young. Pretty. Bored, I guess. She didn't have a job or children to keep her out of trouble." Miss Beulah's lips curled, as if the words tasted bad. "Reynolds hired her to decorate the offices. The first day she came and I watched them together, I saw the writing on the wall."

Keeping the rage out of his voice was impossible because it required much more control than Andrew was capable of at the moment. "That doesn't prove he was my father."

Miss Beulah was unfazed. Only the hard flash of her eyes revealed any emotions. "He left me. Just like that." She snapped her fingers. "Said she was the one for him—"

Arnetta wailed, the sound raw, primitive and unbearable, but for once she wasn't the star of the show. Miss Beulah didn't pause in her bitter recitation.

"They went for lunch and stayed gone for the whole day. Stayed locked in his office for hours. Went on trips to Paris and London to buy furniture." She laughed, making a choked, sickly sound. "Didn't even try to hide it. After about a year he got tired of her, and that was that. He came right back to me."

"What has this got to do with me?" Andrew was out of patience and didn't have the stomach to listen to more of this disgusting narrative without vomiting. "I haven't heard you say anything that tells me—"

"Nine months after they started, when you were born, Reynolds went to the hospital to see you, and then he came to the office. Floating on air. He had a cigar. Opened a bottle of champagne. Toasted his grandson, Andrew *Reynolds* Warner. Said he'd be the best Warner yet."

Andrew stared at Miss Beulah while common sense and denial battled for supremacy inside him. Denial won. "I don't believe you. She could still have been sleeping with my father, with Charles, I mean, and—"

"Charles was sterile. From when he had the mumps as a boy."

This new voice was as unexpected as a July visit from Santa Claus. Disbelieving, Andrew swung around to see Arnetta sitting straight and proud again, watching him through eyes that were red, but clear and dry.

"It's true, Andrew," she told him. "We all knew what was going on—"

"No," Andrew said. *"No."*

"I knew…Charles knew…the help knew. It wasn't a secret, but we pretended it was. No one talked about it because appearances had to be kept up. But…I'm tired of not talking about it."

"No," Andrew said again. "I don't believe this."

This was a lie. He *did* believe it. This was *exactly* the kind of amoral behavior that could have been expected of his so-called grandfather and his so-called mother. The two of them, from all accounts, had never denied themselves anything, had never cared about consequences, and had never given a damn about other people's feelings.

Typical, really. So predictable it was boring.

"I found this. It's how I knew."

Andrew looked around to see Viveca holding something in her hand, offering it to him. A photograph, he realized. As if he wanted to see actual proof that he was the product of an adulterous affair between two of the most spoiled people who'd ever walked the face of the earth. He took it anyway. After several deep breaths, he had the courage to flip it over and look at it.

It was an old black-and-white, a crowd scene from one of the countless balls at Heather Hill. In the front stood Arnetta, laughing in her white gown, a Diana Ross wig on her head and a cigarette dangling from her fingertips. She was the subject of the shot.

But behind her, a little to the right and a little bit apart from the rest of the partiers, standing much too close to each other, and clearly unaware that they were being photographed, stood Reynolds and Barbara.

Reynolds wore a tuxedo, Barbara a low-cut, glittery sort of gown like the ones Cher used to wear, the kind that needed only a strategic tug or two to fall to the ground in a pile of sequins.

They were looking at each other like lovers, not in-laws.

It was a sexy, smoldering look, the kind that screamed

of plans to rip off clothes and take each other, hard and fast, at the earliest opportunity. Lowered lids. Knowing smiles. Heat and desire.

Stunned, Andrew waited for it to sink in—the realization that he was the son of a Warner after all, even if it wasn't the Warner he'd always thought—but it never did.

No one spoke. Maybe everyone sensed he needed a minute to rearrange his family tree and memories, to realign his life.

Bishop, he thought suddenly.

Bishop loved him. Bishop had no hidden agendas. Bishop would tell him the truth. If Bishop said it was so, then it was, and that would be the end of it. Andrew turned to the old man and opened his mouth.

"It's true, Scooter," Bishop said.

Andrew shut his mouth. That was it, then. All the fight and anger went out of him, and only sorrow and bewilderment were left. He thought of the terrible day he'd realized Charles wasn't his father, the day Bishop had found and comforted him.

"Why didn't you tell me, man?"

Bishop held out a gnarled, beseeching hand, begging for forgiveness without saying the words. "If you'd asked," he said, "I'd'a told you. But you didn't ask and I knew it was because you couldn't handle it. You weren't ready, Scooter."

Again Andrew opened his mouth, ready to argue, but what was the point? Bishop was right. Andrew hadn't been ready. Hell, he wasn't sure he was ready even now. That was why he'd never, this whole time, tried to find out who his father was. Maybe on some level he'd always known that the information would make him feel worse, not better.

Another thought occurred to him. He couldn't seem to

stop them from coming. "Is this why you always hated me?" he asked Arnetta. "I've always wondered."

"I've never hated you," Arnetta said, "but you need to understand. Reynolds had his eye on Barbara from the second Charles brought her home to meet us. That woman caused me more pain than—"

She broke off, shot an angry glance at Miss Beulah, and then dropped her head. Miss Beulah had the decency to hang her own head. It took Arnetta a minute of dabbling at her eyes with her handkerchief before she was ready to speak again.

"You look like them, Andrew." Arnetta's laugh was cold and ugly. "You look exactly like Reynolds and Barbara. When I look at you, I see them and I feel that pain all over again."

Andrew nodded. He understood. There was no point being angry with Arnetta anyway. The people he should be mad at were dead, but he didn't want to waste time with bitterness. What point was there to that?

What a family. He looked at them all, then. Eric, stunned and silent, collapsing on one sofa, Arnetta and Bishop, looking old, tired and shell-shocked, on another. Viveca, still hovering nearby, watching him with worried eyes. How could he ask her to marry into this mess? The poor woman would be safer if he pushed her into the crocodile pit at the zoo.

Viveca looked at her watch. "The board meeting will be starting soon, Andrew, but you can cancel it. You don't have to quit now. There's no reason for it. And your inheritance belongs to you. That's why I brought Miss Beulah here. You *are* a Warner, and you don't have to—"

"Yeah." His decision came without hesitation. "I do."

"What?" Eric looked alarmed, as though the reprieve he'd been hoping for had been snatched away.

"Well, I'll keep the inheritance. Don't get me wrong." Andrew managed a smile. "But I'm still resigning from the company. I need a new challenge. Something different. And I need a minute alone with Viveca."

Viveca stilled but met his gaze head-on and that chemistry, as powerful as ever, surged between them. He'd meant to give her more time to come to terms with their relationship, but she'd had enough time and his nerves were fried enough as it was. Today was a day for answers and new beginnings, and he intended to have both from Viveca. As soon as he could get rid of everyone.

Muttering now, Eric stood and shook Andrew's hand. "What're you now? My uncle? Can I call you Uncle Andy?"

Laughing, Andrew pulled him in for a hug. Leave it to Eric to bring a little levity to any situation. "Get the hell outta my office."

They all filed past, Miss Beulah first. He took her hand. "I forgive you," he said in response to the questioning look in her eyes, and she sagged with relief. Andrew hugged her, grateful that she'd had the courage to tell him the truth when no one else ever had.

Bishop was next. "I'm sorry, Sc—"

Andrew hugged him, too. "Don't be sorry, old man. And don't call me Scooter."

Arnetta was last, and hardest. They studied each other, both cautious and unsure. Arnetta finally spoke. "Maybe we can try—"

"I'd like that," Andrew said quickly.

Nodding, looking satisfied, she reached up and patted his face, something he could never remember her doing before. Emotion tightened his throat and he tried to swallow it, but then she pulled his face down and kissed his cheek.

Nearly undone—he'd always kissed her, and she'd never, *ever,* kissed him—he pulled her into a tight hug that lasted a long time. He held on, savoring it, because it had been over thirty years in the making.

At last everyone was gone, the door was shut and he was alone with Viveca.

"Are you okay?" she asked anxiously.

Grabbing her hand, he pulled her closer but not into his arms. "I am now."

"I don't see how you could be."

"Maybe I'm in shock." He paused. "Or maybe I'm not really that surprised."

The funny thing was…nothing had really changed for him. Before the meeting, he'd known he had a promiscuous, self-absorbed mother and a biological father who had no interest in fathering. After the meeting, he had the same thing. The only new element was that now he had a name for his nonfathering father: Reynolds Warner. And his feeling was…*so what?*

He wasn't anything like his father. Hell, he'd already lived his life trying to be nicer than Reynolds Warner, trying to undo the damage Reynolds had done to and with the company, trying to make the Warner name stand for something ethical and good. That wouldn't change.

"You know," Viveca said, squeezing his hand, "you're not your father. Or your mother. You're so much better than either of them ever were. I hope you know that. You've made yourself better than that."

God, he wanted to be worthy of the precious faith she had in him. If she gave him the chance, he'd make it his life's work to never let her down. "I'm working on it, I guess."

They stared at each other. Viveca still looked worried,

as though she expected him to collapse to the floor in a delayed reaction or something.

Thinking of Viveca chasing down Miss Beulah and getting the truth out of her, he had to grin. "That was some crack reporting, Lois Lane."

"You think?"

"Oh, yeah."

"I had to do it. I couldn't stand by and let you lose *everything*—"

"I haven't lost *everything*." He pulled her closer. "Unless I've lost you."

She smiled a heavy-lidded woman's smile, the kind that spoke of secrets in the dark, the slide of skin against skin and, more than that, of futures, children and *family*.

She tilted her face up a little, just enough to torment him. "You haven't lost me."

His heartbeat galloped straight into the red zone but he worked for nonchalance. "No? Why's that?"

"Because I love you."

Weak with relief, dizzy, he grabbed her face and kissed her, over and over again, hot, wet, deep kisses that lacked any of the finesse he'd learned over the years, and she laughed every time his lips left hers. The sound of her joy went straight to his head, intoxicating him, and he wondered if she could possibly be as happy as she'd just made him.

"Does this mean you'll marry me?" He leaned his forehead against hers, trying to catch his breath and to take it a little slow so he didn't misunderstand anything or imagine signals that weren't really there.

"Are you asking, or is this another one of your statements of intent?"

"I'm asking."

"Well, then… *Yes*."

This kicked off another round of laughing and kisses, at the end of which he felt it was fair to warn her. "I don't know why you'd want to be part of this family. You've seen what you're getting. If you were smart, you'd say no."

"Yeah." She nodded somberly. "I'm not that smart though."

"What about the book? We gave you about a hundred pages of material in the last ten minutes alone."

"Ah, the book." She tried to look serious and disappointed, but didn't do a very good job of it what with all the grinning. "I hope you're not too upset, but I quit the whole book project. Sent back my advance. Looks like I've got a conflict of interest."

"What a shame."

"I know."

"We'll have children and adopt Nathan," he informed her."

"God willing. But I want to keep working."

"Will your job keep you from having sex with me every night?"

"*Nothing* will keep me from having sex with you every night."

"Then you have my blessing," he told her, and they both laughed. "We can live in New York and keep my house here for weekends."

"Really?"

"Really."

Life, Andrew thought as he held her close, caressing and kissing whatever parts of her he could get his lips and hands on, *is strange.* Fifteen minutes ago he'd had his world blown out from under his feet, and now he was the single happiest man who'd ever lived or ever would live.

"Don't think," he said, stroking Viveca's hair, "that

you're going to get out of this. You're stuck. Even if you're only saying yes because I've had a rough morning. You're still stuck."

Those glittering brown eyes smiled at him. "Good."

"*Viveca.*" The name was a prayer, a blessing, three syllables that held all his dreams and hopes for the future. "I'm going to be a good husband. I'm going to love you so much for so long, you're not going to know what hit you."

"Promise?"

"Just wait."

Epilogue

Viveca pushed the blue curtains aside, looked out the window across Fifth Avenue, which was relatively quiet for this time of day, and down at the treetops. They looked, from this height, like great clumps of broccoli, but the sky was clear and beautiful, the sun bright.

Still doing that dance-sway routine that mothers did the world over, and patting his little cushioned bottom, she looked down into her six-week-old son's sleeping face. He had, if possible, gotten more adorable in the last hour or so. He was a perfect miniature of his father, down to the silky black hair, enough for a nice baby wig or two, and the piercing blue-eyed gaze.

He'd also inherited his father's enormous appetite and

love of her breasts, the little piggy. Andrew Ryan Warner, named for his father and hers.

She'd never thought she could love anything this much.

Humming absently, she swayed over to the crib and wondered if she dared try to lay him down. Every other time in his life that she'd done it, he'd instantly woken up, but what the heck. Maybe this time she'd get lucky. It had to happen sooner or later, right?

She'd just started to lower him when she heard the distant open and close of the front door and the sound of heavy, determined footsteps in the hall.

Straightening, she looked around in time to see the nursery door open and her husband poke his head in. *"Andrew."* Remembering, too late, the sleeping baby, she winced, clamped her jaws shut and prayed she hadn't woken him. Undisturbed, he slept on, his little rosebud mouth sucking reflexively. "You're early."

Andrew unleashed the full grin on her as he came inside, a sight as devastating today as it had been the first time she saw it. "I missed you." Careful not to disturb the baby, he leaned in and kissed her.

Gingerly taking Andy out of her arms, he settled him against his own chest and began the dance-sway. "Where's Nathan?"

"Soccer practice."

"How'd the meetings go with the investors?"

"Good." He kissed Andy's little head, nuzzling him. "How's the diaper rash?"

"Since you called three hours ago to ask?"

Andrew laughed, looking sheepish, then swayed over to the crib. Seeing him start to put the baby in it, she cringed but, as always, Andrew did it perfectly and Andy didn't stir.

"How do you do that?" she asked sourly.

Andrew grinned, loosened his tie and turned to her, a new light smoldering in his eyes. Something low in her belly tightened with anticipation.

"Did you have your checkup?" he asked.

"I may have." Viveca watched him toss his suit jacket on the rocker and creep closer, feeling her knees weaken with every step he took. "Why do you ask?"

"Because." Unsmiling and unhurried, he took that last step that put him directly in front of her and held her gaze. "I haven't made love with my wife in six weeks and it's killing me."

Need roughened her voice and made her hands shake as she reached for him. "Come here."

He didn't need to be told twice. Locking her into his arms, he swung her off her feet and onto the love seat in a dizzying burst of movement. Words poured out of his mouth between his deep, biting kisses and his jerky movements as he ran his hands all over her body told her how urgently he needed her.

"I missed you, Vivi. *Missed you.*"

"I missed *you.*"

His hands slid under the fluttery cotton of her summer dress; he yanked the bodice down and buried his face between the lacy cups of her bra, inhaling her. A shudder rippled through him, and she clutched at his heavy shoulders, trying to hold on even as sanity slipped away.

Zeroing in, too far gone for much foreplay, he slid his fingers under her panties and stroked over her core. "You're so wet," he murmured. "Open for me, baby… Let me in, sweet baby."

Another well-placed stroke made her eyes roll closed with ecstasy, her toes curl. Forgetting that they should be quiet because of the baby, she moaned, long and loud, and arched beneath him. That did it.

Cursing, frantic, Andrew tore her panties off her legs. In another half second he had his belt undone and his pants unzipped, and then, with one relentless surge, he was inside her, moving, and they were both making enough noise to wake the long-dead. Wrapping her legs around his waist, she took him deep inside, welcoming him back.

Pumping hard and furious, he clamped his hands on her butt and rode. "No more kids," he panted against her mouth. "I can't do without this for another six weeks of my life."

"One more baby. One more."

"No."

"Please?" She clenched her inner muscles in the way she knew drove him insane, and he cursed again but didn't answer. "Please." She raked her nails across his back. *"Please."* This time she licked his lips, tugging at the bottom one with her teeth.

Andrew gave up the fight. "One more. *Only one.*"

That was all the talking they managed to do until, with three more hard thrusts, he sent her over the edge and followed immediately after. Trying to be quiet at that point never entered Viveca's mind, baby or no baby.

For a long time they lay together in a tangle of arms and legs and she gloried in his weight and the heavy muscles that pressed her so deep into the cushions. There was nothing in the world like making love with her husband. And to think she'd almost missed the chance to do it for the rest of her life.

At last he lifted his head and smiled down at her, the picture of male satisfaction. "This is a new one. We've never done it on this love seat before, have we?"

"No." She grinned. "We're still not that good at making it to the bed, are we?"

"Vivi," he said, "we never will be."

Tyson Braddock was not a man to be denied....

Second Chance, Baby

Book #3 in The Braddocks: Secret Son

A.C. ARTHUR

Except for one passion-filled night, Ty and Felicia Braddock's marriage has been cold for years. Now Felicia is pregnant. Unwilling to raise her baby with an absentee workaholic father, Felicia wants a divorce. Ty convinces her to give him another chance. But as they rediscover the passion they'd lost, will it be enough to make them a family?

THE BRADDOCKS

SECRET SON

power, passion and politics are all in the family

Available the first week of October wherever books are sold.

KIMANI™
ROMANCE

www.kimanipress.com

KPACA0841008

Will being Cinderella for a month
lead to happily ever after?

A
Gentleman's
Offer

DARA GIRARD

Wealthy Nate Blackwell offers dog groomer Yvette Coulier
an opportunity to live among the upper crust if she'll let him
pose as her valet. But it's not long before their mutual passion
forces them to take off their masks...and expose their hearts.

Four women. One club.
And a secret that will make all their fantasies come true.

Available the first week of October wherever books are sold.

Was her luck running out?

GAMBLE ON
Love

The second title in The Ladies of Distinction…

MICHELLE MONKOU

"Black American Princess" Denise Dixon has met
her match in sexy, cynical Jaden Bond. But as their
relationship heats up, she knows their days are numbered
before her shameful family secrets are revealed.

THE LADIES *of* DISTINCTION:

They've shared secrets, dreams and heartaches.
And when it comes to finding love, these sisters
always have each other's backs.

Available the first week of October wherever books are sold.

KIMANI™
ROMANCE

What Matters Most

ESSENCE BESTSELLING AUTHOR

GWYNNE FORSTER

Melanie Sparks's job at Dr. Jack Ferguson's
clinic is an opportunity to make her dream
of nursing a reality—but only if she can keep
her mind off trying to seduce the dreamy doc.
Jack's prominent family expects him to choose
a wealthy wife. But he soon realizes he's fallen
for the woman right in front of him…. Now he
just has to convince Melanie of that.

*Coming the first week of October
wherever books are sold.*

ARABESQUE®

www.kimanipress.com
KPSKI040908C